OTHERWORLDS

Second Edition

A Story Collection By:
M Todd Gallowglas

M Todd Gallowglas

OTHERWORLDS
Copyright © 2012 M Todd Gallowglas
Cover design Alyxx Duggins and Ed Litfin

This is a work of fiction. Any similarity between real names, characters, places, and incidents is purely coincidental.

No part of this book may be used, reproduced, or transmitted in any manner without written permission of the author, except in the case of brief quotations for critical articles and reviews. All rights are reserved.

This Second edition of OTHERWORLDS is dedicated to:
Laura and DJ
For standing in the front ranks of the #Gallowglasarmy since day one.

Acknowledgements

This is where I talk about people who have helped me to get to this point in my career. Well for this book, I'd like to thank you, the individual reading this, or at least the one who came to my show and stayed to the end in order to get this particular book. Thank you for being part of keeping oral storytelling alive in the world. If not for people like you, I won't have a great career as a storyteller, and if I didn't have that, I wouldn't have had nearly as successful a beginning I've had as a writer. Thank you. I truly hope you enjoy this collection of stories.

First Edition Dedication:
Marti and Bill:
You guys gave me the best platform I could have asked for in launching my career.

Ace:
For daring me to open my eyes and see what I could accomplish.

M Todd Gallowglas

Table of Contents

Introduction to Second Edition	7
Jaludin's Road	9
Chaos Factor	39
Paradox Loop	43
Paladin	51
Prophesy	73
Writers' Block	77
The Dragon Bone Flute	89
Familiar Choices	129
The Half-Faced Man	133
Excerpt from First Chosen	149
Excerpt from Halloween Jack	163
Excerpt from Dead Weight	171

INTRODUCTION
to the
SECOND EDITION

After the first edition of *Otherworlds* went out of print, I planned on that being it, no more. Since I gave away the very last copy at the 2012 Folsom Renaissance Faire, I've had people coming up asking me when I'd have them again. I went through the entire 2013 Renaissance Faire season without offering *Otherworlds* at my shows. Since I began publishing my books, I've become an international bestseller. I've had people come up to me and tell me how much they love my books in much the way people at Renaissance Faires come up to me and tell me that they like my stories. Truth is, if it weren't for my audiences at my shows, I probably would have never even tried this self-publishing thing, and without that, my world would be a much different place. For the people who come and support my storytelling show, I decided that it was time to bring this book back. It's only available to people who come to my live events: my storytelling shows, readings, and speaking engagements. Whether you've been coming to my shows for years, or you decided to pick up this collection of stories the very first time you saw me, I consider you a part of a very special community of people who changed my life and allowed me to pursue and live my dream.

For the second edition, I've added a few stories and cleaned up errors in the others. I considered taking two of the stories out. I've changed both significantly. One I sold to an anthology, the other, I put into a bigger project because it just fit in so well. After much consideration, I decided to keep those two stories in the collection as they originally were so people could have a bit of "before and after" of the evolution of my writing.

So here it is: the second edition of *Otherworlds*. Thank you for helping keep the oral storytelling tradition alive.

May all of your stories have happy endings.

JALUDIN'S ROAD

For David B. Coe
A.K.A
D. B. Jackson

Thanks for giving the title and some good advice for playing Risk.

"Jaludin's Road" originally started as a typical Northern-European fantasy adventure. It was originally a song that I wrote and performed at bardic circles in the SCA. In my early twenties, I wrote it out as a story. Later, while working on the world of Tears of Rage, I rewrote the story and set it on a continent to the south of where the events of Tears of Rage unfold. It's gone through about a dozen iterations and rewrites, until I became happy with this story.

For those of you who decide to pick up my other books, especially the Tears of Rage sequence, a character makes a veiled reference to Jaludin in book four, Judge of Dooms.

I've got more tales of Jaludin and the Lands of Endless Summer waiting in the wings. Some of the characters from these stories will show up in future Tears of Rage.

I like pretty much every story I put out into the world, but I'm rather fond of this one. I like Jaludin and the companions that join him. I hope you enjoy them as much as I do.

> *There's a race of men that don't fit in,*
> *A race that can't stay still;*
> *So they break the hearts of kith and kin,*
> *And they roam the world at will.*
> *They range the field and they rove the flood,*
> *And they climb the mountain's crest;*
> *Theirs is the curse of the gypsy blood,*
> *And they don't know how to rest.*
>
> Robert Service
> "The Men Who Don't Fit In"

The camel-riding nomad tribes of the deep deserts have a saying, *The dunes are never the same on the return journey.*

I never really understood what that meant until I looked down on my childhood home. I had just crested the last dune when the light of the setting sun forced me to shield my eyes. In all my travels, few sites could match the holy radiance of the desert sun shining down on the village of Bhaklah. The sunlight came from the southwest, as it was close to dusk, hitting the white-stone buildings so that they seemed to glow. Taking in the sight of it, a cold sweat that had nothing to do with the sun's heat ran between my shoulder blades.

This particular talent of my body reacting to things before my conscious mind notices them has saved my life on more than just a handful of occasions.

I closed my eyes and drew in a deep breath. I held the heat of the desert air in my lungs for a moment, and then slowly let the breath escape as I opened my eyes.

No firelight shone from the All Flame that should have burned atop the town's temple; no one stood on the four watchtowers.

The moment those details registered in my mind, I was scrambling down the dune. I felt the sand working its way into my clothes and I might regret it later, but there really isn't any way to get down a sand dune easily without getting sand everywhere in your clothes. Had someone followed me home? No. Impossible. Only one man knew that Jaludin Wanderer was the Ghost Between the Shadows and that he came from Bhaklah. That one man was dead. His death had inspired my decision to return.

Soon the sand gave way to rock. I stumbled several times as smaller stones skittered out from under my feet as I approached the outer walls. Plants grew where the wall met the ground; some even showed hints of green, evidence of Bhaklah's ample well.

At the eastern gate, I nodded to the symbols of the five gods carved into the stone archway. True, tradition required that I kneel and pray to each of the five greater gods, but I'd ignored greater traditions than that in my life as a wanderer. That, and no one stood at the gate to call this lack of proper piety into question.

"Hello?"

My echoing voice was the only response.

I chewed my lower lip – a habit I still fall into occasionally when heavy questions weigh upon my mind. Could it be plague or bandits? I dismissed both thoughts. If a plague had found its way here, the desert sands would have shown the black marks of burn piles. If bandits had struck, then bodies would litter the street and many houses would be burnt-out husks.

I turned a corner and progressed through the town square. The well was here. At this time of day, the sound of laughing children should echo from the high walls as they played while wives and eldest daughters fetched water to prepare supper. A flock of sheep scattered before me as I ran through their midst.

"Watch where you're going, stupid human!" the ram bleated after me.

I started. In my travels I had gathered quite a collection of blessed items, and while I'd been wearing the ear clip that allowed me to understand the speech of animals for several years, it still surprised me when my mind wasn't specifically set to the task of speaking to the animals. That ear clip, along with the other items I'd gathered, helped me a great deal in my career as a thief – a career I'd come home to abandon. Let some other fool take up the mantle of the Ghost Between the Shadows.

Less than a hundred heartbeats later, I came to my parents' house. The door hung partially open, and I drew two curved-bladed knives behind my back. Letters in the spiderweb script of Grandfather Shadow's divine language glowed darkly on the blades. I do not draw those enchanted weapons without good cause, but I have never tossed the bones without tipping the odds in my favor.

From years of practice, I made no sound as I crept from room to room. Nearing my parents' room, the stench of urine and excrement wafted into the hall. I covered my nose with the back of my left hand, taking care not to scratch myself with the blade. That would have done me no good.

I moved the woven curtain aside and entered the room. Both Mother and Father lay on Mother's large mattress. By tradition the house belonged to the husband but the sleeping room belonged to the wife. A curtain on the southeast corner closed off Father's sleeping pallet. Any time a married woman grew angry or annoyed with her husband, she could banish him to that small alcove for the night – or even out of the room if he had offended her enough. Each wall except the south had a window. No wall facing south had a window. That would let in too much sun during the hottest part of the day.

Mother's bed was a mattress stuffed with wool and encased in four boards a single hand high. The blankets were woven of wool and showed patterns of squares and triangles, the shapes sacred to All Father Sun and Mother Earth. Father lay with Mother on top of those blankets. Father's crotch was stained with waste. I shifted the hand that covered my nose and turned a bit so that I could not see Mother in such a state.

Father lay on the mattress as if relaxed, with no tension in his limbs. His eyes were sunken deep into their sockets, his face appeared flushed, and his breath came in deep, rapid gasps that echoed slightly in the stone room. Father's lips were so dry that they were cracked and bleeding, and his skin looked dry and brittle like parchment left in the sun too long. Unable to keep my curiosity at bay, I glanced at Mother. She was much the same as Father. It was as if they had lain down for a midafternoon nap, except that they stared glassy-eyed at the ceiling.

The small fireplace in the northwest corner of the room held no fuel, not even embers. No one would let their embers burn out in both the sleeping chambers and in the kitchen. A thin layer of sandy dust lay across my parents, the bed, the wooden chest of drawers that sat next to Mother's side of the bed, and the baskets woven from river reeds and palm branches that were arranged against the south wall. Those baskets held clothes and other personal belongings. The chest of drawers was new. My parents must have risen in status since I left. Wood was usually reserved for weapons, tools, and buildings. A brass pitcher rested on the table, as well as the silver lamp that Father had given Mother as a bride-price.

Choking down bile that rose from the stench of waste, I approached the bed. I waved my hand in front of Father's eyes but got no reaction. I wanted to reach out to him, to shake him awake, but I could not for fear that this strange affliction might take me, also. Instead, I screamed, first standing above them, then right next to their ears. I shook the bed as hard as I could. Father's walking stick rested in its usual place next to his alcove. I prodded Father with it, lightly at first, then with more vigor. After that, I couldn't think of anything else to do, so I went to the kitchen, to the clay pitcher Mother used to fetch water from the well every day. The vessel contained barely one mouthful of water.

Holding the pitcher, I glanced from the small bit of water to the fading light of day. How long had they been without water? I took the pitcher to my parents and sprinkled a few droplets of water into Father's mouth. Nothing happened. Then, a moment later, Father licked his lips, then drank the water down in earnest. Mother did the same. They slurped at the water with greedy need. Again, I wondered: how long had they been lying here without food and drink? It couldn't have been more than a few days, or they would likely be dead. Was the whole village like this?

That question spurred me to movement. I fled my parents' home at a brisk walk, but as my throat tightened and threatened to choke off my quickening breath, my feet sped up to match the pace. Minutes later, I burst through the front door of another house. Caution had left me as I raced up the stairs three at a time. At the top, I pushed a curtain aside and stopped short.

Safia wasn't there.

Throughout my travels, dreams of her laughter pulled at me no matter how far I'd wandered. When Safia laughed, I felt as if the sound banished all darkness and evil from the world, even if for only a few moments. It wasn't true, and that description also didn't do her laughter justice, but nothing would really do to translate the magic of that sound into words. These last few weeks the memory of her laughter had plagued me more than usual, calling to me as I'd journeyed across the sands.

I stood there, staring blankly at the sight of the room absent Safia. That meant she was married or dead. I didn't know which would be worse.

After a few moments – at the time it seemed longer, but everything seems longer seen through the eyes of youth – I made my way through the rest of the house.

Safia's parents were in their room, though unlike my parents, her father lay behind the curtain on his sleeping pallet. That didn't come as a surprise. Those two had been in one never-ending argument for as long as I could remember, and there seemed no end to it in sight when I'd left. The rest of the town pretended not to notice as best they could because, as far as anyone could tell, their fury with each other had not come to blows. This bickering had tempted me to take Safia with me five years ago, but traveling the ten deserts was foolhardy enough for a fourteen-year-old boy. It would have been suicidal for a fourteen-year-old girl.

Ishara, Safia's older sister, wasn't there either, but that did not come with the same shock. She was three years our elder and should have married and gone to live with a husband long before this.

I searched through the town. Every home was the same. People lay in their beds, staring at the ceiling, wallowing in their own waste.

Finally, I found Safia. She lay in a bed next to another man. I recognized Ashamel's large frame and bulbous nose. Safia had a the circular symbol of the world tattooed in the center of her forehead while Ashamel had a sun tattooed on his. Only married couples adorned themselves with these matching symbols of Mother Earth and All Father Sun. My parents had the same markings, but I'd always seen them that way so it wasn't something I took note of. I noticed this change.

A finely crafted clothing chest sat in the corner, though nothing as fine as Mother's chest of drawers. This was likely the thing that Safia's husband had used to bribe her into marrying him.

In childhood, Ashamel had been my chief rival for Safia's attentions, though the rivalry had more to do with Safia's parents' desires than due to Ashamel's own virtues. He had been well-liked by many of the adults in town for his simple honesty and willingness to bend his back to any task requested of him. The other children had a completely different view of him. He was honest to a fault and spoiled many plots for adventure by speaking to another child's parents if he heard even a whisper on the wind of them doing anything that offended his sense of good behavior. He'd had no ambition other than to take over caring for his father's herds and doing the hard and laborious duties no one else in town wanted.

I appreciate the need for men like that in every community, but I despised how everyone always compared me to Ashamel and found me wanting for any number of reasons. There was a need for adventurers as well. Adventurers created the stories — even though I had learned that those stories were always exaggerations, at best — that allowed people to dream, and a man was lost without his dreams. And that's the moment I realized that dreams could also die. The tattoo on Safia's forehead proved it.

I reached out to Safia, wanting to touch the symbol of Mother Earth. I watched my hand as if I were watching someone else's hand, wondering why the man who owned it would slip to such blasphemy. When I realized I wasn't actually reaching for the mark on her forehead, I took control and stopped myself. With only the smallest space between my fingertips and Safia's lips, her breath tickled my fingers. I'd committed many sins in my travels, but as much as I yearned for her, I could not allow myself the sin of touching another man's wife.

Before leaving, I spared a glance back to Safia. I felt the years fade, and I was back on the night I'd run away, having snuck up to her window to watch her sleep. Even then, I'd displayed aptitude for the skills that would serve me in my travels. I's crept inside her room and placed a note underneath her pillow. "I'll never be a man worthy of you while trapped in Bhaklah. I'll return with my fortune. — J."

Before leaving Ashamel's home, curiosity got the better of me. I went to Safia's clothing chest and rummaged through it. The note lay carefully folded at the bottom in a corner. I took the note and slid it under her pillow, being careful not to touch another man's wife. Then I fled from Safia's husband's house.

I returned to my parents. Pacing their kitchen, my mind raced in a dozen directions at once. I had to discover the cause of this affliction and somehow cure it.

"Stop," I said. Then I reminded myself of an old desert proverb, "Each journey is only a series of single steps. Take each with care and surety."

Everyone needed water, or many might not survive the night. Collecting all the water skins from the neighboring houses took some little time, but as my chore continued, trips back to the well grew further and further apart. I took skins from every house I went to. The fewer trips I had to make back and forth to the well, the faster I could water my people. That thought brought a cough of laughter. *My people*. Would they be so willing to accept me now? I could not shake the feeling that my return had somehow brought this doom down on Bhaklah.

During my errand, I discovered several of the elders and infants already dead. The dry desert heat showed no pity. The young and old usually suffered from the desert's cruelty first. With each corpse, I prayed to Old Uncle Night, asking the god of Death to ease each soul's passing into the mystery that came at life's end.

In the home of Safia's husband, I chewed my lower lip as my heart quickened. If Safia's husband died of dehydration, Ashamel would just be another corpse. Safia would be free to marry again after a suitable mourning period.

Then Sahlbak's face appeared in my mind — that almost too-narrow face ending in a ferret-like snout of a nose — screaming. His screams echoed across the weeks and the miles through the deserts. "Run. Run Jaludin. No. Save me. Don't you leave me to this. Ten upon ten curses upon your head." Even to this day, even across great time and more miles, I still hear those words, and he was hardly an innocent man. Allowing Ashamel to die would damn me forever.

"What are you thinking?" My stomach sickened at what I'd just contemplated.

I knelt down next to Ashamel.

"I don't know if you can hear me, but I want to tell you, not letting you die is the hardest thing I've ever done. I've done many things shameful in the eyes of gods and men, but I could not bring myself to kill a helpless man. I pray that you can forgive me for what I considered doing."

I gave water to Ashamel and his wife, then fled to the next house.

As I worked, my words *I could not bring myself to kill a helpless man* echoed in my mind. The memory of Sahlbak's cries for help soon followed. The slight, rodent-faced man hadn't been completely helpless. He'd been fighting for his life when I left my companion to die at the claws of some other-worldly creature.

"What could I have done?"

"Nothing."

But the twin knives with Grandfather Shadow's script etched in the blades hung heavy on my belt. They could cut the skin of anything not from the natural world.

I did my best to ignore the voices. By the time I'd gone through the town twice, my neck, shoulders, and back ached. Gods and goddesses how I wanted to retire, especially with All Father Sun nearing the end of his westerly decent; however, the desert would not wait while I rested before claiming more lives.

I returned to Father's home and knelt toward the fading daylight and prayed to each of the gods in turn. "Aunt Moon, give me the luck I need to find a cure for my people. Grandfather Shadow, send me the knowledge to find a cure for my people. Please Mother Earth and Father Sun, forgive me for the sin I allowed into my heart today. Uncle Night, pass over this town tonight without notice. I beg you to look on the House of Ashamel with favor. Give them a long and blessed life together."

With my prayers completed, I refolded my prayer mat and placed it inside my satchel and ate a dinner of cheese and bread without tasting any of it. This was not the meal I'd expected.

After finishing, I returned to my parents to do what I should have from the very first. I brought from under my shirt my silver amulet with the five clear stones set into it. As I approached my parents, one of the stones glowed with a bright light. I thanked all five of the Greater Gods that this strange malady was magical rather than infernal or some natural affliction. If it were natural, I might catch it, and if it were infernal… well, I might have been able to bargain with the Daemyn, convincing it to release the town, however I did not want to consider what the Daemyn would ask of me in exchange.

Well then, with it being magical, I had something to try. I swallowed hard when I pulled the ring protecting me from magic from my finger and placed it on Father's finger. It took about fifty heartbeats to summon enough courage to let go of that ring. Nothing happened. Father's condition did not change, and I did not descend into that strange slumber. I began breathing again once I returned the ring to my finger.

Like most of my enchanted items, I wished I'd known more about the ring. I'd obtained them all either from theft or from dealing in the shadow markets of the northern port cities. Some were straightforward, like the bracelets and anklets that let me climb any surface as if it were a ladder, while others, like the ring that resisted magic and the ear clip that let me speak to animals, contained some mysteries. The ring didn't seem to work on some magics, and the ear clip wouldn't allow communication with reptiles and certain types of birds.

After learning nothing from examining my parents, I sought the animals to see what they might be able to tell me. I ignored the sheep. They were skittish of anything not part of their herd, and getting them to stay still long enough to have a conversation wasn't worth the effort.

Instead, I approached a cat. Cats were at least occasionally inclined to converse. "Excuse me."

The cat looked at me, head cocked to the side. "You speak."

"Yes," I replied. "Can—?"

"The others like you can't speak," the cat said. "They only spout gibberish and strange noises."

"We just speak differently than you."

"Oh. Do you have milk?"

"No."

"Then you're not worth talking to." The cat raised its tail and walked away.

Every cat I came across treated me much the same way, at least all the ones who acknowledged my presence. One cat was different. It was a kitten.

"Will you play with me?" it asked in a squeaky voice.

"If I do, will you answer a few questions?"

"Of course."

It was better than any of my other offers. I found a long strand of wool in a nearby house and dangled it above the kitten. It began to jump and paw at the wool.

"Have you noticed how the people like me have been acting strange?"

"Yes. They've never slept this long before."

"How many times has the sun risen since they became like this?"

"Twice."

"Did anyone new come to the town right before this happened?"

"Someone did. It was just before this long sleep. He had lighter skin than you. He made pretty sounds with his voice. Even though I couldn't understand him."

"Did he use anything to help make the pretty sounds?"

"Yes. A box with strings. I wanted to play with it, but he was mean and wouldn't let me."

"Have there been any other strange things going on lately?"

"There's a mouse we can't catch. It's only been here a few days. Normally mice are stupid. Not this one. Not even old Sanddevil can catch it."

"Thank you." I dropped the yarn. The kitten promptly tangled itself within it.

I learned nothing else from the other animals. Several goats and a hen verified the presence of a minstrel just before the townspeople fell into their strange sleep.

Did the minstrel have anything to do with this? Had he been a wizard in disguise? His lighter skin made me think he might be from across the northern sea. There was much trade between the infidels across the sea and the northern ports, and while some came this far south, it was a rare enough occurrence to cause notice.

The time had crept well past the witches' hour. I leaned against a wall and rubbed my eyes with my palms, wondering what to do next.

"Jaludin, is that you?" a voice asked just behind my ear.

I gasped. Only years of conditioning kept me from screaming. Even still, sound echoed through the empty town as I leapt away from the wall and drew my daggers. At first I saw nothing, but then a mouse poked its head out of a small crack.

"Did I scare you?"

When my breath returned to normal, I asked, "How do you know me?"

"I'm Ishara."

"Really?" Even with all I'd seen, this was a little much to accept. "Convince me."

"It's me, you wayward dog. We convinced my parents that it was Ashamel and not you who had trampled my mother's herbs, and if I could, I'd take my father's sheep whip to you for breaking Safia's heart."

"Ishara! What has happened to you?"

"I was changed into this form by Najib Faq'hara, a wizard who has taken residence nearby. I went to be his apprentice. He turned me into a mouse when I refused to let him into my bed. I think he wanted his cat to eat me, but I escaped and came home."

I thought for a moment. "Get on the ground and hold out one of your hands – front feet."

"Why?"

"I want to try something,"

I slipped the ring off my finger.

Ishara climbed down the wall and held out her front left foot. I placed the ring around her foot. A flash of light blinded me for a moment. When my vision returned, Ishara stood in front of me, in her human body, and very naked.

First my ears burned. I snapped my eyes shut. Then I spun around. I couldn't get the image of her out of my mind, so I opened my eyes again.

"How—?" Ishara asked.

"The ring protects against spells and enchantments." My words came out in a terrified rush. "I've collected a small assortment of enchanted items in my travels. I figured that one might be able to remove your enchantment. Guess I was right. Ummm."

"This ring alone makes you the wealthiest man in Bhaklah. Well, I guess it makes me the wealthiest woman in Bhaklah."

"You have to give it back, Ishara."

"You greedy dog!" she screeched. "You'd leave me as a mouse just so you could have your precious ring?"

I almost spun to confront her, but then I recalled that she was naked.

"No. The ring can only protect one of us from the curse that's befallen Bhaklah while we're both human, and the curse doesn't affect animals. Besides, I'm going to need the ring if I'm going to confront this wizard."

"What? Najib Faq'hara is too dangerous. I don't want to think about what he'd do to you."

"I've known many dangerous men." One of them had been a friend until I abandoned him. I would not abandon Bhaklah in the same way.

"You are a fool, Jaludin."

"Perhaps, but I'm a desperate fool. If you don't come, it will take me longer to find him, which means more of our people will die."

"Fine." There was a short pause, then Ishara's next words echoed through the ear clip. "Take the ring back. I'll take you there."

I turned. Ishara was a mouse again, and the ring lay on the ground beside her. I picked it up and slid it back on my finger. Breath came easier.

While I gathered food for traveling, Ishara continued to warn me of the danger of dealing with wizards. This only firmed my resolve. Soon, we left Bhaklah, Ishara riding on my shoulder. When I reached the top of the first dune, I glanced back at the still dark All Flame. I took a deep breath.

"What is it?" Ishara asked.

"I'd meant to leave the road behind me, and now, a day after returning home, I'm leaving. The gods are cruel sometimes."

"But they are also kind," Ishara replied. "If they hadn't brought you back, the whole town might have died."

"They still might," I said.

"Perhaps, but with you they have a chance."

"That they do. And I mean to give them the best chance I can."

With that, I headed back into the desert. For weeks and weeks I'd been planning on leaving the desert behind me; now after less than a day, I was returning to the dunes.

After an hour, I left the road, circled a dune, and fell into my bedroll. I pleaded with Aunt Moon to guard my sleeping mind from nightmares. Even with my exhaustion, sleep did not come easily. Memories of my people crawled up from the depths of my mind, begging me not to leave them to the merciless desert heat.

*   *   *

I woke when All Father Sun's early morning light crept over the tip of a dune. Habit brought me instantly awake, scanning my surroundings. When I saw all was clear, I laid my prayer mat on the sand and knelt to the east, thanking the gods for granting one more day of life and supplicating them to send a cure for the town.

"Why did you leave?" Ishara asked, as I breakfasted on bread, goat cheese, and figs.

"One of the minstrels that came to Bhaklah convinced me that I would find a happier life as a wanderer. He didn't mean to. I believed that his stories about wandering heroes were true, and I wanted to be like them."

"You should have come back a year earlier," Ishara said. "She waited for you as long as she could, but Father finally arranged a marriage."

"All things happen as the gods will." I thought I'd kept my voice even, speaking as any man should when accepting the will of the gods, but it felt as if a stone had formed in the pit of my stomach.

As we traveled, I told her stories of my life after I'd left Bhalkah, that I'd been a thief and that I'd come home to seek some semblance of redemption. Ishara told me of things that had happened in the town. We stopped for a few moments at every marker stone to give thanks. Marker stones were one of the few remnants of the Empire of the Sun and Earth. Those enchanted stones kept the roads clear no matter how much sand the wind blew across them.

When the sky darkened, we stopped for the evening. I'd considered continuing longer into the night, but it was a new moon and the desert sands could be treacherous enough on nights when Aunt Moon blessed her luck upon the sands. Traveling without her smile was suicidal at best. I found a place a short way from the road where three date trees grew amongst some desert shrubs. I prayed before setting up my bedroll, collecting wood from dying shrubs, and using that wood to make a small fire. Then I brought a small kettle out of my satchel and filled it from my water skin.

As I rocked back and forth on my feet, waiting for the water to boil for tea, a voice called out from the darkness, "Hello, the fire." The voice spoke in the trade language of the Lands of Endless Summer, but the accent was strange.

My hand was at a dagger as I spun around, peering into the darkness. A human-shaped shadow stood at the edge of the firelight.

"Name yourself and state your intentions," I said.

"My name is Rief van Aldemeer," the voice said. "I am a minstrel from Heidenmarch across the Northern Sea. I saw your fire and thought I might share it for a story or a song. It would be a great honor to be your guest."

"Step into the light," I said.

The silhouette came closer and I took in the sight of this stranger. Rief possessed all the telling signs of a minstrel from across the seas. He wore plain, yet strange, clothes in brown and green which contrasted with his black and white striped cloak: black for Grandfather Shadow, god of Secrets and Knowledge, white for Aunt Moon, goddess of dreams and luck. A leather harp case hung off one shoulder and a bedroll off the other. His eyes possessed the roguish twinkle that most traveling performers seemed to develop. He had dark hair and a mustache. His skin showed no wrinkles. He looked between five or ten years older than my nineteen summers.

Could this be the minstrel the kitten had mentioned? Could he have had a hand in the curse? Rief had requested to be a guest, and since Rief van Aldemeer had not made himself unworthy, I could not honorably refuse. Normally I might have refused anyway, as honor did not mean as much to me as it did to other men, but he was also a minstrel, and it is bad luck to deny a minstrel your fire — I felt I was going to need all the help I could get.

"I am Jaludin. Be welcome at my fire."

I touched my heart with both hands and gestured outward with both palms to the sky. Rief returned the gesture. Few Northerners cared to adopt the customs of the People of Endless Summer. To further test this outlander, I offered both hands. Rief grasped my wrists. We each squeezed with tight grips. After we released each other, Rief went to the other side of the fire, gently lowered his harp case to the ground, unslung a back satchel I hadn't seen, dropped it next to the harp, and then crouched by the fire. Rief warmed his hands while I finished the tea.

"What brings you to travel after sunset?" I asked, handing a small cup to Rief.

"There is a town not much further to the south," Rief replied. "I was hoping to perhaps arrive there before witches' hour."

"You will not want to go there. The whole town is cursed."

"Really?" The minstrel's eyes glimmered in the firelight. "What kind of curse?"

"Do you take me for a wizard or a priest? I know nothing of the workings of magic. I only know that the people of my home are under some strange enchantment. I'm on my way to the nearest wizard to do something about it."

"Perhaps the wizard placed this magic in the first place?" Rief suggested.

"If he is responsible, I'll get him to set it right."

"You think it will be that easy?"

"I know it won't be easy, but I've faced more difficult tasks."

"I wish I'd had your confidence when I was your age. Oh, well. I'll not be having any regrets. I promised you a song, didn't I?" Rief took a harp from a tooled leather case and began drawing notes from it. "I'll sing for you about another lad who had dealings with a wizard."

I hardly listened to the song. In my travels I'd had many people try to warn me in many different ways: stories, proverbs, and yes, songs. I hadn't heard this particular song before, but I had heard its like again and again. The song told the tale of a young man who thought too much of himself and began trying to manipulate a circle of wizards. I listened with only half an ear. I wasn't trying to be rude; I'd just heard at least half a dozen like it. The minstrel's song taught me nothing new.

In reply, I sang:

"Never trust your senses to what instinct will unfold,
And luck is much more valuable than a sultan's hoard of gold.
Keep one hand on your weapon's hilt, the other hand on your purse.
Live your life one day at a time and laugh in the face of a curse."

"You've traveled far in your life," Rief said. "There is another man rumored to wander the sands who lives by those words, the Ghost Between the Shadows. It is said that he is a thief so blessed by the gods that it would be easier to catch and hold the wind."

I forced my face to appear bored. "You of all people should know the truth behind stories. He's likely as much a myth as the Queen of Stories."

Rief produced a flask from somewhere in his baggage. "Oh, but I have met her." He took a drink, coughed, and continued. "She is quite the seductress, but her stories were no match for my songs."

The minstrel offered me the flask, and I politely declined with a raised hand. Only the gods knew what foul northern concoction that flask held. Rief shrugged and continued drinking. For a long while, only the crickets, the wind across the sand, and the snapping of the fire broke the silence of the night.

At last Rief spoke. "I should just follow you." His words were slurred just a bit.

"What?" I asked.

"Even if you aren't the Ghost Between the Shadows, I could gain a lifetime of songs from you. Provided you don't get yourself, or me, killed in the process."

"I hate to disappoint you, friend," I said, "but I'm unlikely to be much of an inspiration. I am not the Ghost. Besides, once I deal with this wizard, my travels will be over."

"Are you the Ghost Between the Shadows?" Ishara asked from inside my blanket. "That sounds like a name you'd make up."

I sent a bit of sand flying at her with a flick of my finger.

"You may say that now, but the road will call to you again," Rief said. "You may be content for a few months, maybe even a few years, but eventually you'll journey once again. Traveling is in your blood."

"Perhaps I'm tired of wandering," I said. "I plan to find a wife and raise a family."

"You could have had one now if you'd come to this realization a few years ago," Ishara said.

I flicked sand at her again, hoping Rief would take it as a habitual gesture.

"I suppose it's possible," Rief said, "but I can see it in your eyes. You will never be happy unless you're standing at a stretch of road leading away from you in at least two directions." He took another drink. "And I'll tell you, Jaludin, the longer you ignore that call, the harder it will be to resist."

"It's late." I said flatly. I was done listening to this man's drunken ramblings. Did all Northmen get drunk so quickly? "May Uncle Night ignore you, Mother Earth protect you, and All Father Sun shine his blessing on you when you wake."

With that, I wrapped my blanket around me and lay down with my back to Rief. Instead of closing my eyes, I stared into the distance. I counted stars to occupy my mind. Soon, my patience was rewarded when I heard the minstrel begin to snore. Once Rief's snoring settled into a steady rhythm, I counted a hundred heartbeats before leaving my bedroll.

Rief lay on his back, wrapped in the cloak declaring his profession. His head lay on his satchel, tilted up toward the sky, and his mouth hung open. A small stream of spittle rolled out and down his cheek. His eyes shifted from side to side inside his eyelids, the sign that he was in a deep sleep. Rief's choice of pillow ended my thoughts of going through the Northman's pack. However, the bedroll lay next to his side, tied and rolled. I'd known men who thought themselves to be clever to hide valuables inside seemingly innocuous places like bedrolls. However, it raised suspicion in even more clever men when the bedroll remained tied while the bedroll's owner slept in his cloak.

The bedroll was tied together with a series of intricate knots. I smiled at Rief's cunning. Perhaps he was almost as clever as he thought himself. Almost. If anyone untied those knots, Rief would know. Fortunately, I had a way to bypass such a simple, yet clever, deterrent. I waved the ring on my left hand over the knot, and it unraveled. I opened the bedroll just enough to see the hilt of a sword. A red gem set into the pommel gleamed in the fading firelight. Pulling my pendant from beneath my shirt, I passed it over the sword. The pendant glowed bright yellow. This weapon possessed a strong enchantment of All Father Sun.

So, Rief van Aldemeer was more than what he seemed. But how could a man like this come to possess an enchanted sword? It might have been a gift, but I doubted it. The sword was too fine a prize to be wasted on the buffoon that slept before me. Perhaps Rief had stolen it. Well, it was a mystery I was unlikely to unravel. The minstrel and I would part ways in the morning.

I rewrapped the bedroll and then waved my ring over the leather thong that had bound it. Like a snake, the thong slithered together, binding itself in the same knots as before. Clever enough to stop most people, but not clever enough for the Ghost Between the Shadows.

As I crept back to my blanket, part of me wanted to flee into the night, but that would arouse suspicion when Rief woke. If the minstrel –

if he really was a minstrel – owned one enchanted item, he might own more. I didn't want to gamble on Rief not being able to find me. I considered staying awake, but that would also be a poor choice. I'd need to be as rested as possible once I reached the wizard's tower.

"Ishara," I whispered.

"Yes?" she asked from beside my satchel.

"I need you to watch over me through the night. If the Northman wakes, bite my ear."

"When will I sleep?"

"Tomorrow. You can sleep while I carry you."

"Very well. You sleep. I'll watch."

* * *

I woke with a start. For a moment I thought a wild creature was attacking the camp. When I realized it was only Rief snoring, I relaxed. Father Sun was just showing himself over the eastern horizon.

"Why is it that all minstrels feel the need to snore at the top of their lungs?" I asked to no one in particular.

"Maybe it's part of some northern mystery," Ishara replied.

"It could be one of those things civilized folk will never understand." I laughed.

Ishara and I broke our fast with bread and cheese from my satchel and dates from the trees. I tore pieces of each into what I thought were mouse-sized portions. The minstrel was still snoring when we started north along the road.

"Jaludin," Ishara said. "Are you—?"

"Yes." I didn't bother waiting for her to finish the question. "I am one of the men who has been called the Ghost Between the Shadows."

"How many others are there?"

"There were two."

"Were?"

"They are dead now. I don't want to talk about it anymore."

"But how can you… The stories we've heard…"

"Sometimes stories lie. Let's leave it at that."

We journeyed in silence after that.

Sometime later, a faint noise grew from back the way we had come. Someone was shouting my name. A moment later, Rief came into view on the road as it wound between and over the dunes. I crouched by the side of the road, waiting. Rief ran as if Old Uncle Night himself were dogging his heels.

Rief finally caught up. From the wheezing and the color of Rief's face, it appeared that such physical exertion was not a friend to the minstrel. It seemed a small miracle that he did not collapse.

"What do you want?" I asked.

Rief managed a few words in between gasps. "Want... to... follow." After a few more puffs he continued. "Write... your... adventures."

"I told you," I said. "I'm done traveling. All I'm going to do now is set things right and then return home."

"Can... follow... this... time."

I sighed. So much for parting ways.

"I suppose." It seemed faster to agree than to stand there arguing the point. "But the moment I think you're becoming a danger, either to you or myself, I leave you behind. Agreed?"

Rief's lips curved upward in an impish grin as his head bobbed up and down. I was going to regret this, I felt it deep in my bones, but the bargain had been made.

"So what is your plan?" Rief asked.

"I don't have one yet," I replied. "Be quiet so I can think."

We journeyed onward. I thanked whichever god or goddess made Rief actually remain silent. It likely took the power of several gods to hold the minstrel's tongue still.

As All Father Sun neared the end of his daily journey, the tower appeared on the horizon. The structure looked as though it was an hour's walk from the road, which meant an exhausting trek over the sand.

"Let's go." I stepped off the cobbles and onto the sand.

"I think I'd just get in the way." Rief's eyes never left the tower.

I bit the inside of my cheek to keep from smiling. "So be it."

Were all minstrels like this? Always bragging about where they had been and all they had done, but in truth nothing more than cowards? I had heard of the northern idea of the warrior poet, but after all the minstrels I'd met, I suspected that myth was created to make the northern minstrels seem greater than they were.

I shrugged to myself and marched across the dunes. By the time I reached the base of the tower, my legs burned from the effort of walking across the loose sand.

I looked up at the tower and chewed my lip. I'd only dared to steal from a wizard once before, and that had inspired my return to Bhaklah. The ghost of Sahlbak's voice whispered in my ear, "Coward. We could have been rich beyond a sultan's imagination if you'd saved me. We only had one more door to go."

I shook my head. Sahlbak had never been one to realize his own limitations.

"What is it?" Ishara asked

"Just thinking. More thieves get caught because they don't take the time to think their robberies through."

"And what do you think right now?"

"Mostly, I'm wondering why wizards always seem to live in towers."

I slid my satchel to the ground, then I undressed down to my pants and sleeveless small shirt. I put my clothes in the satchel and began digging in the sand with my hands.

"What are you doing?" Ishara asked.

"Taking steps to ensure that this will still be here if I come out again." If Ishara noticed my suspicions that I might not be exiting the tower, she said nothing about it.

Before long, I'd buried the satchel under a thin layer of sand. That last task completed, I crouched on the balls of my feet, peering up at the tower. High up, higher than any of the houses back in Bahklah, were the tower's only windows.

"The door to the tower is just to the left of us," Ishara said.

"I'm not going to use the door," I said.

"How will you get in?"

"Through one of those windows." I gestured with my chin.

"But…"

I scooped Ishara onto my shoulder and began to scale the tower. The enchanted bracelets and anklets allowed me to scale the wall; however, I had to rely on my own strength and stamina to make that journey. My hands, feet, arms, and legs all strained to carry me higher and higher. With every inch I prayed that the wizard, like most people, had not thought to place any protection on the outside of his home.

Finally, I stopped next to a window. Glancing upward, I saw only one window higher than this one.

"What is this room?" I whispered.

"I don't know."

"You said you'd been here."

"Just because I was here doesn't mean Najib Faq'hara let me wander anywhere I wished."

My muscles ached and cried out for rest. Still, years of habit and caution quelled the temptation to hurry into the room beyond. I used my pendant to check for magic around the window. Confident there were no magical traps, I looked for more mundane deterrents and saw only a simple latch on the inside. I waved the ring on my left hand over the window where the latch met the frame. Clenching my teeth and holding my breath, I slid into the room. Crouching, tensed to spring, I waited. And waited. Crouching beneath the window sill, I waited as my eyes adjusted to the darkness that shrouded the room. Over the span of one hundred heartbeats, I did nothing but be prepared to move. When no-thing had happened by the time I reached the hundred and first heartbeat, I forced myself to breathe again.

Even after my eyes adjusted, only the faintest bit of moonlight came through the window and revealed the vague outline of dark shapes through the room. I couldn't see a door, but did see a line of flickering light where the opposite wall should meet the floor.

"Can your mouse eyes see anything?" I whispered.

"Yes," Ishara replied. "It's a small room, roughly five by ten paces. The wall to your right has a bookcase. To the left are a cot and a small table. There's a lamp on the table and a chest at the foot of the cot. The door is right across from us."

"What do you think is on the other side of the door?"

"Either a hallway or the wizard's main chamber."

I crept toward the bed and the table. "Where's the lamp?"

"Step half a pace to the left. Good. Now, lower your hand so it's level with your birth scar. Reach out another hand's length."

My fingers brushed against something cold and metal. Picking it up by the handle, something sloshed inside. I switched the lamp to my right hand and went to the door.

"Why?" Ishara asked.

"I don't want to leave a weapon behind."

"A weapon?"

I ignored the question and knelt down where the bottom of the door met the floor. Placing my cheek to the cool stone, I looked through the slim crack to see a short hallway lead to another door on the far side. Clear and empty. I don't know why, but that made me more nervous than if I'd seen something guarding the hall. I took in a deep breath, let it out slowly, and then stood and opened the door.

My feet barely made the whisper of a sound as I padded down the hall. I paused once to light the lamp.

"Why—?" Ishara started, but I silenced her with a sharp, "Hsst." The sound came out only slightly louder than my footsteps.

At the second door, I hesitated just for a moment, took a breath, and slowly opened the door.

The large room beyond held two huge tables and two smaller ones. Many jars, vials, and bottles holding a variety of powders, liquids, and parts of animals – some of which I couldn't identify and wasn't sure I wanted to – were scattered about all three tables. Strange symbols, from what might have been half a dozen different languages covered the walls, floor, and ceiling. A man lounged on a huge bed of pillows on the far side of the room. He was huge. His skin hung off his face in fat, meaty rolls. Dark pouches hung beneath his eyes, which were shot through with red. He wore robes almost entirely of black and gray, though there were trimmings of white at the sleeves and hem. From the symbols and his choice of colors, the wizard practiced the magic of Grandfather Shadow, Old Uncle Night, and just a bit of Aunt Moon. The wizard reached out with a thick hand, easily twice the size of mine, snatched a pastry from a floating platter full of delicacies, and popped it into his mouth.

"Now you can see why I wouldn't let him into my bed," Ishara whispered.

"Welcome, Jaludin," the wizard said, as he chewed. "Or should I call you, the Ghost Between the Shadows. I am Najib Faq'hara, Knower of Secrets, Proclaimer of Sultans' Fortunes, and master of all the divine sciences."

"How do you know my name?"

"I study the teachings of Grandfather Shadow, god of Knowledge and Secrets. The world has no secrets that I cannot learn with but a minor ritual." Najib chuckled. The rolls of his cheeks and chin wobbled. The laugh turned into a gagging cough. After the fit died down and he could breathe again, the wizard continued. "I know why you are here. You desire to save your village from the curse. It is only logical for you to seek me out."

"Well, that saves me the trouble of explaining myself." I shifted from foot to foot. Of all the scenarios that had played out in my mind, not one had come even close to this bit of banter. "Will you remove the enchantment?"

Najib smiled. The expression seemed so foreign on that bloated face. "Stupid whelp. I placed the curse myself."

"Why?"

"For two reasons. First, I needed a test for a new spell. I wished to divorce myself from the need to sleep in order to devote more time to my studies. I placed all the sleep that I will ever need on the people of your home. Second, I knew that it would draw you here. You are one of those rare individuals whom all the gods smile upon. I wish to utilize this blessing for my own ends. Do you think it is a coincidence that you have accomplished many of the things you have, despite being lazy, stubborn, and of mediocre intelligence?"

"Grandfather Shadow must hold both you and me in high regard to reveal these secrets."

"Oh, he is not the only source that reveals information about you."

A door on the other side of the room opened, and Sahlbak entered. He wore fine clothes of velvet and silk. His fingers, ears, and neck were adorned with the finest jewels.

"Greetings, my friend," Sahlbak said. "I told you he would come home if he thought I died."

I wanted to say something, perhaps scream or maybe throw out a clever quip to fill the surprised silence, but I couldn't find the breath to utter even a whimper.

"Right you were," Najib said. "And you have earned every reward I promised you.

"Don't look so shocked and wounded boy. He's not the only one who betrayed you. Ishara told me about you and the bond you shared with her sister. I used that weakness to draw you home, and I wanted to ensure that you would seek me out."

I almost asked how Najib Faq'hara's magic penetrated the protective ring, but I resisted. I should never have expected the ring to protect me against every kind of magic, and just because the ring hadn't protected me from one thing the wizard had done, that didn't mean it wouldn't protect me from others. No need to give him more information than he already possessed.

"Well, you have me," I said. "There must be all sorts of things you want me to do for you."

The wizard nodded and rolls of fat rippled on his chin.

"If I agree, will you remove the spell?"

"No."

"You said you would!" Ishara screeched. "You said if I helped you bring Jaludin here, you'd change me back and release the town."

"I lied," Najib Faq'hara said. "I find my life far more productive without the need to sleep."

"So be it." I slid a throwing knife out from the small of my back.

The wizard began chanting. I tossed the lamp so that it sailed through the air toward him. The flame sputtered but did not go out. Just before hitting the wizard, the lamp stopped and bobbed in the air as if floating on water. I couldn't stop the smile from creeping across my face. I had seen this sort of enchantment before, and had anticipated it. This was only a distraction. My knife flew and struck Sahlbak in the chest. He coughed blood and dropped to his knees. His eyes widened as he took in the sight of the thin hilt sticking out from between two ribs

Drawing two more throwing knives, I dove to the side. Ishara flew off my shoulder.

A spout of flame erupted where I had just stood. I threw both knives as I rolled behind a table. One blade hit Sahlbak in the throat. The other struck the lamp with a sharp *clang*. Though the lamp remained in place, it spun, spraying flaming oil on the wizard. The wizard shrieked.

I drew two more knives and stood, intent on ending this. Sahlbak had pulled the knife from his throat and was trying to staunch the blood. His eyes seemed to look at everything and nothing at the same time.

The wizard's skin was now a deep shade of scarlet, but he seemed no worse off from the burns. He held a wand of black wood encrusted with red gems, likely rubies. The tip of the wand flashed.

A shower of fire sprayed across the room. My ring might protect me from the magic, but it wouldn't help me if my clothes caught fire.

Sliding across the floor, I made it to a table and tipped it over. That would give me cover and a moment to collect myself. Glass shattered on the other side as jars and beakers hit the floor. Something exploded on the other side of the table, pushing it a few inches toward me. The last thing I wanted was to get caught in another explosion, so I leapt from my hiding place. A moment later, the table burst into flames.

I threw the two knives roughly in the direction of the wizard. They were a distraction. The moment the weapons left my hands, I raced toward the door I'd entered through. Halfway to reaching it, something struck my head, knocking me sideways. Stars danced across my vision, and I tried to roll with the fall. The effort did little to soften my collision with the floor. Only instinct made me scramble for the shelter of a table as I rolled.

"Is it too late to change my mind?" I called over the crackling fires.

Pushing the pain aside, I drew my last two throwing knives. Once these were gone, I'd be reduced to fighting knives, and getting close enough to the wizard to use them seemed somewhat problematic.

Ishara skittered across the floor toward me.

"I'm sorry, Jaludin," she squealed. "I didn't know how evil he really was."

I grunted something and waved her to silence. I didn't need her distracting me right now. I had also already forgiven her. There were people that had taken advantage of my innocence when I'd first left Bhaklah, and it seems they still were. It amazed me that even after everything I'd been through and done, people could still play upon my naïveté, but I wasn't the only one to suffer that humiliation. I imagine Ishara still has trouble coming to terms with putting me in that situation.

"Do you honestly think I could believe anything the Ghost Between the Shadows would tell me?" the wizard asked. "The man who leaves a friend to die? Who threatens to kill another man so he can possess his wife? Such a blackened soul can be put to better use once its body is dead." The wizard began chanting in that strange tongue again.

Then he went silent. I waited for three slow breaths. I didn't hear anything, and my skin didn't peel off my body. I leapt up, ready to throw. The air between us shimmered like a heat mirage. I threw a knife, aiming for the wizard's throat. A Daemyn with a bat-like head, ram's horns, and leathery wings appeared between us. My knife struck the massive chest. Its fiery eyes glanced first at the hilt protruding from its chest, and then at me.

And I thought this couldn't get any worse.

The creature roared as I landed. The sound of it grated on my back teeth. I didn't waste any time before fleeing back the way I'd come.

Three steps brought me to the door leading to the hallway. I pushed through the door, slammed it shut, and raced toward the window.

An explosion rang out behind me. Splinters of wood sailed past me and pelted my back. I reached the second door, slammed it shut, and ran to the window. I reached it without hearing the door open. I calculated a moment, hoisted myself outside the tower, and scrambled above the window. Thanking the gods for my anklets. I drew my enchanted fighting daggers.

Back in the tower, the door crashed open. A moment later, the Daemyn's head appeared out of the window. Its head twisted from side to side, searching. When the creature stretched out enough to expose its entire torso, I dropped onto its back, straddling its neck and shoulders like a horse.

Air whistled in my ears and whipped my hair as the ground rose toward us. Not for the first time, I questioned my sanity as I held my knives poised to strike. The Daemyn's wings billowed outward, and its snarls replaced the whistling air. As our descent slowed, the creature sank its teeth into my thigh. Its fangs felt like shards of ice, but its spittle scalded like boiling water.

I bit back most of a scream as I slashed both wings with my knives. Gray fire burned along those long gashes. Hissing and growling, the Daemyn released its hold on my leg.

The monster beat its wings, but the harder it worked to stay aloft, the more it shred its wings, speeding our decent. When we neared roughly five paces from the ground, I kicked my feet up and rolled off the Daemyn's back.

The sand cushioned my fall a little, and as I rolled, some sand ground into my leg wound. Gritting my teeth against the pain, I got to my feet. The Daemyn had come down on all fours and scurried to face me, every inch of the creature moved with the grace and speed of a predator. Its orange eyes burned like dying embers.

My breath came in short gasps that had nothing to do with my pain. How had I ever imagined I could face this creature? The only thing I could hope was that the gods gave me the courage to die well.

The Daemyn leapt. I dodged to the side. The Daemyn flew by me, and quicker than I could have imagined, it twisted, landing to face me, poised to leap again. The air between the creature and me shimmered with another heat mirage. Rief appeared between us. The minstrel held the enchanted sword out before him. The blade pulsed with a yellow light.

Rief darted forward and slashed the Daemyn's arm. Fire erupted along the gash. The Daemyn gripped the wound with its other hand and bounded backward.

"The wizard wants the whelp's soul, so it is safe," the Daemyn snarled. "But I'm free to feast on yours, once I water the sands with your blood."

"I thought you might need some help," Rief said, without taking his eyes from the Daemyn. "I wish you had heeded my warnings, but no changing it now."

Rief circled to the right. Not being one to question a blessing from the gods, I moved to the left.

"This could get dangerous, Ishara," I muttered under my breath. "You might want to get off and hide somewhere."

Her tiny weight left the place where she grasped the collar of my shirt.

With Ishara away, I slid a finger into the secret pocket in my sleeve. When the Daemyn glanced away from me to look at Rief, I tapped the stone hidden there seven times, activating the enchantment blessed upon it by a priest of Grandfather Shadow. An illusionary image of me appeared a short way to my left. I prayed that if the Daemyn pounced on the image, it wouldn't hit me with one of its wings before I got a chance to strike.

When the Daemyn looked back toward me, I rushed forward. The Daemyn sprang and flew right through the illusion. Its arms and face struck the sand. I drove one of my knives into the Daemyn's back.

With an ear-piercing scream, the Daemyn whirled around. I let go of my knife as the fiend slashed a clawed hand through my illusionary double. Fire burned around the blade. As the creature spun, clawing at my knife, trying to reach it to pull the weapon free, Rief lunged through the illusion. The minstrel's sword pierced the Daemyn's side. A shower of sparks and tiny lightning bolts sprayed from the wound. As the Daemyn howled in pain, I flipped my knife in my hand, leapt at the creature, and slammed the knife into its exposed neck all the way to the hilt. Again, fire erupted from the wound, scorching my hand. I pulled back, this time pulling the knife free. I wasn't about to leave myself completely defenseless. The Daemyn dropped to the sand, thrashing about, trying to reach the knife I'd left in its back. Together, Rief and I hacked and stabbed at the foul thing. When it stopped moving altogether, I took my other knife back.

With the fighting over, my leg throbbed and my throat burned from heavy breathing. Sometimes the cold air of the desert night burns the chest more than the heat of the day. *Please, gods, let me have just a sip of water.*

"My thanks," I said between breaths. "You must tell me the story of how you came by that sword and why I'm so lucky to have met you."

"Evil men are not the only ones interested in those blessed by the gods," Rief replied. "Now, shall we make a hasty retreat?"

"I cannot," I said. "This wizard placed the curse on my home. I must force him to remove it."

"He said the town has been cursed with all the sleep he'll ever need," Ishara called from the ground. "If you kill him, the curse should end."

"Should?" I asked.

"Should what?" Rief said.

"It's the only chance," Ishara replied. "I don't think you'll convince him. His heart and pity seem to be gone."

"Very well." I looked to Rief. "I have to kill the wizard."

"It is easier to look down some roads than to travel them," Rief said.

"I have no—" I felt some force pulling at my clothes. My illusionary double vanished.

Najib Faq'hara's cackling laughter echoed across the dunes. "I know all about the stone you have hidden in your sleeve and the ring that protects you from my magic. Fortunately, it doesn't protect your clothing, making it far too easy to keep you under control. You move quickly, and I underestimated you in the tower."

I rotated in the air and something pulled my knives from my hands. An archway had opened in the tower. Najib Faq'hara still lounged on his bed, which floated several feet off the ground. I scanned the ground. I needed to know where my knives were if I ever broke free of the wizard's power. Instead of my knives, I saw Ishara scurrying across the sands. Thank the gods for my nimble fingers. I worked the protective ring free from my finger. *Please let Ishara be clever enough to use it.*

Rief charged. Najib chanted, and fire erupted from his fingertips and flew toward the Northman. Rief's sword spun in a wide arch. The fire dissipated. With the wizard's attention focused on Rief, I flicked the ring toward Ishara.

"Interesting blade," Najib said. "I look forward to studying it."

With one hand, the wizard continued to send fire searing toward Rief, with a flick of the other, I spun through the air toward the tower.

The pressure on my clothes disappeared, so I twisted as best I could so that when I hit the tower, I wouldn't crush my skull. I managed to absorb most of the impact with my left shoulder, but it still felt like I'd been crushed under some massive weight. The sensation lasted a moment, and then I slid to the ground in a crumpled heap. After a few short breaths to steady myself, I raised my head. Najib flung a continuous stream of fire at Rief. The minstrel's sword spun in dizzying arcs, forming a barrier between him and the wizard's magic.

While Rief made slow progress toward the wizard, I inched toward the throwing knife I'd dropped when I'd climbed out the window. I reached the knife just as Rief approached striking distance. Suddenly, the sand beneath Rief's feet gave way. The Northman sank up to his shoulders, making it impossible for him to swing his sword in defense of the wizard's spells. Aiming quickly, I threw the knife.

The blade sailed through the air. Najib Faq'hara lifted a hand and the knife stopped inches from his neck. A flash of light from behind the wizard blinded me for a moment. When I looked back, he was turning. Ishara stood there in all her naked beauty with one of my enchanted fighting knives in her hand. She thrust the blade into Najib Faq'hara's chest. The wizard pitched off his floating bed and fell face-first to the sand.

With a groan, I picked myself up from the sand and limped over toward the wizard. I turned the wizard over with my foot. My enemy's breath came in gurgling gasps as blood pooled in his mouth, his eyes pleaded for something.

"Please, boy." Blood burbled as the Najib spoke. "Do it. I brought you here to kill me."

I blinked, looking first to Rief, then up to the stars.

I knelt down next to the wizard. "Is there any way you can come back from the darkness that has surrounded your soul?"

"No. I dealt poorly with a Daemyn. This life belongs to him. If you don't kill me, the Daemyn who owns my soul will force me to do worse things than what I did to your town. Please, do what I have been forbidden to do myself."

"If you wanted me to kill you, why fight me?" I asked.

"I must, as part of my bargain."

Again, I looked into the stars. My chest felt empty and my face tightened. I'd been manipulated every step of this journey, and I hated myself for that. I understood that I could never have known, but that didn't make the realization that I'd been played for a fool any easier. Now, the last thing I wanted to do was give this Najib Faq'hara what he wanted, but there was no denying the truth of his words. I pulled the dagger out of the wizard's chest, and with a quick slash, I cut his throat.

"Are you alright?" Ishara asked.

"No."

My body ached. My leg hurt so much that standing was becoming a challenge. I just wanted to crawl somewhere far away from anything and anyone I'd ever known and sleep. Instead, I knelt down and started digging Rief out of the sand.

Rief opened his mouth.

"One word and I leave you here."

Rief closed his mouth.

*   *   *

Three days later, I sat with Mother and Father drinking tea after the morning prayer. The tea came from the enchanted teapot I had brought for Mother.

Ishara, Rief, and I had returned to Bhaklah to find the curse had ended. Over the course of those days, the people of Bhaklah had burned and mourned their dead and made progress on returning to their normal lives. Ishara, however, had remained a mouse any time she wasn't wearing my ring. Rief and I wondered if the town had returned to normal, why hadn't the enchantment on Ishara ended with Najib Faq'hara's death. Ishara explained that the wizard had taken the people's waking hours, and when he died, those hours returned to their original owners. Najib hadn't taken anything from Ishara, he had transformed her. In order to return her to human form, we needed to find someone capable of transforming her back.

"Are you absolutely sure you won't stay?" Father asked, not for the first time. "Your mother has missed you so much."

I sighed. It was always about Mother. Why couldn't he admit that he was afraid that this would be the last time he saw me?

"I can't," I replied. "It wouldn't be fair to Ishara. Besides, I'm not ready to see Safia walking next to her husband every day."

"But there are other young ladies in Bhaklah who would make a fine wife," Mother said, pouring him more tea. "Any one of them would be honored to have you now."

I swallowed the tea in one gulp. Every moment I stayed made it harder for them to see me go. I moved toward the door where my satchel waited. Every moment I stayed made it harder for me to say goodbye.

"I'll return as soon as we find a cure for Ishara. I promise."

"Will you stay then?" Mother asked.

"Perhaps, but I don't know for sure." I hoisted the satchel onto my shoulders.

Father came to the door. He opened his arms, with palms raised to the sky. I returned the gesture, and we gripped forearms.

"I'm proud of you, Jaludin," Father said. "My son left little more than a mischievous boy, but returned a man of honor. Carry your head high and keep your footsteps light."

"I will, Father."

We embraced, and I left.

As I made my way through the streets of Bhaklah, people greeted me, wishing me well on my journey. Thanks to Rief, everyone knew about my "adventure," due to the song the minstrel had composed about the ordeal, with no small amount of embellishment. The Northman must have sung the piece at least a dozen times a day. Now the whole town regaled me as a returned hero. The only small blessing is that he'd not named me as the Ghost Between the Shadows.

Rief and Ishara were waiting by the town well, Ishara now fully clothed. The two of them had developed a fast friendship on the way back to the town. Ishara had decided to remain a mouse for that journey because we could not find clothes to fit her. I had given Rief my ear clip and let the pair of them walk well ahead of me. I was in no mood for conversation and had quickly grown weary of translating for them.

On seeing me, Rief and Ishara gathered their packs and bedrolls and fell into step beside me.

"Gods and goddesses, Jaludin," Rief said. "If we have a few more adventures like that, I'll be the richest minstrel in all the Lands of Endless Summer."

"I'm hoping we don't have any more adventures like that one," Ishara said.

"I agree," I said, "with Ishara."

Rief and Ishara continued speaking, but I didn't hear their words. Safia walked toward us from the other direction. Her dark eyes met mine for a moment, and my heart pounded in my chest. I wanted to turn away, to walk down another street, but my feet disagreed and carried me toward her.

"Jaludin."

"Safia."

Even though All Father Sun was still low in the east and had not chased away the coolness of the night, sweat ran in streams down my back. Had the day grown so warm so fast?

Safia took a step closer. She did not meet my eyes now.

"Jaludin," she said in a voice barely above a whisper, "I—"

"Stop!" My voice almost came out as a growl. "I've seen you looking at me when your husband isn't watching. There are some things that should not be spoken under the light of the Sun. I know, and you know. Let Grandfather Shadow be the only other who knows this as well. Congratulations on your marriage."

Her head snapped up. "Well, doesn't All Father Sun just rise and set with you?" Her voice came out in a hiss between her clenched teeth. "Both Ashamel and I heard what you said about you letting him die. The rest of the town may think you are a god made flesh, but Uncle Night can take you for all I care. I was lucky to get a good man like Ashamel."

She stomped off down the street. I'd seen her several times over the last few days as she'd helped clean the town, as she collected water and walked with her husband. Apparently, I'd misjudged her sidelong glances.

"Who was that?" Rief asked as I rejoined Ishara and him.

"Nobody."

"She wasn't *nobody*," Rief said. "I can see that in your eyes."

"Rief, do you want to have to worry about having your throat slit every night when you go to sleep?" Ishara asked.

"No."

"Then leave off," she replied, "or I think you might."

Rief stood there for a moment, looking between Ishara and me. "Very well."

I gave Rief a wan smile. For someone who spent so much time talking, Rief had a talent for understanding when to remain silent. The minstrel reached out and squeezed my shoulder.

We walked in silence until we stood atop the first dune that led out to the desert. The whole world beyond glowed with All Father Sun's golden light reflecting off the dunes. I glanced back. When I'd left the first time, five years ago, I never wanted to see Bhaklah again — so much that I hadn't looked back then. Now I could hardly wait to return.

"Are you sure you still want to leave?" Ishara asked. "Rief and I could do this by ourselves."

"No. If I stayed now, it would only cause me heartache and grief. Besides, someone has to keep you two out of mischief."

Ishara snorted a laugh at that.

"I thought you wanted to stop traveling." Rief said.

I couldn't help but smile. "I still have a few miles I can force out of my feet. Besides, this is my home. No matter how far I travel, it will be here, waiting."

With that, I turned toward the desert. The ancient cobblestone road that brought me here stretched out into the dunes, leading to uncertainty and the unknown. At my back, the town offered security and comfort.

I took a step on the road, then another, and our journey began.

Chaos Factor

"Chaos Factor" started as a two-page flash fiction assignment for my class, The Short-Short Story back in my time in the Creative Writing program at San Francisco State University. I needed something fast, as it was about an hour until class, and I still didn't have anything. This is one of the stories that helped me realize that writers wlock is a completely fictional condition. You can always write something. It might not be good. It might need some edits and rewrites, but hey, most writing does. I cranked the original draft of this out in fifteen to twenty minutes. Then came the rewriting and redrafting. This is not the final version of this story. I sold another version of this story under the title, "Just Another Day in the Butterfly War" to the anthology Bless Your Mechanical Heart *edited by the incomparable and just darn awesome, Jennifer Brozek. I changed some characters, added others, and changed the outcome of the story...all at Jennifer's guidance. I've gotten my copy of the anthology, and it has some amazing stories by some of the fantastic writers.*

The eighteen-year-old Laphroaig single malt scotch slid down Agent Maxwell Chaos's throat just as smoothly as Ella Fitzgerald's silky vocals slid into his ears. The combination of early Twentieth-Century Jazz and Islay single malts helped his mind wander away from the rigors and trials of the job. He leaned back in his favorite chair, an antique – almost a relic of soft leather from the early twenty-first century – with the massagers set on the lowest speed rolling up and down his back. Chaos closed his eyes and let out a contented sigh as he lay back and did his best to become one with the recliner.

In the midst of his reverie, a beep from his wrist interrupted Ella. Chaos's fingers tightened around the thistle-shaped snifter glass (the only way to properly drink single malt with the possible exception of metal pocket flask) and chewed his upper lip. He sucked in a deep breath through his nose, held it for a three seconds, and let it out slowly.

"Stop music."

Silence, then another beep.

He looked at the amber colored drink that remained in the snifter, bobbed his head from side to side, contemplating. The Cybernetic linkup on his wrist beeped again. Not wanting the single malt to go to waste, Chaos tossed it back. He allowed himself five seconds to revel in the sensation of that descending into his stomach, then he looked at his right wrist.

It flashed:

DATE: Good Friday, April 14, 1865 LOCATION: Ford's Theater.

Chaos put down the now empty snifter, pressed the red button to the left of the display screen, and went to his office. Upon entering, Chaos reached over and took a healthy swallow straight from the bottle of blended whisky. It burned his throat like swallowing charcoal briquette.

The stark blacks and grays of his office contrasted with the rest of his apartment. Like the Laphroaig, jazz, and chair the apartment's decor had been carefully selected to project an essence of calm. Soft colors, soft lighting, and softer linens took away any semblance of a harsh line, and every piece of furniture had been arranged according to the foremost Feng Shui experts. The effect was so subtle that it wasn't really noticeable until Chaos left it to come into this hateful place.

He went straight to the rectangular black locker, opened it, and started to gear up. When he'd first began with the Temporal Anomaly Patrol (or TAP for short) this ritual took nearly thirty minutes, but now, after four years, three months, one week, and two days, Chaos had re-duced that time to between seven and eight minutes. Going through this also used to make his hands shake so much that he would almost always drop a thing or two, but now it was just as rote as taking a shower. He had come to terms with the understanding that sometimes good men just had to die.

Chaos glanced at his wrist again. One of the most notorious dates in all history flashed up at him. Before he pressed the blue button that would alert headquarters that he was ready for the assignment, Chaos slipped a metal flask into the left breast pocket of his fatigues. Some-times, even the very best of men had to die.

* * *

John Wilkes Booth crept toward the presidential box. He didn't see the rift open in reality behind him as he crept toward the presidential box. His gun hand shook a little more with each step. Deep down, Booth knew he had a job – no, a duty – to do. The South would benefit in so many ways if the President, Vice President, and Secretary of State all died in the same night. However, the rational knowledge of this could do nothing to slow his heart, dry his palms, or wet his suddenly parched tongue. Had he noticed the swirling hole of pixilating colors about twenty feet back, it would have might have destroyed what little nerve he had left. Seeing a man step out of that hole wearing a Union army officer's uniform would have stunned booth to inaction.

* * *

Agent Chaos took a healthy swallow of blended whiskey, this was even worse than the swill just inside the door of his office. The liquor burned his throat like the worst kind of prostitute and settled in his stomach like a jalapeño brick. There were some guys in TAP who developed an enjoyment for their work. The bad booze was just one of the ways Chaos reinforced the unpleasantness of his work. It was the third time this week his linkup had beeped. It used to be once or twice a month, but between the escalating hostilities, high turnover rate, and agency deaths, Chaos got called for an assignment more and more often. He took another swallow of whisky – just to be safe – and waited.

*   *   *

Booth didn't see the rift open in reality behind him. Had he noticed the swirling hole of pixilating colors about twenty feet back, it would have destroyed what little resolve he still possessed. His gun hand shook a little more with each step. Deep down, Booth knew he had a job – no, a duty – to do. The South would benefit in so many ways if the President, Vice President, and Secretary of State all died in the same night. However, the rational knowledge of this could do nothing to slow his heart, dry his palms, or wet his suddenly parched tongue.

*   *   *

A door opened – not the one from the president's box. Chaos slid the flask back into his pocket. A woman came into the hall wearing a silk and velvet evening gown. She looked first at Booth, then to Chaos. Chaos met her eyes, bared his teeth, and stretched out his neck as far as he could while scrunching up his shoulders. Any normal lady (read: human lady) attending a play at Ford's Theater in 1865 would, at best, have been taken aback by such a display; at worst, she would have cried out or possibly fainted. Instead, she mirrored Chaos's expression. Booth stopped when she did this, and Chaos imagined a look of confusion contorting the assassin's features.

A moment later, the creature who wore a very convincing human disguise recovered from the instincts of its species and cried, "Booth! Behind you!" It was a common enemy tactic to set someone that could not die yet against an agent. The hope was that the agent would kill that person before they got around to doing whatever it was that he or she needed to do.

Booth spun, but Chaos was a professional. He tossed a neural inhibitor with each hand. The one from his left was set for humans. The one from his left wasn't. Two golf-ball sized silver orbs arched through the air, and each hit its mark. Booth froze in place. The woman crumpled to the floor, shimmered, and in her place lay a creature that resembled a reptilian orangutan.

*   *   *

Booth struggled to move, to raise his gun hand, to pull the trigger. He couldn't. Only his eyes seemed capable of movement, and he shifted his gaze flittered the Yankee Officer and the vile thing that lay in the hallway. Even if he could move, he didn't know which to shoot first.

"I know you're scared," the Yankee said. "I also know you've been having second thoughts. Unfortunately, humanity can't afford for you not to do this. The War of Northern Aggression may be over, but there's another war going on. It's us against them." The Yankee gestured toward the creature. "And if you don't go in there and kill Lincoln, all mankind will turn out like that. You kill Lincoln, you'll be a hero for centuries." The Yankee touched the ball attached to Booth's neck. Booth felt some of the rigidity leave his neck. "Can you do that for your species?"

Booth nodded as much as he could.

"Good."

*   *   *

Turning away from Booth, Chaos and fitted a temporal locator to the Repsapien and hit the transmit button. The alien vanished in a shower of light.

Chaos grabbed Booth under his left arm and drug the assassin toward the President's box. True, Booth had acknowledged that he would kill Lincoln, but Chaos knew that men would make almost any promise or break any agreement under stressful and frightening circumstances. And this was too important to be left to chance.

When they reached the door, Agent Chaos looked at the count-down on the cybernetic implant in his wrist. Less than three minutes. Chaos loosened the inhibitor just enough to make Booth malleable, fitted an army knife into his hand, and took his firearm. Less than two minutes. Chaos took a healthy swig of the vile scotch.

This was Chaos's least favorite part of the job. He didn't really want Lincoln to die. He was a good man, and lots of good would come to the United Sates and Earth for the next hundred and fifty years if he lived. However, if allowed to live, Lincoln and his wife would have another child, a daughter this time. In the middle of the Twenty-Second Century, a direct descendant of Lincoln would come along who would make Hitler seem like a spoiled Sunday school student.

When it was time, Chaos kicked open the door to the president's box, and shot Lincoln in the back of the head. As pandemonium ensued, Chaos removed the inhibitor from the back of Booth's neck, shoved him through the door, then slammed it shut.

Chaos's wrist beeped. The cybernetic link up flashed:

Date: Friday, November 22, 1963. Location: Dallas, Texas.

He took healthy drink from his least favorite prostitute.

Paradox loop

Two things inspired this story. First: the question all writers get, and most dread, "Where do you get your ideas?" The second, the fear that even if we get a good idea for a story, will it be any good?

The most frequent comment I get about this story is, "I think I've read that before." Once you see the other side of it, you'll see why.

Jason made his way through the lobby of the hotel hosting the World Science Fiction Convention. He'd just come from the bathroom to empty the half a dozen or so drinks he'd already had that night. Even though it was only just after 10pm, he concentrated on firmly planting each foot on the floor before taking his next step. The convention had already been embarrassing enough. About ten feet from the hotel bar, a trio of Klingon warriors, complete with authentic armor and prosthetic head ridges, argued with a pair of Jedi Knights toting lightsabers over the merits of warp drive over Hyperspace. Only their mundane membership badges disturbed the authenticity of their costumes. If Jason's weekend had been better, he might have stopped to listen. He loved eavesdropping as the geeks and nerds debated each other over theories that had no basis in the physical universe. However, tonight he just wanted to get back to the bar.

Entering the bar was like stepping through a portal between worlds. While the fans might make a quick foray into the bar, they rarely lingered. The bar was for pros, the people with pressed clothes and shined shoes: editors, agents, and writers. It could be any other business convention; the only giveaway that these people had anything to do with the fans outside who supported them was that the pros also wore World Science Fiction Convention membership badges.

Jason wove through the crowd and returned to his seat at the bar. His shot of Jack Daniels and the Captain and Coke remained right where he had left them. He'd graduated from a regular Coke chaser two shots before heading to the bathroom.

He was considering killing these two drinks and calling it quits for the evening when someone squeezed in next to him. Whoever it was jostled him, splashing a bit of Jack over his fingers. He released his grip on the shot glass and sucked the booze up before turning to the offending individual, from whom he intended to extract an apology.

That was before he saw the name tag. It was an editor from Penguin. Next to her was an editor from Del Rey, owned by Random House. They both glanced at his name tag. Recognition showed in their eyes like an epiphany at the end of a James Joyce story. Without ordering drinks, they snickered their way back to a long table filled with other editors and five big-name authors. Any given year, at least three of those names would top the best seller lists. When the editors sat down, Penguin leaned in and whispered to the rest of the table, as if sharing some bit of playground gossip. Random House nodded vigorously the whole time. The rest of the table looked over at Jason. They had the expression of the cool kids in high school watching and wondering why one of the nerds had actually showed up to the homecoming dance.

Jason turned back to his drinks. He slumped forward a few more inches. He picked up the JD and put the glass to his lips.

Joycian epiphanies? High school dances?

Jason had heard that the quality of a writer's fiction reflected the quality of his thoughts. Even though drunk, these ideas struck him both cliché and trite.

Maybe he should just go back to his hotel room. He tossed the shot back. Maybe he should pay the extra hundred bucks to change his plane ticket. The Captain and Coke joined the other drinks that mingled in the cocktail party taking place in his stomach.

"Looks like you're in the same boat I am," some guy said as he sidled next to Jason.

"What boat's that?" Jason asked.

"The pros won't take me seriously either."

"Yeah, well, that's not really my problem." Jason tossed back the Jack Daniels in one swallow.

"What's the problem?"

Jason looked back and the table of editors and writers. Two of them averted their eyes quickly. Jason took a healthy pull off his Captain and Coke.

"What the hell. It's not like it's any real secret. They," he waved at the table currently gossiping about him, "think I'm trying to rip off one of the most famous science fiction writers of all time."

"Which one?"

"Isaiah Harlison."

"Wow. That's a pretty hefty charge. Are you?"

"No! When I first started, I had never even heard of this Harlison. Now he seems to be everywhere."

"Well, I haven't heard of him either. Let me buy you another drink and you can tell me about it."

The guy waved the bartender over and ordered two drinks to replace two empty glasses in front of Jason. Jason took the opportunity to give this guy the once over. He looked familiar, but Jason couldn't quite place him. The guy might be in his early or late twenties. He had close-cropped, short, dark hair with just a hint of gray here and there. Some pretty hefty sideburns graced his chin, and might have been dignified if he had been a few years older. He stood a good half a foot shorter than Jason and might weigh in at a buck twenty with wet clothes. He wore a white turtleneck and a black suit coat.

Jason tried to place him in the drunken haze of his memory, but couldn't. He wasn't wearing a membership badge, and Jason decided he was grateful for that. Jason wanted to talk, and while some little piece of his logical mind thought that this might be someone playing a joke on him, Jason would just enjoy another human being that showed interest in his problems.

"Where should I start?" Jason asked.

"Why don't you tell me about the stories people say you stole from this writer?"

*   *   *

The ritual was always the same, because the Self-Addressed-Stamped Envelope was always the same. Jason traced his finger around the edge of envelope that had his home address scrawled across the front in his own handwriting. Once, when Jason was in college, a magazine accepted a story written by one of the other students in the creative writing department. It paid one quarter of a cent per word, but it was a sale. That SASE was thicker than any other envelope Jason had received back from a magazine. But that was years ago, before graduation, before moving back in with his parents, and before the string of going-nowhere jobs he'd trudged through while pursuing his writing career.

This envelope seemed a bit thicker, or was that his imagination? His chest couldn't seem to decide if it wanted to suffocate or hyperventilate. As always, this could be *the letter*. It wasn't like he hadn't received envelopes like this before. He had. Dozens of them. But this was in response to a story that all his friends said was really good, that this was his breakout story.

He carefully opened the envelope so as not to harm the letter inside and slid the single sheet of paper out.

Dear Mr. Klark

The three dozen or so previous letters had all begun with, "*Dear Contributor.*" They might have well begun with, "*Dear Unworthy Hack.*" Jason's mouth went dry and his breath quickened.

He took in the whole page. A personalized note had been written in at the bottom in something that resembled a cross between Sanskrit and hieroglyphics. His lungs stopped working. Even if this was a rejection, this editor's personal attention represented a new jump in the quality of his writing. He'd always heard that when editors took the time to add personal notes to rejection letters, publication couldn't be far behind. His eyes scanned the note several times as his brain translated the communiqué into something intelligible.

>   *P.S. I wonder if you truly thought we wouldn't recognize Harlison's work.*

Jason closed his eyes, shook his head, and read the letter from the beginning to make sense of that strange note.

>   *Dear Mr. Klark,*
>   *I must reject your thinly veiled plagiarysm of "'Will You Change, Clockwork?' asked the Jesterman." It is very unprofessional to claim another's work as your own. Please consider Horizon Events closed.*
>   *Editor,*
>   *Horizon Events Magazine*

"What the—?" Jason crumpled the letter.

Science fiction had been his passion ever since junior high school, and he had never heard of this Isaiah Harlison. He spent the next hour pacing around his apartment trying to conjure the title of any single Isaiah Harlison story to mind.

Sitting at his computer, he pounded I-S-A-I-A-H H-A-R-L-I-S-O-N into the search field at google.com. Hundreds of matches came up. Jason blinked at the screen. He clenched and unclenched his fists to keep from pounding his keyboard into oblivion.

"I will not fear," he said to calm himself down.

It must have been just a really weird fluke, a coincidence of astronomical proportions. In order to avoid this Twilight Zone-like situation again, Jason cross-referenced the titles of all his stories currently in circulation with the titles that came up in his Harlison search. There were no other matches. No-thing even came close.

He grabbed a beer and decided that it wasn't that big a deal. Horizon Events was a decent 'zine, but it didn't have the clout of the big three. So he'd lost a market that only paid a penny per word as its top rate. In the grand scheme, he'd still make it, and now he'd have a kick ass story to tell while he was at cons and signings once he did get published. To make himself feel even better, Jason pulled the editor's business card off his post-it board, ripped it up, and tossed it in his recycle basket.

Two weeks later, another letter came.

>   *Dear Mr. Klark,*

> *I must reject your story, "I Can't Scream Without A Physical Mouth." This is nothing more than a poor imitation of the Isaiah Harlison story which was nominated for both the Hugo and Nebula awards. Please, do not send us any further material.*
> Editor,
> *Future Speculations*

    Another Google search revealed dozens of references to Isaiah Harlison's story, "I Can't Scream Without A Physical Mouth." He went to the neighborhood library and checked out a collection of Isaiah Harlison short stories. After a reading just a few of Harlison's stories that shared a title with his own work, Jason flung Harlison's book across the room. Harlison used words to paint the picture that Jason had envisioned when he'd sat down to write those stories. Jason paced around his room, kicked the book out of his way a few times, and then got a beer. After a few sips, he calmed down and picked the book up. He'd learn from Harlison. He'd study Harlison's choices of language compared to his own, and then editors wouldn't have any choice but to accept his work.

But the rejections kept coming:

> Mr. Klark,
> *I cannot accept your story "Visions of Robots Dreaming." Although you offer some interesting twists on the classic story by Isaiah Harlison, it is still plagiarism. If you ever decide to write and submit ORIGNIAL stories, you might do well to consider a nom deplume.*
> Editor
> *Fantastic Visions Magazine*

> Jason,
> *I remember meeting you at last year's World Con. And while, I have heard about the "Isaiah Harlison conspiracy," I hoped it wasn't true. I find your involvement even more disappointing. You seemed intelligent and well spoken. I even gave you the benefit of the doubt and read your story, "Aye, Robot" despite its' title's similarity to Harlison's story. Unfortunately, that is not the only similarity between your work and Harlisn's masterpiece. If you really want to be a writer – and from our conversations at World Con, I believe that you do – I urge you to try your hand at finding your own voice, perhaps a story that comes from your own unique perspective or experience.*

Editor,
Virtual Realities Magazine

The ritual changed. The reverence for these letters was gone. He'd toss each one on his desk, grab a beer or two, take the darts out of his pen and pencil drawer, and flop down in his chair. When he saw the comparison of his writing to Harlison's, the darts flew across the room and pieced the already significantly-perforated picture of the late Isaiah Harlison, white hair, sideburns, wrinkles, and all.

> *Mr. Jason Klark,*
> *I represent the estate of Isaiah Harlison. I must request that you cease and desist all submissions plagiarizing Mr. Harlison's intellectual property. Further infringement of copy write laws will result in legal action.*
> *Sincerely,*
> *Kurt Richards*

*   *   *

And so Jason told the stranger his story. He talked about his stories and the inspiration behind each one, and how they all, months or years later, because Isaiah Harlinson stories, written with such much more clarity of voice and artist vision than Jason could ever hope to have. The guy listened all night and bought each round. They closed out the bar and moved to the hospitality suite and kept talking over coffee. They parted ways at four, and as Jason lay down in his hotel room, he realized that he never got the guy's name. The only detail Jason could remember the next day was showing the guy his driver's license.

When Jason returned home from World Con, his apartment was a mess. Not the same cluttered mess that it normally was, but a someone-has-gone-through-all-your-stuff kind of mess. After a bit of cleaning and taking a quick inventory, the only things he could find missing were hard-copies of all his stories. Jason didn't call the cops; he sat down at his desk and started writing.

> *Dear Editor,*
> *I realize that it is not normal to query a short story, but mine is a bit unusual. My story, "Paradox Loop," is about a guy who travels to the future in order to learn stories from hopeful science fiction writers. Then he returns to his own time and publishes those stories as his own. The twist is that the original writer doesn't know about this until his work comes into contact with the*

work of the guy stealing his ideas, because the future writer is stuck in a Paradox Loop.

> *Yours,*
> *Jason Klark*

Dear Mr. Klark,
I must reject your story proposal. Theme and plot wise that is exactly the same as Isaiah Harlison's final published story.

> *Editor,*
> *Heinlein's Science Fiction*

Paladin

I wrote the first version of this story in my early twenties. I can't actually recall which story I wrote the original draft of first: "Jaludin's Road," "Paladin," or "The Dragon Bone Flute." Each has changed and grown over the years, "Jaludin's Road" most of all. "Paladin" is much the same as it was way back then; however, a slightly modified version of this story wandered into the DEAD WEIGHT world. For the longest time, I didn't think I was going to do much with this one besides add it to some personal collections, because, while I love it, I think I'd have a rough time finding a home for it as it is here. Then, back when I wrote some of Boy Scout's first flashback entries in the instalment which has become DEAD WEIGHT: Seek and Destroy, I realized that I had mentioned a character who needed a back story – or maybe it's a side story...hard to tell with things of faerie nature – and "Paladin" was a perfect fit. This means I've been working on DEAD WEIGHT longer than anything besides my SPELLPUNK project. Anyway, I'm leaving this story in here, unmodified, as a bit of an example of the growth of my writing over time. To see the latest version of this tale, check out DEAD WEIGHT: Paladin. And don't worry; I've changed enough so that you'll still probably be surprised by that version.

"We don't like yer kind around here," ten feet of gnarled, red-and-black-checkered-flannel-wearing troll snarled in my face.

Great, I thought, as the heat and stench of its breath burned my nostrils, and I choked down bile as my eyes watered, *of all the trolls in Arcadia I had to get one of the ones that embraced* Deliverance *as its paradigm for existence*.

My partner, Morgan Freesong stepped up next to me, and said. "Frankly I don't care."

The troll's head swiveled away from me, and I sucked in a breath of sweet, contaminant-free air.

"What about you, partner?" Morgan continued. "Do you care if big, dumb, and inbred likes our kind around here?

"Can't say as I do," I replied in an over-exaggerated drawl.

I've already introduced my partner, Morgan Freesong; I am Roland the Bold. We are Paladins. We serve the lords and ladies of the Seelie Court of Arcadia.

"Look," I said, "we don't want any trouble, but there's a faerie inside who has greatly offended the Duke of Avalon."

"Well, ain't dat sweet," the door troll growled. His head swiveled back to me, and kept my feet planted in place rather than step out of the blast of its breath. "I give less crap than a goblin's black ass." I blinked a second trying to wrap my mind around that metaphor, but shrugged it off. Better not to try and fathom the inner workings of the trollish thought process. "I'd turn away Oberon his self, iffin he came here. So any changeling fetch dog can piss the hell off."

Typical response from the Unseelie slums. Avalon is one of the nicer cities in Arcadia, but there are still some undesirable elements in the Unseelie neighborhoods.

"Don't make this harder than it has to be," Morgan said.

She was giving him one last chance to be civil about this. That surprised me. Normally Morgan would have started breaking bones by this point.

"Go bother some one else, *changeling*," again the word came as a curse. "You ain't gettin' in."

"You expect to stop me?" Morgan asked. "Better pixies than you have tried to stop me and failed."

The troll snarled and reached to for Morgan. Morgan dropped to her knees, forcing the troll to lean further over to grab her. Its hand barely touched her shoulder when Morgan dropped, braced against the ground, and kicked the troll where its foot met its leg. I pulled my pistol crossbow. Morgan rolled out of the way to avoid the toppling behemoth. The troll rolled over, and as it got to its knees, I had the quarrel an inch away from its nose.

The troll froze.

Arcadia is timeless, but it's not truly real – the realm is formed of the dreams and nightmares of humanity. Nothing in Arcadia can truly change as a direct action from any other aspect of itself. Thus the two great factions of Arcadia, the Seelie and Unseelie courts, cannot directly affect each other. They require something that has a spark of reality to wage their eternal war: the Seelie call their humans knights Paladins; the Unseelie call their human slaves Rogues. Each court calls their enemy's humans changelings. Changelings are the only thing that can change things permanently in Arcadia, including killing faeries.

"Now," I said, "I'm going to go inside. Morgan is going with me. Will you kindly open the door? If you don't, I'll be on my way. I'm sure my patron would be more than happy to let me close the bar. Permanently."

I could see, and unfortunately smell, the sweat on the troll's forehead as it opened the door. Threatening a faerie with permanence usually gets things done.

"Yes, sir Paladin," it growled.

I replaced my crossbow in its holster under my cloak. Then I carefully walked around the ambulating landmass with Morgan trailing me. While the troll gave a slight bow as it held the door open, its eyes tracked us as we passed. One more enemy made in the Unseelie slums.

"Quick hands as always," Morgan said.

"One of these days I'm not going to be quite as fast as you need me to be," I replied.

Just because changelings can alter things of faerie, it doesn't make us all-powerful. While the fey can (and do) commit horrible and violent things to each other with no serious repercussions, humans die just as easily in Arcadia as they do on earth. The only thing that keeps most enemy Fey in line, is our potential to kill them, even with the fey being bigger, stronger, faster, sneakier, et cetera, ad infinite, we changelings can always get in a lucky shot, and that's all she wrote.

The bar was dark and grim, even for an Unseelie dive. Morgan and I had to tread carefully through the chains hanging from the ceiling. Sharp barbs and hooks protruded from the chains, threatening to shred our skin. I breathed through my mouth, trying as best I could to avoid inhaling the odor of the clientele. The sound metal grinding, completely devoid of rhythm, surrounded us and I don't mean metal rock music; I mean grinding metal.

The patrons watched us weave through the chains. Several smiled at us, though not with anything remotely near humor or good cheer; one ghastly thing that looked like a cross between a iguana and a miniature sumo wrestler actually licked its lips. Many of the darker fey develop taste for human blood and have no problem attacking Paladins – if the fey thinks it can win. Morgan and I pushed our cloaks back, revealing both the crossbow and the sword we carried. The patrons still looked hungry after that, but they didn't look quite as eager.

I saw our target across the room. He was hard to miss, even amongst the congregating dregs of Unseelie. He had no hair, his muscles rippled in odd ways as he swayed back and forth in his chair, and his sunken eyes scanned the room.

"Hello, Caliban," I said, stepping up to him.

"Roland." Caliban's voice was like a knife being pulled across a stone. "You got here faster this time."

His defiant smile showed twin rows of sharp canines, a crisscross of scars marred his lips. When he laughed, sometimes Caliban's teeth would cut his own lips to ribbons.

"You've done something that not even your fellow Unseelie scum would," Morgan said. "You aren't exactly subtle and must have known the Duke would want your head."

"Well, isn't that something," he said with a chuckle. A small cut appeared on his lower lip. "I'm not going to bother denying it. It was fun to watch those two Sidhe brats writhing on the floor, twitching like pixies at a mushroom dance in their death throes. But if you kill me, the Duke is only going to be half satisfied."

"What do you mean?" I asked, as my hand went for my crossbow.

"Think, changeling," he snarled his contempt. "I got into the palace somehow."

"Did the Rogues help you find those human drugs you spread throughout the royal house?" Morgan asked, pulling her sword free from its sheath.

"No," said a familiar voice behind me. "He's saying that a Paladin *and* a Rogue helped him."

I heard a thud and a soft moan, and Morgan fall to the floor. My hand shifted from my crossbow to the hilt of my sword as I spun. I've been knocked unconscious many times, and it's never pleasant, but it's even less pleasant when it comes with the bitter stab of betrayal.

* * *

The black cloud surrounding my mind lifted.

Blinking, I shook my head to clear my vision. For a moment it looked as if everything was upside down. I must have gotten hit harder than I thought, so I shook my head again. After a moment, I realized the world was in the right place; I was upside down. A rope or something cut into my ankles, and my pulse pounded in my ears.

An angel of a woman sat in front of me upon a black demon of a warhorse. Golden hair fell behind her shoulders like a waterfall of sunlight. Her sea green eyes sparkled with a humor that never left them. She wore the silver armor given to her by Morgan.

"Good morning, sleepy head," she said in her musical voice.

Fiona Loin's Mane had been my student, my greatest student. We had bonded like father and daughter while she grew up in the Avalon Royal House. I loved her more than any save Morgan and would have sworn her to hold honor above all other things. Apparently, I didn't know her as well as I thought.

"What's going on?" I asked her.

"Only what should have been done a long, long time ago," she answered.

"Poisoning members of the Royal House is something that shouldn't be done at all!"

She laughed. Her eyes took held an edge of contempt, such as I've seen from many Unseelie, though I'd never thought possible from her. A strange new fear drenched my spine in ice. If even she could be corrupted, could I trust anyone?

"You think this is about some noble brats?" Fiona smirked. "This goes so much further than that. Those children were a test to see if we could bring drug to Arcadia."

"Why?"

"It will make taking control of Arcadia so much easier."

Not even the vilest of Rogues would dream of attempting such a scheme. All changelings knew their place in Arcadia. We were the champions of balance in the battles between the courts. If either court, Seelie or Unseelie, gained a permanent advantage over the other, the repercussions across the dimensions would be devastating. The last time it had happened was around the time of the last ice age, or so the elder Paladins and Rogues tell us.

"Don't look at me like that Roland," Fiona said. "Have you ever wondered what it would be like to be free, to not have to play out of these games just for the courts' amusement, and have a life where you didn't have to follow the demands of someone else? Or maybe, when the lights are dim and you stare up at the ceiling when you're trying to go to sleep, you've even dreamt of controlling the games."

"Why would you enslave or destroy those who have given so many honors?" I asked.

"Wake up, Roland," she snapped. Her eyes bore into me with fury and hatred. "No matter how much praise and titles they lavish upon us, we are nothing more than glorified slaves. Many changelings have gathered together, both Paladins and Rogues, to stand for our race. It is time for humans to rule this world."

"What of Earth?" I reminded her. "Will you risk the damage to our home by upsetting the balance?"

"If the Fey had any truth to themselves, they would have been able to stay there rather than flee to this stagnant realm. We are the only real beings here and it is our right to stand over those who are not."

"I can't believe I'm hearing this from you, Fiona."

"Believe it, Roland," she hissed. "You're only alive because I hoped you might see the truth of my words. I have some errands to run. I'll leave you to think on what I have said. When I return you are either with me, or you are dead."

"What if I lie to you?"

"You would be a terrible liar, Roland. Don't try to start today. Be honorable with whatever choice you make."

"There is no honor in the path you have chosen," I said.

She turned the horse and rode away, leaving me to think.

"What have you done with Morgan?" I yelled at her retreating form.

"Don't concern yourself with her anymore," Fiona called back, laughing wickedly. "Worry about yourself."

Then I was alone.

*   *   *

After what seemed like hours of twisting, turning and straining I was no closer to being free. It couldn't have been that long, or I would have passed out again from my blood flowing to my head, but that didn't do anything to make me feel better about it.

I stopped my efforts when I heard something tromping through the woods. Branches snapped, and animals cried out in fear.

Again, I fought against my bonds. I pulled as hard as I could with all the strength my arms held. I felt blood dripping down my fingers from where the rope cut into my wrists.

A tree to my left fell to the ground with a crash. A bright red hat came bobbing into the clearing. The hat rode on a squat creature dense as stone, with stubby legs and arms. Its face looked like a wax-museum replica of mafia-movie tough guy, only the wax had melted just enough for the face to slide weirdly out of proportion. That odd face and stubbly body didn't scare me nearly as much as that bright, red, damp hat.

Think of all the things you might have been afraid of coming out of the closet at night after your parents tucked you in. Well, those things are afraid of Red Caps. Even the worst Unseelie, and that would include Caliban, refuse to deal with Red Caps, because Red Caps are too dangerous and unpredictable. They terrify changelings even more. Red Caps earned their name from the hats died red with human blood. Since Arcadia severed almost all ties with earth, changelings are the only source of fresh blood for Red Caps to keep their hats from fading. The only times Paladins and Rogues work together is order to hunt the Red Caps down and put an end to them.

The Red Cap chuckled wickedly as it stalked toward me at a slow determined pace.

I struggled even harder, even though I knew I couldn't break my bonds. I wasn't about to hang here passively while it slit my throat and soaked its hat. On the bright side, at least I wouldn't have to face Fiona again.

"Try facing something that can fight back, monster," Morgan's voice rang out in the clearing.

Morgan stood on the edge of the clearing. Blood ran down her armor, and she had a bruise darkening under her left eye, but she was alive. She'd never been more beautiful.

"Stay put," the Red Cap growled. "I'll eat you after I play with your pretty friend."

Morgan smiled and waited while the Red Cap ambled toward her. After he crossed half the distance, she reached under her cloak and raised crossbow. Taking careful aim, she fired a bolt. It landed right between the Red Cap's eyes.

The Red Cap howled. One of the earliest lessons Paladins and Rogues learn about fighting Red Caps is never attack the head. It only makes them mad. Then they hurt you a lot more before killing you.

Morgan took out another crossbow from behind a tree and fired. That time she hit just next to the left ear. Then she ran, weaving between the trees.

"You dye your hat in rabbit's blood!"

The monster screamed and lumbered after her. The only real adventage any creature has over Reds Caps is speed.

I hung there and wondered what game Morgan was playing. Early in our career, she and I had gone on a Red Cap hunt. Five other Paladins and three Rogues went with us. We'd spent a month of planning, going over our strategies and how best to use our skills and talents together. Two of the Paladins and one of the Rogues never fought again.

In the midst of my pondering, I realized I should be moving. Morgan had given me precious time in order to act. Some claim that fear is the greatest motivator to accomplish the impossible. Many times I had faced death as a Paladin. However, I had never *known* that if I failed in one small thing, I *would* die. If I didn't free myself from my bonds, the Red Cap would return and kill me. The sensation was empowering. I focused every ounce of my being on one task, getting free of the ropes.

The ropes holding my wrists split as I strained against them. My strength was not my own, for I was a mere passenger in my own body. I swung myself up to the rope holding me to the tree and began to work on the knot there.

A glint of metal flashed above me, cutting the rope. I hung there for a moment that felt longer than the time I spent struggling, and then gravity, that harsh mistress, took hold of me.

"Are you all right?" Morgan asked, as she resheathed her sword.

I coughed and wheezed to get enough air into my protesting lungs.

"Fine," I groaned through gritted teeth as I stood

"Good," my partner said. "I left several false trails for the Red Cap, but he'll figure it out eventually. I'd rather not be here when he does."

"Agreed," I answered, as we made our way in the opposite direction of crashing trees. "I thought you were dead. Glad you're not"

"Well, it's not for lack of Fiona and Sandtrap trying."

"Sandtrap?" He was a Rogue I'd fought with several times. There's a nasty scar in my upper-right thigh thanks to him. I'd have never thought he'd betray the Unseelie. Then again, I'd have said the same thing about Fiona when I'd woken up this morning.

"Sandtrap got careless and won't be able to betray anyone again."

"Did Fiona talk to you about her plan?" Morgan asked. "To recruit you?"

"She did." I shook my head at the thought of it. "Guess you too?"

Morgan spat, "I told her what to do with her plan and that she'd better kill me, or her plan would die with her."

"We need to tell the Duke," I said. "Fiona sounded like this was going to get really nasty before it's finished."

"Good thought."

Morgan led me to a small grove where two horses waited for us. We mounted, and started toward Avalon.

"Thanks for saving my life," I said. "When the Redcap showed up, I really thought I wasn't going to make it."

"I'm not about to let anyone kill you, yet," Morgan laughed. "I still need you. If you died, who could I trust to rescue me when I get myself in trouble?"

"Well, you rescued me this time."

"That I did," she punched my shoulder. "I'm catching up."

I shook my head, and we kicked our horses into a walk.

"What?" Morgan asked.

"You've got a long way to go before we're even close to square," I said.

She punched me again. Harder. I laughed, just happy that Morgan was alive.

The ground rippled around us. The horses stamped and spun in panic. Three trees to my left sunk into the ground, and a tree ahead of me e-rupted and the splinters transformed into wasps.

"What the hell?" Morgan asked.

"Fiona and her fellows must have gotten another Fey," I called out as I tried to calm my horse. "Probably more, considering how far we are from anything. It's going to get worse the longer they are left unchallenged."

The rippling stopped, and we got our mounts under control. We kicked them into a canter. We couldn't get to Avalon soon enough.

* * *

Even riding our horses as hard as we could without killing them, it took us several hours to get back to Avalon. Fiona had taken us far out into the Wild Lands. We made straight for the Duke's palace.

"Do you know any Paladins who specialize in mind magic?" I asked, as we rode into the courtyard.

"Yes," Morgan answered. "Why?"

"Odds of Fiona giving over her accomplices is pretty slim," I replied. "I suspect the only way to get what we want, is to have someone go into her mind."

"It'll take some time. The only ones I know are in Tir'Nog'Nough. As soon as I can, I'll send off a few messenger sprites."

We dismounted. I thought about how long it would take Morgan's mind magic Paladins to arrive from the capital. Maybe a day or two if we were really lucky, but most likely closer to a week. I hoped to have Fiona in custody by the end of the day. That meant holding her long enough to give her allies a chance to flee justice, or attempt a rescue.

"Where are we going?" Morgan asked, as I turned down a side corridor.

"I need to get something in my quarters," I said.

"We don't have time for a side trip. We have to warn the Duke."

"Trust me," I said. "It's something that will aid us greatly. If it will make you feel better, go on ahead. I'll be right behind you."

She gave me a strange look, and then hurried off toward the Duke's study. He was usually there at this time of day, relaxing before an evening of stately functions.

My quarters were not far, so it took me little time to get there. Once inside, I went straight to my desk. There I opened my jewelry box and took out a small pendant on a gold chain.

The pendant was my favorite and most useful magical device. Because it could track anyone I I had physically touched almost anywhere in all of Arcadia. There were a few limitations, such as wards of protection and such, but for the most part it was fool proof. Only the Duke knew I had it. He gave it to me upon my graduation from the Paladin Academy.

I put the pendant around my neck and tucked it into my shirt, just as my door burst inwards. Two hulking Seelie brutes lumbered into the room. They looked like Mafioso tough guys. The Duke had recently rediscovered his love of hardboiled detective fiction, and his court had altered their look accordingly.

"Stand down, forsworn," one said, waving his billy club at me. The other started rifling through my room, searching for something

Two more toughs pushed their way into the room. Behind them, I saw the Duke and Fiona in the hall.

"Fiona was right, boss," said the tough searching my room. "We found the contraband right where she said it would be."

I turned. Mr. Wiseguy held a glass vial with a white powder in it. My heart sank.

"Take him," said the Duke, "and hold him until we can have a proper trial."

"You can't believe what they've told you about me, Your Grace," I pleaded.

"I don't want to, Roland," the Duke said. He turned his back. "I don't want to."

Fiona gave me a wink as the gueards searched me for any hidden weapons.

"Worry not, Your Grace," Fiona said. "I'll make sure he does not escape."

One of the tough guys lifted my pendant. "What of this, Your Grace?" he asked.

"Your Grace," I said, "for my past honor, I ask that I may keep it."

He looked at me with all the hurt in the world.

"I should send you swimming with the fishes," the Duke said. "Just to make an example of you."

"I understand you have to place me under arrest," I said. "But everyone knows I'm a terrible liar." I glanced at Fiona; she glared back at me. "Please, Your Grace, I don't know where that vial came from. I'll go peacefully, and you know it will do me no use in the prison."

The Duke nodded. "Roland may keep the token."

He turned and walked away. His shoulders slumped forward and his slow steps echoed the betrayal he must have felt. I wondered how much Fiona's lie crushed him.

"Why are you doing this?" I asked her after he'd gone.

"I am a Paladin," she said, in a mocking tone. "It is my duty to deal with traitors like you."

"I am no traitor."

"Enough," Fiona snapped. "Take him to the tower."

As they led me away, prayed Fiona didn't know Morgan was alive. That might be my only chance.

* * *

I sat in the cell for about two hours when I heard the sounds of fighting in the halls outside. I took the pendant off my neck and swallowed it. Just afterward, the door to my cell burst inward in a shower of splinters. Fiona stood in the frame, grinning like an idiot. Only her sword kept me from leaping at her.

"Welcome to your rescue," she said.

"First you capture me. Now you're freeing me. Why?" I asked.

"Well, your capture was just dumb luck," she said. "The Red Cap was supposed to kill you. How did you manage to get away?"

I gave her a blank stare in response.

"No matter," she continued. "I had already put the drugs in your room, and had told the Duke you were trying to recruit me. Imagine my surprise when I saw you there."

"But why bother freeing me? What's your game?"

"So you can look even guiltier," Fiona answered. "We both know you are innocent, and so will everyone else if the wrong Paladin gets here to scan your mind. I can't take the chance that that Paladin won't be in with us. So, think of how it will look when all of the prison guards were killed and you are nowhere to be found."

"How do you know I'll leave?"

"Because I've brought an old friend of yours to make sure you do," she said with a wicked smile.

Fiona stepped aside and Caliban stepped into the cell. There was no contest between us. Without my weapons, I proved no match for the Unseelie brute. He picked me up and dropped me into a large sack. I struggled, trying at least to be irritating. Caliban dropped me, then beat me into unconsciousness.

*   *   *

I blinked as the darkness gave way to light. My head pounded in time with my pulse.

Rolling over, I looked around. I lay in a dark alley. The scent garbage and spilled booze filled my nose. This was not a Seelie neighborhood. Despite the pain, I pushed myself into a sitting position. Aside from a few rats, I was alone. That could change at any moment, so I had to get moving. My first priorities were to get a weapon and find a place to hide. After that, I would have time to come up with a plan.

I had an idea who might help me. I even suspected he might not be in league with Fiona. But I had to get to him before the Duke's guard, the Paladins, or just some Unseelie toughs who wanted to beat on an unarmed Paladin found me.

I shoved my finger into the back of my throat and wiggled it vigorously. Between my throbbing and spinning head and the stench of the alley, it didn't take long to heave up the Duke's pendant. After shaking what bile I could off of it, I put the pendant around my neck.

I sent the image of who I wanted to find into the pendant. I felt it tug toward the center of the Unseelie district. This did not surprise me.

The pendant led me deep into Unseelie territory. Dodging groups of Unseelie was relatively easy – it was still daylight, so the worst of them weren't about yet. However, the trouble came as the cityscape changed around me: out-of-place walls, massive rocks, and brambles burst up from the ground, walls, and sometimes even out of a rippling in the air. Once an entire tower of pearl and silver shot up in the middle of a square. I might have laughed at watching the Unseelie scramble in confusion, if not for knowing what was causing these strange occurrences.

Eventually, I came to the door of a flat that looked very well kept for this part of the city. I knocked on the door three times, waited ten heart beats, and knocked three times more.

The wait wasn't long. The door opened and someone in a deep gray hooded cloak pointed a crossbow at my head, and by crossbow, it was more like a small ballista.

"What do you want?" asked a voice from under the hood.

"I need your help, Whisper," I said.

"Why would I help a Paladin?"

"Because I need your help with something worse than hunting a Red Cap," I replied. "If you don't help me, it might mean the end of both the Seelie and Unseelie courts."

"How do I know you're not lying?" Whisper asked.

"Come on," I said in exasperation. "How long have you known me? When have you ever heard even a *rumor* that I've told a lie? I have no weapons, no allies, just me, asking for your help."

We stood there a few moments, Rogue and Paladin, looking at each other. What was going through his head? How close was he to pulling the trigger and skewering my head? Something that sounded like tearing cloth came from behind me. I glanced back. Twin rows of cherry trees lined the street. I raised an eyebrow at Whisper.

He lowered the crossbow. "Come in."

I entered. Never before, to my knowledge, had any Paladin seen the inside of a Rogue's lair. After passing beyond the front hall, I stood in awe.

Abstract paintings covered every wall. I don't have words to describe them with any justice, but most of them were more beautiful than any work in the Duke's private museum. Each painting was a swirl of colors and patterns that evoked raw emotions: joy, sorrow, regret, whimsy, the entire spectrum of what it is to feel as a human being. In the far corner, I noticed a painter's easel, two shelves filled with painting supplies, and a stack of untouched canvases.

"Surprised?" Whisper asked, removing his cloak.

"I would never have guessed you would be such a master of art."

"Contrary to the propaganda they feed you, we Rogues are more than spies and assassins. When we are trained we are given extensive schooling in the arts. Our masters understand our lives are grim. Art helps to ease our hearts."

"I have learned something about the honor of the Unseelie."

Whisper laughed. "Never forget that we are what we are and will always oppose you. You are still alive only because I want to hear why you think I will help."

I told Whisper my story from the beginning. Then I spoke of the reasons I sought him. I knew of him not only from the times we faced each other over a disagreement by our masters, but also by his reputation of unswerving loyalty to the court he served.

All through my story Whisper sat taking everything in. When I finished my tale, he said nothing. He got up and walked over to a cabinet. He opened it and brought out a sword.

I tensed. Had I misjudged him?

"What's that for?" I asked.

"If we're going to stop this Fiona you might need a weapon," Whisper said, as he tossed the weapon to me. "I don't intend on doing all the fighting by myself."

"Don't you need one?"

"I am a Rogue," Whisper said. "I already have all the weapons I need."

"Thank you," I smiled, taking a few practice swings.

"Don't think for a moment this changes things," he said. "Once this is over, we're right back in the same place. Your masters and mine will always be at odds, and so must we."

"At least we understand each other," I said.

*   *   *

Whisper and I decided Fiona's quarters were a good place to start looking for some way to uncover more of her plot. However, getting into the palace unnoticed was going to be nearly impossible. Whisper said he knew a secret way into the palace, but would not show it to me unless I swore never to reveal it to anyone.

"You have a way into the palace, and you expect me to do nothing about it?" I asked.

"I did not say that," Whisper insisted. "You may not reveal it to anyone. Once this quest is over, do with it what you will. Only remember, whatever use you make of it, you must do it alone."

"What if I will not swear?" I asked.

"I will use the passage alone, and you may enter through the gates. I wish you luck."

I swore his oath, and he led me to his passage. As I have sworn not to reveal its details I'll not describe any part of that journey here.

Soon I stood within the inner walls of the palace. Since I knew the guards' schedule and their patrol routes, we made our way through the palace undiscovered. Whisper voiced concern that they might have changed the schedule. I pointed out that they weren't likely to expect me to come sneaking back into the palace, all things considered. Not long after that, we stood at Fiona's door. After Whisper picked the lock, I burst inside.

The smell of human blood filled the room. Fey blood smells like sweet brandy, where as human blood has a very pungent odor all its own. The smell always reminded me of my own mortality. All Paladins are trained to recognize the smell. Sometimes in the heat of battle, we do not feel pain because we are caught up in the frenzy of combat. Once you learn the smell of your own blood, you never forget it.

Whisper smelled it also. His body tensed. He looked ready to strike the first thing to move.

"Would that be Fiona?" he asked.

Whisper pointed to the corner. Pinned to the wall with her sword was the young Paladin we sought.

"Yes," I said. What little hope I'd possessed died with her.

"This is interesting," Whisper said.

"What is that?" I asked, wondering how he managed to remain so composed.

"This murder matches the style of one of the greatest Rogues in Arcadia," he answered. "Have you ever heard of, Black Rose?"

"Of course," I answered. "Every Paladin has though none of us know who Black Rose really is."

"Neither do we. The identity of Black Rose is a mystery to all save the rulers of the Unseelie court."

"How do you know this is Black Rose's style?" I asked.

"Each Rogue develops a style for his or her work. We do this so we know to stay out of each other's way. I don't know every style, but every Rogue knows this style."

"What does that mean?" I asked.

For the first time, Whisper looked unsure. "We are in way over our heads."

"And with her dead, we have no way to find anything new," I said.

"What about Caliban?" Whisper asked. "He seems to be a part of this. If we find him he might be able to give us some information."

"I should have thought of that," I said.

"That's what you get when you're trained to use you're muscle and not your mind," Whisper quipped.

I almost responded, but thought better of it. He was obviously trying to bait me.

"Do you know where we might find Caliban?"

"Yes," he said. His tone indicated I'd passed some kind of test. "Let's get out of here before the guards find us."

*   *   *

I followed Whisper deep into the worst Unseelie slum I had ever seen. I'd only ever been this deep into enemy territory once, and that was with a host of paladins and Fey soldiers.

"Would you relax?" Whisper said. "Nothing is going to happen. Nobody here is stupid enough to risk true death by facing us together."

As we walked, the air grew colder, until Whisper stopped in front of a house. It stood out from the surrounding buildings as being darker, seeming to suck up the light from around it. The walls seemed to be made of undulating shadows. When we got to the door, I thought I saw some of those shadows reach out for me. Only Caliban would live in a place like this.

"We're here," I said.

"We're here," Whisper confirmed.

"What now?" I asked.

"We go in and talk to Caliban."

I knew life was getting to me when I didn't bother to knock. With one motion unsheathed my sword, and smashed the door inward. I kicked the remains out of my way as I stepped into the house.

"Bad day?" Whisper asked.

"Worst in my life," I growled.

"Cheer up," he said, "it could always get worse."

"It probably will," I said, and walked further into the Caliban's dwelling.

Inside, I found Caliban's remains. His swamp green colored blood painted the walls, where he had been pinned to the wall. In death Caliban smelled even worse than in life.

"It got worse," I said.

Whisper entered the room. "We are in way over our heads, Roland."

"Yeah," My despair made the words come out at a whisper, "you said that."."

"What do we do now?"

I sighed. "You warn the nobles of your court about this threat."

"What about you?"

"With Fiona dead, I'm a traitor," I said. "I've no way to prove otherwise. The only thing I can do is try and make it to earth before I'm captured again."

"Earth," Whisper said in disbelief.

Most changelings fear earth more than death. To live on earth meant forsaking feel the magic of Arcadia. During their training every Rogue and Paladin is taken to earth and shown its bleakness. Exile is one of the most severe punishments for a changeling.

"It's better than the alternative," I said.

With that, silence fell. We would not speak of the worst punishment.

Whisper was the first out the door. He cursed, and I heard the ring of steel on steel. I pushed my way outside.

I watched Whisper move as he fought the attackers. The only weapon he had was a large straight razor. He wove and dodged between the attacking Fey and Changelings. Each time the razor cut flesh, the area echoed with angry whispers. As the attackers swarmed on him, I thought he would be overwhelmed. In a heartbeat, a cloud of inky blackness enveloped Whisper and several attackers. The violent whispering increased within that cloud.

I screamed a battle cry, and charged. I knew that razor by reputation, and knew that Whisper would be all right. All my rage went into my fighting, as I cut down fey after fey. I did not see them; I merely fought them.

Suddenly, it was over. I stood in a mound of dying fey and Changelings. Never before that moment had I reveled in battle. I had seen it as a duty to my lords but never as something to enjoy. In this battle. I felt the rush Morgan claims to get. I liked it. That feeling frightened me more than anything in my life.

"Roland," said a voice behind me.

I spun, hoping to find more enemies. I saw only Whisper. For a brief moment I did not see him as anything more than another body to kill. The instant before I lashed out, I saw him as Whisper and held my thrust back.

"What?" I snarled.

"Look at this," he said and handed me a parchment. "It seems as though you have attracted the attention of some very powerful people."

I took it from him and read.

Gabrielle,

I need you to dispose of Caliban. He is the only link to us Roland has. If he should find a way to make Caliban speak, our plot is lost. Take as many commoner Unseelie thugs with you as you deem necessary. There is a chance you may be able to rid us of Roland. He might appear to find Caliban. I know I can rely on you.

Black Rose

I let out a slow breath and crumpled the paper.

"What's wrong?" Whisper asked.

I don't know what he saw in reading my expression, but it didn't surprise me that my face betrayed my fury, or my hurt, or any other of the whirling emotions that letter stirred in my breast.

"Where are we going?" Whisper asked, as I started walking.

"To the Duke's palace," I said calmly. Finally, I knew where to get my answers. "I have some unfinished business there."

"What kind of business?"

"You'll see," I said. "I don't want to talk about it.

* * *

We made it to the palace. My anger made me want to run all the way there, but I stayed at a quick walk. All the way, Whisper tried to get me to say what I had planned. I ignored him all the way. No amount of urging could get me to say anything.

We entered through Whisper's secret way. Again, I steered us past the patrolling guards. This made me realize how much damage a group of changelings from both courts could be if they joined together, and why we needed to stop them.

I stopped outside a door. I looked at it for several moments before opening it and entering. Whisper followed me and shut the door.

"What are we doing here?" he asked, looking around at the living quarters.

"We are here to stop the enemies of both our courts," I said.

"Why here?"

My heart sank even further when I said, "We will find the leader of the movement here very shortly."

"Care to explain?"

"No."

Thankfully he did not press the matter further. We waited in silence. I ignored everything as I prepared myself for what I had to do.

The door finally opened, and Morgan entered. She saw me standing in her room. She tried to leave, but Whisper slammed the door shut.

"Well, this is interesting," she said, "seeing the two of you together."

"Hello, Black Rose," I said between clenched teeth.

"What?" Whisper asked.

"How did you find out?" Morgan asked, far more calmly than I would have thought.

I threw Gabrielle's letter in Morgan's face. She snatched it out of the air, read it, and shook her head.

"I can't believe she took the letter with her."

"You have always over estimated everyone but me," I said. "I have to stop you."

"Your duty to your lords would demand nothing less," Morgan answered, her voice dripping with sarcasm. "I knew this would happen if you found out who I really am. The only problem is you also have a loyalty to me. Which will you chose?"

Whisper snorted. "I have no loyalty to you. You have also betrayed my lords as well. I have no such moral dilemma as Roland."

"My dear, Whisper," Morgan said, "don't you think I've been prepared for the eventuality of facing Rogues as well as Paladins."

Morgan became a blur. I'd forgotten how fast she was – her sword and crossbow were out and ready before Whisper and I could react.

She loosed the crossbow, and the bolt took Whisper in the shoulder. His razor was already out, and he let the impact spin him around, turning the momentum into a spinning attack. Morgan ducked under his cut, and threw her crossbow at me. And damn it, I dodged it rather than press an attack.

"We need her alive," I said.

Morgan attacked whisper again, and he spun as her sword lashed out. The attack was a ruse. Morgan's free hand grasped the crossbow bolt in

Whisper's shoulder. Whisper screamed in pain as Morgan wrenched the bolt, dragging Whisper around so that he blocked her from me.

My former friend looked me straight in the eye and smirked as she slid her blade into Whisper.

When whisper collapsed, I slashed at Morgan. She ducked and spun away past where Whisper lay. When she came up, she held Whisper's razor in her left hand.

My gaze went from her eyes, to the razor, and back to her eyes.

Morgan smiled. "You know this, don't you?" She spun the razor in her hand so that the blade appeared as a blurred circle. "The Ripper's razor. Stand down, and I won't use it on you."

I said nothing. I wouldn't stand down, and she knew. She was bating me. I didn't bite. We just stood staring at each other over the tips of our blades. The problem with knowing each other so well was that we'd practiced together so often that whichever of us attacked first would open themselves up for a counter attack. This fight would probably kill me; I just had to make sure it killed her as well.

"What will you do, Roland?" she asked. "I am the only one who knows of your innocence. Everyone else in my rebellion thinks you're in this with me. Kill me and you will never have your honor returned to you."

"I will pay that price if I must."

I attacked before I finished speaking – a completely Morgan-like tactic. She didn't seem surprised at all. In order to win, I needed to fight completely unlike me and unlike her – something I wasn't could achieve.

The fight raged across the room as we tested and taunted each other. It was obvious Morgan was overconfident in her abilities and my weakened state. She chose to play with me, rather than fight as seriously as I was. The thought came to me. I needed to fight like a fey might fight another fey.

Morgan took the openings I gave her, giving me small cuts and slashes to my arms and legs from her sword as I shied away from Jack's razor the few times she close enough to hit me with it. Each time Morgan cut me, I redoubled my effort to attack, spilling more blood from my wounds. I wouldn't last long, but I was a dead man no matter what I did.

"You're too hurt to last, Roland," Morgan taunted. "Give up now and I'll let you walk out of here."

All I did was grunt. I wanted to believe it was part of my ruse, but as you've heard, I'm a terrible liar.

My guard went down just a bit; my arm was so tired, I let my fatigue take over for just a moment. Then, I shook my head, and brought my sword back into line as I backed away. Only, I brought the weapon just a slight bit too high and left my leg out a half a second too long. I've always been more of a defensive than an offensive fighter, and not very creative in the heat of combat; so, just as I expected, Morgan went for that opening. She had intended a small cut, but I pushed my leg into the thrust, and wedged her sword between my kneecap and thigh bone. A streak of lighting danced across my vision, and someone nearby was screaming. Oh, that was probably me.

Morgan smiled, and brought the razor up toward my face. On the edge of my hearing, I heard a whisper saying, "I'm so thirsty; let me drink."

That whisper hit me like being submerged in ice water. I dropped my swords and caught Morgan's wrist with both hands. That razor was *not* going to touch my flesh.

We struggled. She tried to slide the razor's blade across my throat. Unfortunately for Morgan, I've always been stronger. She's never beaten me in hand to hand combat. I wrenched her wrist around and turned the Ripper's razor away from me and toward my oldest friend. She let go of her sword and brought her other hand into the struggle, but it was too late. I had the height and weight advantage. She kicked at my injured leg. I screamed. And even though my leg buckled under the pain, I did not release my grip Ripper's Razor. I toppled over, taking Morgan with me.

Morgan gasped in surprise as the razor blade slid into her throat

"*So fresh.*" A hushed tone echoed through the room. "*So Warm.*"

Morgan coughed up blood. Her arms went slack. She tried to say something, but only managed to cough up more blood. After I watched the light leave her eyes, I pulled the razor from her throat.

"*No,*" the whispers protested, "*Still thirsty.*"

I put the blade against my wrist. Even coated with Morgan's blood, the blade was cool against my skin.

"*Yes. Thirsty. So thirsty. Let me drink.*"

A hand grabbed my forearm and pulled Ripper's razor away before I could make the cut.

"Don't be an idiot," Whisper said.

*   *   *

My name is Whisper. I'm not the first Rogue to wear that name, and I'm not the last. Someday I'll be just a second's breath too slow, and another young Rogue fresh from Earth will get Ripper's razor along with my name. Too my knowledge, I am the first Rogue to willingly aid a Paladin outside of a Red Cap hunt. No, I don't count that group of traitors attempting to wrest control of Arcadia from our Faerie Masters as Rogues or Paladins. Those ungrateful bastards aren't even worthy of the name changeling.

Two days after our encounter with Black Rose, or as she is known in the Seelie court, Morgan Freesong, Roland the bold and I stood at a gateway to Earth.

We had spent the last two days in my lady's care. My patroness, the Countess of the Bitter hearts of Spurned Affections attempted to lavish Roland with favors and gifts, but the Paladin would have none of it. He spent most of those two days in a room, speaking to no one. Our wounds were healed, but I suspected Roland's spirit ever would. The Seelie did not work to protect their vassals from the bleakness of the world as the Unseelie did; I suppose it had something to do with their obsession with the idea of the tragic hero.

On the third day, he announced his intention to leave Arcadia forever. No, I hadn't even considered trying to talk him out of it; he was a Paladin would not spurn that allegiance, and until we found a way to clear his name, returning to his court would only mean his death.

So I came to the gateway to see him off. A pair of heavily armed trolls and a night hag, a bodyguard courtesy of my lady, waited a respectful distance away. Considering what we had just gone though, neither Roland nor I wanted any Changeling protection. Yet, my lady wasn't prepared to let him be alone until he actually stood on Earth. Roland's court might have given him up as a traitor, but to the Unseelie, he is a hero. He seems very uncomfortable by this ironic turn of events. I enjoy watching him squirm every time an Unseelie lord or lady lavishes attention upon him.

"Are you sure you want to do this?" I asked.

"It's my only real option," Roland said.

"You could become a Rogue?" My patroness had commanded me to try once more before he left.

Roland sighed. "You know I will never be anything but a Paladin. I might as well ask you to no longer be a Rogue."

"But do you have to exile yourself to Earth?"

"They will hunt me forever. Earth is the last place they will expect me to go. If I've learned anything from you, it's to surprise them. Before this mess, I would have charged in, seeking retribution and attempting to clear my name based on the strength of my reputation. I'll be safe there until they figure things out, and by then, I'll be ready to defend myself. Besides, I can see if I can disrupt their organization from Earth. This will give you time to work against them here."

We stood in quiet for a few minutes, staring at the gate to Earth. It was the first, and probably the last, time a Rogue and Paladin would stand together in friendship. Yes, I count Roland the bold among my friends – a very exclusive group of people.

Roland looked at the gateway. A tear rolled down his eye. He turned to me and held out a sheaf of papers.

"What's this?" I asked.

"My story," Roland said. "Our story. I've written it over the last two days. See that this makes it through at least the Rogue circles. It'll eventually make it to the Paladins. Some might believe it."

"When they read this, they'll know where you've gone."

"No," Roland said. "I left off after my fight with Morgan."

I nodded and took the papers. The truth needed to get out. He didn't mention that once this began circulating, I would become a target. I didn't argue against it. This was bigger than my personal safety.

"Roland," I said. It was my turn to give him something. "Wear this."

I held a locket out to him. Without even looking slightly skeptical, Roland took it and placed it around his neck.

"What is it?" he asked.

"It will help me find you when the time comes," I said.

"I will be waiting," Roland said, and shook my hand. "Thank you."

Roland turned his back on the gate. He took one last sweeping gaze at Arcadia, the home he'd known all his life. He would probably never set foot in this realm again. The Paladin wept openly. My heart wept just as hard. Nothing I had ever done or seen hurt as much as watching him leave this world behind. Then he turned to the portal, stepped through, and was gone.

To those reading these words, this was Roland's story. He's gone now. Gone to where the traitors of the Unseelie and Seelie courts will have a hard time explaining to their masters why they are going to Earth. To those allies of Morgan Freesong, known also as Black Rose, the truth is out; every loyal Paladin and Rogue will have that nagging question in the back of their minds. From the moment Roland the Bold left Arcadia, you have been living on borrowed time.

While you hunt for my friend, I hunt you. You will not see me coming, but may hear a faint whisper just on the edge of perception.

Ripper's razor is so very thirsty.

Let us begin this dance.

M Todd Gallowglas

Prophecy

The dread sorcerer, Eras Letum, known to the world as The Winter King, stood at his battlements and sighed. Why did it come to this? Why did the people hate him so much?

Lighting illuminated the sky above the fortress with bursts of red, blue, and purple. Thunder followed. Then, a scream echoed from the highest tower. The wind carried that scream out of the tower, across the courtyard, and over the walls to the army of peasants and commoners that waited on the plains outside the fortress.

When they heard the scream, the army shouted, "Chaos is freedom!" It was the heralding call of those who believed the Prophecy of the Destiny Child.

As the rallying cry faded, two of the Gargoyles perched on that tower turned their heads to the Winter King. The movement sounded like a grinding of a mill stone. Lightning flashed, reflecting off their polished black skin. One scratched its claws against the battlements, and growled: *Is it time yet?*

Centuries ago, these creatures were nothing more than statues. Now, hundreds of stone guardians waited for the command that would send them to destroy the army below. He'd created them, not from personal desire, but because of the myth that he'd been forced to become to maintain order.

"Not yet," the Winter King said. *Hopefully not at all.*

He gazed across the vast army that had come to overthrow him. Thousands of peasants and disgruntled soldiers believed that events tonight would set them free. The Winter King hated them all for forcing him to become what had been needed to cow them into submission. Without him, the lands would fall to chaos and lawlessness, as they had been before his coming.

"Chaos is freedom!" they cried again, as if sensing his thoughts.

He gave a short, condescending laugh. No, he didn't want to loose the gargoyles and other creatures that defended his home; however, the Winter King had struggled too long, fought too hard to bring order to his lands, to allow anyone to destroy his life's work

"Master," a voice said behind him. "It has begun."

"Excellent."

The Winter King turned from the scene below. Whisper, his assassin-bodyguard, stood two paces away in all blacks and grays. Over a dozen knives were secreted about him. This man, with a face no one could remember, had protected the Winter King for the last fifteen years. Several times, Whisper had nearly died protecting the sorcerer. And still, the Winter King did not completely trust him, hence, Whisper's proper place, like everyone else, was two paces away. At two paces, gave The Winter King enough time to defend himself against anyone.

"Let us go and end this foolishness."

Together, sorcerer and assassin strode through the halls and corridors of the greatest fortress in the world. At the very top of the highest tower, they came to a cell. Two people were inside: the midwife, and Marigold, the woman pregnant with the Destiny Child. Marigold's broken water saturated her bed of rotting straw. Beads of sweat rolled down her face and intermingled with her tears, joining together as if they were lovers.

The midwife stood and bowed. She could not meet the dread sorcerer's eyes. "She is close, my lord."

"Excellent," the Winter King said. "You have served well."

"Thank you, my lord." Her head bobbed, and she returned her attention to her profession.

Marigold glared at the sorcerer-king. It was death to look on him in such a fashion, but she did not fear this. She carried the means to the Winter King's destruction in her womb.

"I might die tonight," Marigold said between gasps, "but my child will end your tyranny."

The Winter King looked down on her as if she were a beggar covered in filth, pleading for a bit of food or coin. He managed a bored expression, but nausea churned in his stomach. This prophecy was even older than the sorcerer-king himself. It proclaimed that the Destiny Child would dissemble all of the Winter King's magical defenses allowing the Summer Prince to strike him down.

Again, Marigold screamed. The power of destiny caught hold of the cry, carried it through the tower, into the courtyard below, and across the battlements.

Again, the army cheered. "Chaos is Freedom!"

After another earsplitting scream, the midwife said, "I see the head."

As with Marigold, destiny magnified the midwife's voice so that every soul within a mile of the fortress heard. All breathing stopped, save for the mother. The wind seemed to match her gasps, and thunder rolled across the sky as she screamed. Only Marigold's cries and the midwife commands to "Push!" punctuated time's passage.

Scream. "Push!" Scream. "Push!" Scream. "Push!"

Marigold gave on final cry that dissolved into weeping.

The midwife held the baby out. "It's a boy."

Despite her pain, Marigold sat up and snatched the baby from the midwife's hands. She cradled it, pressing its head to her cheek. "Please save us," she whimpered.

The infant child opened its eyes and stared at the Winter King with a colorless gaze, and spoke three words, "I have come."

The Winter King lifted his hand, and a wave of black fire enveloped the midwife, the mother, and child. A voice whispered just above the crackling flames. "This will not save you."

The Winter King stared at the ashy remains of his three victims. He laughed, a deep happy laugh, full of relief. He had done it. He had defeated the Destiny Child. He had outwitted Prophecy.

The Winter King's laughter stopped short as Whisper thrust a knife between his mater's shoulder blades. In his haste and eagerness to kill the Destiny Child, the Winter King had neglected to notice Whisper creeping closer and closer until he was much, much closer than two paces.

"But…" the Winter King began to protest, but had no words to finish.

All his work had been for nothing. He had transformed himself into something what the people needed in order to build an empire to protect the people who needed him. Now it would crumble apart. The laws he had created to ensure their safety would be forgotten. The poor would know hunger again, for who would maintain the food rationings? The people would be overcome by sickness, for who would maintain the college of surgeons?

The assassin known as Whisper, who history would call the Summer King, said, "The Prophecy only said the Destiny Child needed to be born." Then he added in a voice softer than the wind, "Chaos is freedom."

It was the last sound Erus Letum ever heard.

M Todd Gallowglas

WRITERS' BLOCK

This story is one of the few science fiction pieces I've done. When it comes down to it, my brain works in fantasy. Even when teachers told me to leave the fantasy out, I usually ignored them. The few times I listened and did some-thing completely based in realism, the pieces I produced were dry, stale, and lacked any spark of joy. I don't think we should tell anyone what they shouldn't write, at least creatively. Sure we can give parameters, but discouraging their creativity in anyway is counterproductive. I've had people telling me for a long, long time what I should and, more often, shouldn't write. In this story, I address this a little...as well as poking a little fun at the big 5 versus the indie book movement.

I slid into the booth at the coffee shop. The place had that strange, not quite fast food, not quite real restaurant smell. I didn't say anything. I'd learned as a freelance editor to never start talking first. Wait for the client to start, then only ask direct questions if applicable to the target.

Smith – for some reason every contact wants to be called Smith – pushed a microdrive across the table with his pinky. "Smith" is almost always between thirty and a hundred pounds overweight, carrying a disproportionate amount of that extra bulk in his chins (yes chins), jowls, and neck. That's the reason for no small talk; it's too easy to let loose with an offensive slip.

"Welcome to the big leagues, Vince."

Big Leagues. I'd heard that several times before, so I didn't think anything of it when I picked up the microdrive and slid it into my palmtop's USB. The screen lit up. I read the contract and took in the target and his indie publishing history. My breath caught in my throat. This *was* the Big Leagues – BIG LEAGUES in bright, neon, gothic letters.

After a few moments of blinking at the screen, I managed, "Are you sure this is for me?"

I couldn't help breaking the silence rule, but I had to be sure. This must be a mistake. My freelance editing resume was pretty good, I mean, I've handled some pretty hefty indies, but this guy... this guy was... well...

"Yes." Smith said, bringing me out of my shock, at least somewhat. I looked away from my palmtop. He nodded his bulbous head twice, making his jowls and chins ripple. "If you complete this project, there will be a permanent, salaried position for you in our company."

I looked from Smith to my palmtop, back to Smith...and back to my palmtop. He waited for my answer. For each potential freelance editing contract that comes along, I consider three things: first is the money (every freelancer thinks about that first), second is what kind of name the author has (if I started taking contracts on no-names, I would find the amount I could ask for my services dropping), and third is what are my chances of surviving the job? Editing indie authors can be dangerous work, especially if the money and name recognition is worth the time.

I weighed the three variables for a few moments, took a drink of water, and considered whether I had put my affairs in order. I had. I looked out of the window.

"I'll do it," I said, not making eye contact.

"You sure?" Smith said. "You seem hesitant."

I looked him in the eye. I was done dealing with his kind. I wanted to get my assignments from some smoking hot office android, have benefits, and most importantly, an extract team standing by if things got rough on a job.

"I'm sure."

"Excellent," Smith said. "Everything you need is on the microdisk."

Stone Nomad was one of the most elusive indie writers out there. With his name on my resume, I would have no problem finding a salaried editor's position in any corporation in the world. He had been writing freelance free fiction for two decades and had been able to avoid all the editors sent after him to date. He would be the challenge of a lifetime.

RANDOM MEMORY FROM MY CHILDHOOD:

"They can't do this!" Father cried. "What ever happened to free speech?"

"Calm down, dear," Mother said.

I watched from the shadows at the top of the stairs. Their argument woke me up. I loved those stairs because we could afford a two story house, not apartment, but a house. All my friends were jealous.

"Don't tell me to calm down! Those bastards are shredding the Constitution. First they buy free speech. What's next? Corporate appointed presidents? That's what it'll come down to. We're becoming the Incorporated States of America."

"Honey, America needs money so badly that," my mother said, "what does it matter if they regulate the content of fiction a little bit?"

"How can you say that with all the great things my father and uncle have written? Hell, half of their books are on the banned list."

My mother sighed. "It's not like we can do anything about it. The laws have been passed. It's just something that we'll have to accept."

I spent the week after my appointment with Smith following all the rumors of leads: old schools, friends, business associates, and other unproductive avenues. Normally, I'd be a bit more pressed for time, but Stone Nomad was a strange case: everything in his file about his past was conjecture, rumor, and supposition. Common knowledge had him in California about the time of the Indie Writer Uprising, but that's not a surprise. Also, I had plenty of time because this was *Stone freaking Nomad*! I could be on the case for a year before I brought him in and I'd be the golden boy of freelance editing.

Not that I thought any of these would pan out, but I had to try. A freelance editor never knows where a clue might lead to an indie. As I followed these less-than-stellar leads, I sifted through the files of the editors who had picked up Stone Nomad's contract before me. That didn't turn up anything either, most of the reports were incomplete because Nomad killed all the other editors sent after him. Surprisingly, they didn't have time to update their files before he ended their contracts, permanently.

Oh, what I would give to be able to go through his written works. Ah well, better to wish for an end to the war with China. Freelance editors don't get to go through training to resist getting taken in by indie writers. Never working again would have been the least of my worries if I started poking around in any of Nomad's works. I might get lucky enough to get away with the proverbial slap on the wrist, but I could say good-bye to my career.

So, with little hope and less to go on, I kept looking. One of the freelance editor's credos is, "I'd rather be lucky than good," because so many times we get lucky enough to find that one place an indie writer screwed up and didn't cover his or her tracks.

I love Berkeley, California. I've nailed so many indie writers because of that one town. SO many people there want to believe in peace, love, and freedom that they'll open up to perfect strangers despite the dangers. Also, many of the big-name indies lived in the San Francisco Bay Area during the early part of the century. That's part of the reason the Indie Writer Revolution started there. Both my grandfather and uncle had lived there, and had told me stories of people I helped bring to justice. So, with the loose lips and good odds that Stone Nomad had been in Berkeley at some point, I wandered around, hoping, praying to get lucky.

RANDOM MEMORY FROM MY CHILDHOOD:
"Vince, come here."
"Yeah, Dad?" I asked.
"You know about the new laws about free fiction writing?" he asked.
"Yeah?"
"You know the laws are wrong," he said.
"If the laws are wrong, why do we have them?" I asked.
"Because free fiction is a threat to the corporations who control America. It can give people something to look to besides the monotony of their own lives. It can give people the hope they need to make the world a better place rather than living under the sword of corporate law."

"Okay, Dad."

"Promise me one thing, Vince," my father said. "No matter what ever happens, you won't forget what good, decent men your grandfather and uncle are, even though they used to write free fiction."

"Sure, Dad."

With that, he handed me a couple of books. Some of them with my grandfather's name on the covers, some with my uncle's. He smiled at me, ruffled my hair, and went to work.

"So you've read Nomad's stuff?" I asked a young woman in her early twenties.

I had overheard her talking to some friends in a coffee shop. After she was alone, I made my way over and started a conversation. A bit blunt, but most people don't expect an editor to use the direct approach. And most don't. That's why I'm better than most freelance editors are: I don't act like one. Then again, I know from personal experience how to deal with writers and the people who love them.

She looked at me just over the top of her paper coffee cup, eyes half closed, satisfied smirk playing on her lips. "Who hasn't?"

She was one of those attractive girls who knows she's attractive. Her black hair had been gelled and teased in just the right way to make it look like she hadn't done anything at all. Her makeup was so subtle only a pro would see that it was makeup. She'd gone to a lot of trouble to be a girl of the streets. Fortunately, she was also smart, smart enough to think she was smarter than anyone else. My great-aunt was like that, which was why I'd caught her so easily when she'd gone indie. She was my first big break.

Convincing this one I wasn't an editor or just some cop doing the rounds was a fun game. She knew the right answers to the right questions, and she knew the right questions to ask me. Luckily, I knew all the right ways to talk to writers and those who love them, thanks to my grandfather, aunt, and uncle.

"I wish I could get my hands on some of Nomad's work," I said, not lying at all. "It would change my life." That wasn't a lie either.

"What if I told you that I've got everything he ever wrote," she said, very careful not to say she did, "even his early stuff he wrote with some of his friends?"

This was the big test. What would I say if I wasn't a freelance editor, if I hadn't seen those files on my palmtop? What would an underground indie book enthusiast say?

I glanced around the coffee shop, swallowed once for show, and leaned in close.

"He collaborated?" Please, please, please let that be the right answer.

She leaned in even closer, and put her lips right up to my ear. "With several people," she whispered, her breath tickling my ear and sending shivers down my spine to my toes. "One of them was supposedly one of his boyhood friends. The other was one he met while he was still living in Minnesota."

Bam! Rather lucky than good. Nothing in my files mentioned Minnesota.

"Wow," I whispered back. "I feel like this is my lucky day. But we probably shouldn't be talking like this, out here in the open. Dangerous topics for even hypothetical wonderings."

"Why don't we go back to my place?" she asked.

"Not today," I replied. "I heard that the big six are now running entrapment stings. This seems too easy, and you know too much." I stepped away from the table. "Good to meet you, Stephanie. Maybe I'll see you around."

And I left. Her expression was priceless, just the right mix of confusion and self-righteous indignation. I'd see her around. I'd make sure of that.

I planned to be at that coffee shop every day about the same time. The second day, Miss Stephanie, the perfect street-smart girl, came up to me.

"Hello," she said.

"Oh, hey," I replied.

"About the other day," she started.

I glanced at my palmtop. "Yeah, it was fascinating, but I gotta go. I'm... uh... late for something."

I fled the coffee shop before she could say another word.

Another two days went by, and I "bumped" into Stephanie on the street. She grabbed my hand, and said, "Come on," and pulled me along before I could protest. This didn't take nearly as long as I'd thought it was going to.

When we got to her building, I stopped at the door and looked around.

"Relax," she said. "I don't work for the big six. I'm an indie. Stone Nomad is my hero."

"Okay," I said.

Her apartment was a small, one-room studio not far from the abandoned university. The only furnishings were a bed, a small table with an old laptop computer, and a typewriter.

A typewriter!

Even with my experience I had never seen such a device. I had only seen pictures so I could identify one. They were highly illegal because it was impossible for the corporate government to keep track of what you wrote with it. Thus it was the perfect writing tool for a budding indie writer.

Then I saw the bookshelf. I whistled through my teeth at the size of this illegal library. This would be one of the biggest seizures to date, not of just my career, but of any freelance editor's career.

It was hard to tell which was more amazing: the typewriter or the collection. The big-name professional editors dream of finds like this. My career was made even if I never tracked down Stone Nomad. This, in itself, might get me the corporate position.

"Could I use your sweet, old-school board?" I asked, nodding at her laptop. "I need to let my mother know I'm going to be late."

"Your mother?"

"She's sick." That wasn't a lie. "I take care of her when I'm not working." That was.

She smiled at me. "How sweet. Sure, the board's all yours."

I went over to the antique computer while she went over to the bookshelf. I logged on and ran through the net to the local police station. I entered my ID, my location, and the crime codes. I could have done it from my palmtop, but I liked the irony of reporting Stephanie using her own computer. Now all I had to do was keep her busy for about a minute before the police broke down the door.

"Here they are," she said, holding a small pile of paperback novels.

"These are great," I said, as I took them from her. Keeping track of the time, I quickly memorized the secondary names of the writers with Nomad's. I had taken out one in my early years of editing. The second was familiar, but I couldn't place it.

Then I heard footsteps coming up the stairs of the building.

"Don't move," I said, drawing my gun. "You're under arrest for possession of illegal literature and technology."

While I drew my pistol, she leveled a sawed off shotgun at me. And again, proving that it's better to be lucky than good, the door came crashing in. A squad of special ops editors came pouring through. Stephanie turned and fired on the first one through the door.

He had armor. I did not.

I flung myself behind the couch. This was going to get real ugly, real fast.

After the first shot, Stephanie didn't stand a chance. The editors opened fire on her. She'd survive, but she wouldn't be happy about it. It was standard procedure to use rubber riot bullets when doing a book raid. Too many potential sources of information wound up fighting to the death, or their contraband got destroyed.

Stephanie fired three more shots before they finally had her down. Fanatics have always confused me.

An hour later I was sitting in a coffee shop hunched over my palm-top. I had a couple of leads, names of indie writers I thought I'd seen before but didn't recognize.

I logged directly into the editor's sub-web. I entered my user number and pass code. After examining several files and chat rooms, I came to a little known room almost nobody used anymore. When I saw the cursor flashing I entered the password my mentor had given me before an indie killed him rather than get taken in. The screen flashed "ACCESS DENIED." I entered the password again. Again, "ACCESS DENIED." Third time's the charm. This time, a flashing "GO" greeted me.

I typed in the name I had memorized from the books I had seen. For thirty seconds the name went through the database searching for all other aliases. The screen flashed three names associated with the one I had entered. The first two were inconsequential, two minor indie writer "plumes" that were beneath my notice. The final name took me by surprise.

For several minutes I stared at the name Jason Douglas Preston. ISA Senator of the state of Minnesota, Jason Douglas Preston. He was one of the firmest supporters of the Regulated Writing Act of 2029. Senator Jason Preston, who, I had just discovered, was engaged in illegal independent publications.

I logged off the editors' sub-web and went directly to the San Francisco International Airport. I made a reservation on the first sub-orbital flight to Washington, DC. I had a few questions I wanted to ask Senator Preston.

RANDOM MEMORY FROM MY CHILDHOOD:
My face burned where it had rubbed against the concrete of the schoolyard. Someone had pushed me down from behind. I felt blows rain down on my back, shoulders, and head.

"Take that, you traitor," I heard from above me.
"Does your whole family still write that indie crap?"
"Or was it just your traitor grandfather?"

That wasn't the first or the last beating I received because my grandfather wrote free fiction. With each beating, my hatred of the genre grew. I had read everything my father had given me, even though it was illegal. I never got the point of it.

I hate Washington, truly despise the place. It's dirty, smells, and permeates an air of desperation and hopelessness worse than Las Vegas after an energy drought. And that was before the civil riots in the early 2030's; since then the city has been going down faster than the old mid-list death spiral. Only tradition kept that city as the capital of the ISA. Very few of the politicians actually live here. They choose to do most of their work by telecommute rather than enter the city. Still, there are those few die-hards who believe in patriotism at any cost – at least, that's what they want their constituents to believe. Senator Jason Preston is one such patriot.

I sat in the senator's office waiting as patiently as I could. The only reason I had been able to get in at all was Senator Preston is always willing to see any editor, even freelance editors, at almost any time. The Official statement on this is that he's *keeping in touch with the foot soldiers of the war.*

"Good morning, Senator," I said, as he entered.

"Good morning, young man," he replied in a cheery voice.

While I stood and shook his hand, I gave Senator Preston the once-over. He was a tall six-feet-one (yeah, we may have officially gone over to the metric system, but I still measure people in feet and inches) and approaching "Smith" proportions. The senator was definitely on the portly side. He had graying black hair.

Before I let go of his hand, I swung the senator around and slammed his midriff into his desk. He started getting up and I could see the anger burning in his eyes. He stopped when I pulled my gun.

"What the hell are you doing?" Preston asked. "You know this is a capital offense?"

"So is publishing independent fiction without a corporate government license," I replied.

That got him. He stopped struggling.

"How much do you want? My wallet is in my back pocket. I have cash, lots of it."

Of course he did. That way no one could track what he was spending it on.

"I don't want any of your money," I said, knocking the wallet across the room. "All I want is some information regarding the illegal author Stone Nomad. I believe you worked with him a long time ago."

For the next two hours the senator and I sat and talked about Stone Nomad. I didn't learn much about him, but I learned enough to actually track him down. After the conversation was over I got up and started to leave.

"What about me?" Senator Preston asked. "Aren't you going to edit me?"

"I am a freelance editor," I explained, "and a professional. I have not been hired to edit you, Senator. Only governmental or corporate editors could make this kind of call." I didn't add that he'd pretty much helped secure my employment at Smith's publishing house.

After I closed the door I heard the sounds of some hurried packing. I smiled. It didn't matter. The senator couldn't go anywhere that I couldn't follow. His was a face one couldn't hide. Popularity does have some great disadvantages. He was now my first priority after getting the corporate job.

RANDOM MEMORY FROM MY CHILDHOOD:
"I'm sorry about your grandfather," my great uncle said. "We'll all miss him a lot."

"Whatever," I said, and turned to leave. The only reason I was at the funeral was because of a sense of family obligation.

A hand gripped my shoulder and turned me around. My father stared into my face. I could see the rage pushing grief out of the way. I knew his words even before he said them.

"Don't speak to your uncle like that," my father growled, "especially not on a day like this."

I stared defiantly back at my father. "He's not my real uncle. He's just a friend of my dead grandfather. I don't owe him anything. And I am ashamed. I'm ashamed to be the grandson of an indie fiction writer. I'm ashamed to be the grandson of a traitor to my country. I know that he was still writing before he died. I know my uncle is still doing it. I hate all of you for what I have to live with for being related to you."

Before anything else was said, I stormed off. I slammed the door of my car and sped off, ignoring the calls of my parents. I was done with that family.

I was on another sub-orbital. This one was to Scotland. After two weeks of searching and cross-referencing, I'd located the Stone Nomad. It seemed that Nomad had gone to Europe, probably to escape from people like me. Too bad editors have almost as much power in Europe as in the ISA, ever since the collapse of the European Common Market.

I got off my flight at Heathrow Airport in England and took the train up to Glasgow. I would have enjoyed the trip a lot more if I weren't worrying so much about what I was going to face. The closer I got to Nomad, the more insecure I became. A bit of this self-inflicted freak-out was part of my process. But most of my nervousness was because hiding my arrival would have been easier if I had come by train.

When I finally arrived in Glasgow, I had no trouble locating Nomad's residence – a quaint little cottage. It seemed everyone here thought of him as if he was a favorite relative. I'd have been wary, except every story I heard was pretty much the same and each person I spoke to sniffed me out as an editor, most of them telling me to my face.

"If you all know I'm an editor," I asked one young woman who served my breakfast the morning after I got into Glasgow, "why are you so willing to give me information about him."

She smiled at me as if I were some child who had grabbed the pan's hot handle again. "Sweetie, we get editors through here all the time. Not so much anymore, but when Nomad first came to be writing here, editors would come through once a month or more. They all head to that village, and we ain't seen not a one of them come back through. All the time, Nomad keeps writing. Good luck out there, luv, *in nomine padre, et fili, et spiritu sancte.*"

His house was quaint. It had that old-world charm of an age that you just can't get in America. A random thought popped into my head about how much my grandfather would have loved to live in a house like this.

I approached the house cautiously. Freelance editors do not last long in the business by being overzealous and rushing headlong into stupid situations. The myth of the Twentieth Century writer is gone, especially with the indies: they protect their work with an almost religious-like zealotry.

I went in through the front door after picking the lock and snipping the string attached to the shotgun trap waiting for the unwary editor. A coat and hat rack as the only other thing I saw in the hall. From down the hall, I heard a ticking sound coming from a door to my left. Holding my breath, I listened long enough to realize the ticking wasn't at a consistent enough rate to be a timer. Then I heard a bell ring and a dull *thunk.*

Following the noise, I crept down the hall, gun in hand, and carefully peered into the room. My great uncle sat a desk, furiously attacking the keys on a typewriter. He still looked fit, but white dominated his once-dark hair and wrinkles pruned his skin. He looked up at me and then eyed the gun I had trained on him. His expression was calm. Then he did the craziest thing I've ever experienced as an editor.

R*ANDOM MEMORY FROM MY CHILDHOOD:*
"*Get out of this house!" my father ordered.*
"*But, Dad," I said, but he interrupted me.*
"*You shame the memory of your grandfather," he said, and turned his back on me. "You are no longer welcome in this house or this family."*
That was his reaction to seeing my freelance editor's license. It was the proudest day of my life. I had studied hard and fought hard to overcome the prejudice leveled at me because of my family.
"*Fine," I said, "I know that you never approved of me because I didn't turn out like your father. You couldn't write and were hoping that, because I had shown promise, you could turn me into your own little rebel writer."*
If that's how it was going to be, that's how it was going to be. When I got to the door, I stopped.
"*Because I still love Mom, I'll give you a heads up. I'm going to the stop-and-rob down the street. I'm getting a disposable cell phone. The FBI will receive an anonymous tip about illegal works of fiction at this residence. I'm going to throw the phone away, and you'll never see me again. You should have just enough time to destroy all your father's and uncle's books before they get here. BUT. You'll be on their radar even more now. Probably wouldn't be a good idea to get any indie books ever again."*

I closed the door and walked. Damn but that felt good.

"You're here early," my uncle said, as he kept typing. "I didn't expect you for another few minutes. Give me a moment, and I'll be right with you."

What the hell was going on? I had expected an armed resistance, maybe a firefight. As this was so bizarre, I let him continue. Besides, he would be dead in a few minutes and everything in the house would be burned. What would be the harm in letting him finish one last project that was going to go up in flames? I kept the gun pointed at him, and he kept typing.

"This reminds me of something Isaac Asimov once said," my uncle said, still typing.

"I don't care," I replied. "Just finish."

My uncle smiled. "He said, 'If someone told me I had an hour to live, I'd type faster.' Or something like that. Memory's not what it used to be, and I'm not used to composing while trying to talk to someone pointing a gun at my head."

I didn't respond. For all I knew, this was how he'd taken all the other editors – lulled them into lowering their guard.

"There."

My uncle pulled the final sheet of paper from the antique. He placed it on the top of a small stack of papers next to the typewriter. Next to the papers was a stack of notebooks and journals. He arranged them all neatly on the desk and then looked at me.

"I know why you're here, Vince," he said, "I let you find me. I'm tired of running. At my age I don't run, fight, or hide quite as well as I used to. That, and I've just told about all the stories I had in me. I could try and squeeze out another few, but an editor would catch up to me sooner or later, and I'd hate to leave a story unfinished. Too many writers are doing that these days. This last story is for you." He put his hand on the manuscript he'd just finished. "Do with it as you see fit."

He stood and looked at me expectantly. Again I wondered what the hell was going on. I knew I had a job to do, but this was so unlike any editing I had done before. I had never had anyone just stand there and wait for it, much less my own uncle. This whole thing was so weird.

After a few seconds, I did my duty and pulled the trigger. One shot to the head.

I went over the stack of papers he had left me with every intention of burning it. Then I saw it had my name on it. I shouldn't have turned to the first page, but the curiosity gnawed at me. Writing by random strangers was one thing, and I could burn that without a second's thought. I would even burn my uncle's other work, knowing it was the fiction of

Stone Nomad; I'd fire that up and sleep well at night. This was different. He'd written this for me, to me.

My uncle's writing wasn't a work of fiction. It was his life story. From his childhood up until the moment I walked in and killed him. It explained why he wrote and why he defied a corporate government. I read through the rest of that day and into the night, my uncle's corpse beside me the whole time. I stopped and looked at him when I got to the part where he wrote about being the one to hire me to be his final editor and why. He'd included lists of documentation on his previous editors – most of whom hadn't actually existed. Stone Nomad was a shell game that my uncle and Senator Preston created in order to keep the dream of freedom in fiction alive. Even in a country as bleak and grim as the ISA, people needed their dreams. Hell, even I needed my dream of the big catch and the cushy corporate job.

When I finished the book, I flipped through the stack of notebooks. They were some of my grandfather's and uncle's journals. I read the journals. They gave even more details about other writers targeted by several politicians, witch hunts that had never really been pursued in any capacity other than for the media limelight.

A phone rang in one of the desk drawers and I nearly screamed.

I pulled the drawer open and answered the phone.

"Vincent," a familiar sounding voice said, "this is Senator Jason Preston. You have a choice to make right now. You can stay in that house and become a hero to the masses as the editor who brought down Stone Nomad, or you can truly serve your country as the editor who became an indie writer. You have enough time to collect your uncle's writing and his typewriter and get away before ISA agents arrive at the house. Either way, this phone call never happened."

* * *

My fingers poised above the typewriter keys, I was stuck for anything to say. Then I remembered one of the ways the stories my mom and dad used to tell me would start.

Once upon a time…

I stopped. Was that how the stories inside me began? No. I'd try something else.

A long time ago…

That wasn't it either.

I sat there for a long time until I remembered something my grandfather would say before telling me stories as a kid.

Many miles and years away…

The Dragon Bone Flute

For Penny
For helping me see past my rough drafts to the real stories I want to tell.

I

If any one moment could be said to be the turning point in my life, the moment where destiny shifted, where all further actions and choices moved me toward the day when I would be forced to flee my home and give up my music, it would be the time I put my flute on the bench outside my house when my mother demanded I take bread and cheese to my father working in his fields. So much of my childhood was taken up with ways to get out of my chores that should anyone from my childhood see me now, they might not believe it was me. I've grown some, yes, but I also no longer have the music to fill my time. And as music filled so much of my time, I tried to be away from my flute as little as possible, but I also took steps to protect it and ensure its safety. Accidents happen, and when the other children in the town dislike you because you have a gift they do not, and your lazy habits are tolerated a bit more because of that gift, sometimes what seems like an accident isn't. That day, I had chosen to leave my flute on the bench rather than argue with my mother about taking it back to my room. Arguing would have kept me from it longer than it would take to run to my father in the field and back, and run I did, as fast as my legs would move me. Because of trouble I'd gotten into over the years with other village children, I'd learned to put on quite the burst of speed when needed.

Now, if I'd put the flute down on one of the chairs behind the house, or taken the time to argue with my mother, things might have been different. If, after everything, I had the chance to go back and make another choice, would I have? I cannot tell. Most likely not, but I say that with the comfort of not actually having that choice to make.

When I returned home, my flute was not on the bench were I had left it. I glanced around frantically, hoping that it had only rolled off. It wasn't anywhere I could see it. I drew in a deep lungful of air to call to my mother – please, gods and goddesses, let her have taken it inside – when I heard someone cough loudly in the street behind me, the very directed cough of someone trying to get my attention.

I turned and saw Hugh, Eric, and Gregory smiling at me. Those triplets had caused the greater portion of the unhappy moments in my childhood. Hugh stood in the middle, slightly taller than the other two, all three of them easily a head higher than me or any other boy or girl in the town. In that place, in that time, childhood lasted much longer than here, where girls look to marry at fifteen or sixteen. Girls in my hometown were still sometimes playing with dolls, and boys were not yet given the responsibilities in the fields and town reserved for grown men, and most of them still played at being knights with wooden swords. Well, Hugh, the largest boy in the town, held my flute in one hand.

"Give. It. Back." I took a step forward to punctuate every word.

"No," Hugh said. "Your parents obviously don't love you enough to keep you honest about your chores, so we're going to."

I ground my teeth together. Even after all these years, I can still remember the ache in my jaw as I struggled to keep from screaming at him. Screaming would have brought adults, and that was cheating. By the unwritten, unspoken laws of the children in our town, if the adults got involved, you lost status in the eyes of everyone else. I had so little status that I couldn't afford to lose any. Also, if everyone found out what had set me off, and the three brutes looking at me with malicious grins would surely tell them, everyone would know what kind of a reaction stealing my flute would produce. Oh yes, anyone who caused another child to get an adult involved gained standing in the eyes of the other children. Needless to say, Hugh, Eric, and Gregory collectively held as much status in this game as all the other children put together.

"Whether or not I get my chores done has no effect on you three," I said.

"Oh, but it does," Eric said. "Any time any of the rest of us shirk our chores even the slightest bit, we get compared to you." He pitched his voice up an octave or two. "'Well now, since you don't mind your duties, let's get you a fiddle so you can run off and play with Elzibeth.'"

"Maybe if you didn't have a flute," Gregory said, "you'd be able to be a bit more like the rest of us."

My ears grew warm. I ground my teeth together even harder.

"May I please have my flute back?" I said through my teeth.

"Perhaps," Hugh said. He twirled the flute in his fingers. "But you have to do something first."

"What?" I asked, dreading the amount of work they were going to heap on me, or the embarrassing act they were going to make me perform, humiliating me before as many in the town as possible.

"Spend the night in the dragon's cave," they said in unison.

"Fine," I replied.

From the way their faces scrunched up in befuddlement, I'm sure they hadn't thought that I'd actually agree. I would worry my parents a bit, and surely I'd see some form of punishment, but it wasn't nearly as bad as I feared. I spun on my toe, went into the house, and collected my cloak, some food, and one of my father's lanterns with several extra candles. Mother was so busy preparing the stew for dinner that she hardly noticed me. She said something about getting some chore done before getting back to playing my flute, but I hardly noticed her.

"I'll see you tomorrow," I said, pushing my way through the brothers.

I got about twenty or so paces beyond them, when I heard that attention-getting cough again. I stopped and glanced back.

"You have to bring proof," Hugh said.

I gave a sharp nod and left town.

II

Everyone knew generally where the dragon's cave was, but nobody went because it was in the wild hills north of the town. Also, the last man to go to the dragon's cave, in the time when my grandfather was a child, never returned. When people gathered at the tavern, every once in a time, someone would speak of that knight that went into the hills and never came back. People would speculate as to his fate, and even as to why he'd gone up there in the first place. No one had seen any sign of a dragon in more years than anyone could guess at. And even without fear of dragons that probably weren't there anyway, the wild hills contained more than enough real dangers: wild boars, wolves, and the occasional sinkhole. Natives of small towns generally share one common trait, and I've seen many small towns. People who live in them tend to have enough sense not to go looking after trouble.

I scrambled through the hills and crags and brambles for hours. I'd narrowly avoided a wild boar and soaked myself up to the waist by not being able to quite jump across a stream. Scrapes and cuts covered my hands, and I had a large lump on my head from failing to climb the edge of a ravine. Apparently, I didn't have enough sense not to go looking for trouble. Well, in my defense, I hadn't gone looking for three bullies to force me into this. Yes, I could have gone to my parents, but such thinking was impossible in the pride of my youth.

The sun had set, and the shadows between the hills had grown long enough and deep enough that I'd lit the first candle in the lantern. I'd come to the area where people said the dragon cave might be, and I'd been wandering back and forth, searching for it. I was about to give up for the night and find a place to sleep when I found it. I came around a hill, and there it was, a black opening in the side of the largest hill I could see. I'd come here planning to climb to the top and use it as a vantage point.

Now I didn't know if this really was the dragon's cave, but I couldn't imagine it being anything else. In my mind, I'd known that there was a dragon cave. I'd known it was in the wild hills. I just wasn't prepared for the enormity of it. It was somewhere between fifty and sixty paces away from me, and I could tell the top of the cave was at least ten times as high as I was tall. It hung in the side of the hill, dark and gaping, like some mouth waiting to swallow an unsuspecting passerby. Thinking that did nothing to settle my growing nerves, and I froze there, staring at it.

I might have stayed there all night, unmoving, but a wolf howled somewhere in the distance. That got my feet moving again. While a dragon might be waiting somewhere in the bowels of that cave, the cave might also be empty. On the other side of the coin, the wolves were very much real. The dragon, even if it was there, might not devour me whole, but I thought I'd probably prefer getting eaten in one gulp by a dragon than I would getting ripped apart by a pack of wolves. I hurried toward the cave, thinking that if a dragon had ever lived there at any time in the past, wolves and other wild animals would probably stay away from it. Quick death or a safe place, the cave seemed the wisest choice.

Even with all my logic and sound reasoning, stepping across the threshold of that cave was the hardest thing I've ever done in my life. As I write these words, my heart pounds at the memory. My stomach nearly emptied itself of the cheese and bread I'd eaten hours before.

The light of the lantern went before me a few paces and then faded into a gloomy haze. The air in the cave felt heavy, as if pressing down on me and stamping out my light. Still fearing the wolves more than any potential nastiness I might find in the cave, I went further inside.

A gust of wind caused the candle light to flutter a bit, and I thought I saw something move across the floor to my left. I nearly dropped the lantern and ran screaming from the cave. As it was, I gave a squeak of surprise but managed to stay in place. I held my breath and tried willing my heart to slow as I waited for the light to steady. When the wind died down and the candle ceased flickering, I realized it was my own shadow. I had the lantern in my right hand, and my shadow stretched out into the darkness. It weaved and danced every time I moved the lantern a bit. I released my held breath in a long, steady exhale.

It was still light enough to see outside, so I placed the lantern on the floor of the cave and went to gather firewood. This area didn't have as many trees as some parts of the hill I'd been through, but I'd noticed more than a few branches that would make a nice fire and more than enough twigs for kindling. In only a few minutes, I had enough wood to build and feed a nice fire to keep me warm until I was ready for sleep. A few minutes after that, and thanks to the candle in the lantern, I had a fire burning fifteen paces into the cave.

The light of the fire fared much better at pushing back the darkness than my little lantern. Placing another small piece of wood on the fire, I stood up, stretched, and looked around.

And screamed.

III

Even before my mind realized I should be scared, I screamed. I distinctly recall wondering exactly what it was I was screaming about. The scream was definitely my scared scream, which was very different from my angry scream or my sad scream. The fear scream is my highest pitch scream, hurting even my own ears.

Then my mind realized what I was screaming about. It had been too much for my rational thoughts to process all at once.

Silhouetted against the wall, I saw the flickering shadow of a great, gaping maw filled with twin rows of giant teeth. I backed away, shaking my head at the impossibility that there really was a dragon living in the dragon's cave. Then again, if there hadn't been a dragon, that knight probably would have come back. But he didn't. Still backing away, I wondered what happened to the knight.

My voice caught in my throat when I saw what created the shadow on the wall. The flickering firelight revealed the stark, pale skull of what used to be a dragon. Its mouth gaped open wide enough to likely swallow me whole. The shortest of the teeth in that mouth were longer than my forearm. My gaze swept down its long neck until I could take in the sight of its ribs and wings, unfurled out across the roof of the cave. A lance, blackened and charred, stabbed between two of the skeletal ribs. A suit of armor, also black and standing in a scorched area ten paces across, held onto the other end of that lance.

I don't know how long I stood transfixed by the sight of the skeletons of the dragon and the roasted knight, trapped in a moment of mutual murder. Hours had passed. By the time I was able to pull my gaze away, the candle in my lantern had melted away and the fire had burned to embers. I think it was the night's cold that finally overcame my awe. Wrapping my cloak around me, I rebuilt the fire.

Sleep would be impossible. I knew that, so I left the cave to gather more firewood. In the distance, wolves howled in the night, but none of them sounded closer than the first howl that urged me into the cave. Even with the knight and the dragon long dead, I could hardly blame the wolves for wanting to stay away.

When I returned to the cave, I built the fire higher than I needed to. The warmth of it helped to settle my nerves. Every few minutes I turned to warm another part of my body. I'd thought facing toward the skeleton and armor would be bad, looking on them as my back soaked in heat. Not so. Facing toward the fire was the worst. As my back cooled, it reminded me that a massive battle had taken place behind me, one where both combatants had died. Staring into the flames, my imagination glanced over my shoulder from time to time and saw the heads of both the dragon and the knight twisting silently to look upon me, as if asking, "Who is this interloper that disturbs us?" Shortly after that, my actual head would whip around to make sure they weren't stalking toward me. Granted, the thought that a suit of armor and a massive jumble of bones might make a little noise while trying to creep up on me had not occurred to me.

Eventually I nodded off to sleep. I didn't want to. I fought it as hard as I could, pinching myself and slapping my face. It didn't matter what I did, what I tried. The journey to the cave had taxed my body, and what I discovered there had taxed my mind. Both needed time to recuperate. I remember telling myself I would only rest my eyes for a moment. That a moment was all I'd need to be rested again. My eyelids came together. It felt so nice, as if closing my eyes had given my body permission to relax. The fire was so warm. Sleep came moments later.

When I woke, the fire was nothing but ashes and the sun had been up for a few hours at least. I stretched, trying to release some of the stiffness I'd gotten sleeping on the hard rock of the cave's surface. My back popped twice, and I let out a soft groan. Then my mind caught up with my situation, and the realization of where I was hit me as the last of the fog of sleep lifted from me.

I was on my feet at once, heart pounding in my chest, breath coming in short blasts.

Neither of them had moved. I don't know why that surprised me, but the part of me that imagined them turning and looking at me expected them to have gotten a little closer, maybe a lot closer. The mind and imagination play strange tricks on us when covered by the wet cloak of fear. In the months to come, I'd learn that lesson again and again, through pain and tears.

But, I'm getting ahead of myself.

The daylight helped me to calm down sooner than the night before, to get past the momentary fear that came over me, especially with the realization that I'd done it. I'd spent the night in the dragon's cave. I could get my flute back. Then I remembered that Hugh had said I needed to bring back proof.

What could I take that I'd be able to carry all the way back to the town?

I looked around. There had to be something. Perhaps one of the scorched rocks next to the knight? No. They'd be able to say I'd just burned a rock in a fire. Maybe I could find an old scale or something, so I searched behind the scattered rocks and in the corners of the cave. When I came to the very back of the cave, where the daylight barely reached, I saw three large rocks. They came up to about my waist, and each was smooth as polished glass. One was red as any ruby. One was green as any emerald. One was blue as any sapphire. These must be all that was left of the dragon's hoard. They would be the perfect proof, but I couldn't imagine rolling one all the way back to town.

With a huff and a stamp of my foot, I turned away from those stones that must have been worth the ransom of a kingdom. The dragon loomed above me. I followed the curve of its body from its head to its tail and down to its toes. Then I saw my proof. I could take the smallest of its toe bones. It would be easy to carry, probably no heavier than a shovel or other farm tool. My shoulders might ache by the time I returned to town, but I'd get my flute back.

Slowly, I worked my way toward the dragon's forward-most foot. It was the left one. The right was braced up against the wall. The hind feet supported most of the dragon's weight.

Then I stopped.

I'd seen skeletons before, deer and other animals in the woods south and west of town and sometimes livestock that had died alone in one of the further fields. None of them had ever held their shape. Each and every one had come apart as the muscles and sinew rotted away. How then, in all the years since my grandfather's childhood, had this dragon managed to not tumble to the floor?

"Because it's a dragon," I told myself, and that settled it. I needed no other explanation or rationalization.

With that pronouncement, I started toward the foot again. My progress was slow and careful. The thing might remain whole because of whatever lingering magic it had possessed as a dragon, but that did not mean it would stay that way forever. When I was two paces away, I began to hold my breath. I reached down to the smallest of the toe bones, and biting my lips, I took a slow deep breath through my nose to steady my quivering hand. Holding my breath was apt to make me more tense and shaky than not. I closed my eyes and swallowed, despite the dryness that had filled my mouth. My imagination saw the whole thing coming down on me, bones tumbling in a great cacophony that would drown out my scream. Dust settling over my cairn, with no one to mourn me.

I pushed that thought out of my mind, reached out, and snatched up the toe bone.

My breath caught in my throat as a great creaking sound echoed in the cave. My feet wanted to flee, but I forced myself to stand fast. Any further disturbance in the cave might bring the thing down. I waited, not breathing, counting my heartbeats. Ten, the creaking stopped. Twenty, the last echo of the creaking faded. Thirty, silence. Forty, I began to leave the cave, making sure I brought my feet completely off the floor and placing them carefully back down with hardly any jarring and definitely no shuffling.

I didn't take my first full breath until after I had left the cave completely. After my third breath, I laughed and laughed, skipping my way back toward home. I cradled the bone, which honestly wasn't much bigger than my flute, under my arm.

When I came to the place where I would turn out of sight of the cave, I turned back. In the full light of morning, the cave did not look as ominous as it had the night before. It was still huge, still like a gaping mouth, but it no longer held me in the grip of near-terror. I spun the toe bone in my hand and gave a rakish bow a boy might do to an adult's back after having danced out of some bit of serious trouble.

IV

The journey back to town took longer than the journey the day before. Yesterday, I had the passion of my anger to fuel my speed, and I wasn't carrying the extra load of the toe bone. I also had food and water. In my haste to escape the cave, I'd left the basket and what remained of my food behind. My water skin had been in the basket, too. I found plenty of streams to drink from, but my stomach growled with hunger. Despite this, I was also filled with a sense of wonder and awe, seeing the world in a new light. Now that I knew the truth of the dragon's cave, I saw many signs that it had once lived here: a small valley between two hills filled with the sun-bleached bones of what looked like several hundred cows, a grove of burned down trees where no other plants grew, and several places where I imagined I could see the dragon's tracks. This last one was pure foolishness. In all the decades since the dragon and knight had killed each other, the weather would have washed away any fleeting sign of the dragon's passing. On the other side of the coin, the dragon's skeleton had remained together. Who knew what else was possible?

By the time I returned to town late in the afternoon, my feet hurt worse than any time in my whole life. The fog of wonder had lifted. I just wanted to get my flute back, play a few songs, and go to sleep in my own bed. I'd probably receive a stern talking to from my parents. Mother might even yell, and I could live with that. I hoped my father didn't get too quiet. The quieter he grew, the worse it was, especially when he gave me his most I'm-disappointed-in-you look. It always wrenched my insides so much that my stomach and heart seemed to trade places. But mostly, I just wanted to get my flute back.

Hugh, Eric, and Gregory stood in the middle of the road back into town. I adjusted my path a bit and headed right toward them.

Gregory, or perhaps it was Eric – I couldn't tell because I was so tired and fixated on the flute in Hugh's hand – said something. His brothers laughed.

"Did you get to the cave?" Hugh asked, still chuckling a bit.

"Yes." I shoved the toe bone at him. "Here's your proof. Give me my flute back."

They all looked at the bone for a moment, eyes wide with wonder for just a moment. Then Eric laughed and pointed.

"You're trying to convince us that deer bone is your proof?"

"It is," I said. "The dragon is dead. That's a bone from its toe. It's the only one small enough for me to carry."

The other two brothers took up his laughter.

"The only thing you've proven is that you're a liar," Hugh said. "And liars need to be punished."

Before I could do or say anything else, Hugh grasped my flute with one hand on either end and brought it down across his knee. The sound of my flute snapping would haunt me longer than I could imagine. I fell to my knees as the splintered halves of my prized possession fell to the ground.

I grasped one piece in each hand and looked up at the three bullies. In my youth, in my hometown, I hardly knew what that term meant. Sure, my parents used it when describing the tax collector who came once a year, complaining about how he'd bully people around. I didn't understand what it really meant until after I'd traveled far and wide, so that when I call the brothers bullies, I'm speaking in terms I know now, not from any level of comprehension as it happened. They were bullies of the worst sort, because as I knelt in the road, blinking tears of sorrow and loss out of my eyes, I heard gasps from all around. I found out later that the brothers had told all of the other children where I'd gone and what I was supposed to do. Hugh had not destroyed my flute to punish me. He'd done it to solidify his fearful reign over the other children of the town. That much I understood. Even in my stunned state, I knew it hadn't mattered what I had brought back. He and his brothers had decided I was going to be their example, their object lesson. Well they, too, could serve as an example. I was not about to be made a fool of, nor was I going to let them get away with this.

Hugh reached out and placed a hand on my shoulder. His touch was light, almost like a caress.

"Let's get you home," he said in a tone that must have been what he thought of as caring but only came out sounding spiteful. "Your parents must be worried about you."

I met his eyes. I could see myself reflected in them. The dust of the road clung to my tear-stained face in dark-brown strips. When I smiled at

Hugh, my lips thin and pressed together, he blinked a few times. I'm sure that wasn't the reaction he'd expected.

I'm also sure he wasn't expecting me to stab him in the hand with one of the jagged ends of my ruined flute, but I did. Hard. Blood welled from over a dozen wounds in a tight circle. Several of them were rather deep. I twisted my makeshift weapon, hoping to give him splinters.

I tried to get him in the leg with the other half of the flute, but by that time the surprise had worn off Hugh and his brothers. Eric and Gregory grabbed my arms and twisted them behind me. I struggled for a second, but that only made them wrench my arms harder.

Fighting only made it hurt more, but not as much as it did when Hugh slapped me.

I'd been slapped before, but nothing like this. This was no angry child slap. He put his whole body into it. Pinpoints of light and dark circles filled my vision. My jaw ached, and my skin burned. I remember thinking it a miracle that he didn't rattle any of my teeth loose.

Not knowing, or not wanting to leave well enough alone, I kicked Hugh in the shin, then stomped on one of his brother's, Eric's I think, feet. Unfortunately, it wasn't enough to make Eric let go of me, and my kick to Hugh only made him angrier. He balled his hand into a fist and drove it into my stomach. I coughed all the air out of my lungs.

At that point, I was in so much pain and so exhausted from my journey to the dragon's cave that my mind began to shut the world out. I was vaguely aware of other people yelling and the sound of feet stomping. There was more yelling. Someone picked me up and was carrying me somewhere. At some point, I was placed onto something soft and someone put some blankets over me.

I slept.

V

It's been years since I thought of that night, but even now, I can feel the sweat prickling through my pores from the fitful dreams I had. I don't recall the events of those dreams in any semblance of coherence, just images: broken flutes, splinters of wood raining down on me, maniacal laughter, and rivers of blood gushing from the dying bodies of Hugh, Gregory, and Eric. Please don't think me too morbid. I was in that place between childhood and adulthood, and my imagination was trying to balance between both those states of mind after having suffered the worst trauma of my life. Little did I know, it was just the beginning.

At some point in the night, I woke. It was a gibbous moon that night, and the light of it shown in through the window making everything shadowy lumps. I blinked in the darkness of my room. The pain from where

Hugh had slapped my face and struck my stomach was now a dull ache. The burning my cheek had felt was almost gone, and I thought the slight throbbing in my jaw would last the longest of all of them. Thankfully Hugh wasn't much more than a boy, yes a large one, but not at the point where he really knew anything about fighting. The townsfolk weren't violent by nature, but sometimes the young, mostly unmarried, men got drunk at the tavern and settled their drunken ramblings with fists. I sat up, irritated that I was awake, but also thankful to be away from the dreams.

Then I heard a tapping somewhere. Three taps. Silence. Three taps. Silence. I looked around, still trying to blink away the haze of sleep and bad dreams. After a few moments, I stopped trying to see it, closed my eyes, and just listened. The sound was coming from my window.

I crawled out from under my blankets. The night chill hit me, and I shivered as I crossed the room. When I reached the window, I saw the moon first, hanging in the center of the frame. That meant I'd only been asleep a few hours, just long enough to sleep off the shock and initial heartache of my loss. I saw the silhouette of a head in the window – too short to be an adult, not that an adult would be at my window at this hour, but also not tall enough to be one of the brothers.

For a few moments I pondered whether or not to open the window. I was fairly certain I knew who it was, and I wasn't sure I wanted to deal with him. Unfortunately, he would probably keep tapping away at the window until I opened it and dealt with him.

"Hello, Frances," I said as I opened the window.

A blast of cold air hit me as the wind gusted into my room, and I wrapped my arms around my shoulders. Even though my clothes offered a bit more warmth than my nightgown would have, my shivering increased.

"Elzibeth," he said through chattering teeth, "I brought you these."

Frances was a boy of slight build, and though a year older than me, he was shorter by a few inches. He reached up toward the window, holding the two halves of my broken flute and the dragon's toe bone.

"I got them before anyone else could," Frances said. "I thought you might like them, but now I don't know. Maybe not. But if they're going to get thrown away, you should do it. After all, they're your things."

I took them.

"Thank you, Frances. Now go home."

I closed the window before he could say anything else and went back to my bed. Even curling up in the blankets, I couldn't sleep yet. The cold night air had chilled the sleep right out of me, at least for a while. Since sleep would be a little time off, I laid the things Frances had saved for me on the bed, right in the middle of a patch of moonlight. Looking at the remains of my flute, part of me wanted to start crying all over again, but for some reason the tears wouldn't come. Frances' kindness stopped them. At least someone in the village had cared enough about my feelings and what I might want to…well, I don't know, but he did something, made a gesture that helped to draw me away from complete despair.

My eyes wandered away from my ruined flute and looked over the dragon toe bone. It was broken as well. One end had been stepped on, or something like that, because while one end stopped in a smooth knob, the other end had become as jagged and splintered as the broken bits of my flute. I picked it up and turned it around in my hands. When the broken edge faced me, I stopped and lifted it up so I could get a better look.

The bone was free of marrow, as I expected. However, the part I didn't expect was how much empty space there was inside the bone, like a bird's. Growing up in a small community, I'd seen the insides of plenty of bones, and this discovery surprised me to say the least.

I chewed the inside of my cheek, because that's what I've done all my life whenever something intrigues or interests me.

For a long time, I sat with my blankets wrapped around my shoulders staring at the oddity, trying to figure out why exactly a dragon's bones would be hollow. Before I allowed sleep to take me, I went over to my wardrobe and got out my work knife. I used the knife to carve away the dragon bone's jagged edges. When it was mostly blunt, and I wouldn't have to worry about stabbing myself with the edges, I pushed the remains of my flute and bone under my pillow. For some reason, the lumps they made brought me a bit of comfort, as if proving that even in the worst moments, sometimes people still care. I'd have to remember to thank Frances a little more properly the next time I saw him.

VI

Two days later Frances's cheek flared a furious crimson in response to the kiss I'd planted on it. He'd come up to me, awkwardly asking how I was. While he was in the middle of his babbling, I leaned forward and kissed him. Nothing special, just a quick peck, but that was more intimacy than either of us had shared with another human being aside from our parents. Once I'd done it, his mouth opened and closed, trying to find words. Realizing what I'd done, I felt my cheeks begin to heat as well.

"Wha…wha…what?" he managed, at last.

"That was to thank you for bringing those things to me," I replied.

I couldn't say what he'd brought out loud, especially not the bone. In the two days since my fight with the brothers, two things had gotten around to all the other children. The first was that I'd not only stood up to the brothers but actually started a fight with them. The second was that I'd claimed to have found a dragon bone. This collective knowledge had been received with a bit of a mixed opinion. For now, the other children were overlooking the audacity of the dragon business due to Hugh, Eric, and Gregory being much more closely watched by the adults in the town. Oh, of course their parents, especially their boisterous father, had made all sorts of justifications for them attacking me, mostly based on the gash on Hugh's hand. That didn't hold much weight when so many people had seen the two smaller boys holding me while Hugh looked ready to beat me senseless. The result was that they wouldn't be getting away with any of their bullying for quite some time.

"You're welcome," Frances said, and his blush deepened. I'm fairly certain mine did, too.

We stood looking at our feet. After a while, Frances broke the silence

"I need to get back," Frances said. "My da' has things for me to do."

I nodded. "Thank you again."

He nodded back. "Of course."

I watched him walk away, the frail, skinny boy who had done me the greatest kindness of my life to that point.

And that was the extent of our interaction for some time.

I moved from moment to moment in a strange sort of haze. I didn't have a flute anymore. I didn't have music anymore. I'd tried singing and whistling, and these two activities were poor substitutes for my grandfather's flute.

For me, playing the flute had been about more than just making music. It had been an activity that I put my whole self into. My mind had to remember the notes of the melody and make sure that I wasn't rushing or slowing down the tempo of my song. Where most musicians content themselves with the motions of making music with their fingers, more often than not, I would move my body in rhythm to my songs, giving the music physical form. Lastly, or maybe it was firstly, I poured my heart into every piece I did. I can't describe it any more than that, except to say that whenever I played a song, my mood at the time colored the tune, sometimes making the song unrecognizable.

My parents noticed my melancholy, and Father would frequently promise me, at dinner while I was pushing my uneaten food around on my plate, that he'd get me a new flute when a peddler came through the town. He meant well with these promises, but we never had extra money, especially when a peddler came.

After a few months of my moping and listening to Father's hollow promises, a peddler finally came to town. He arrived just between the last of the autumn rains and the first of the winter snows. I never understood how they could tell, but I suppose it's the business of peddlers to know these things, just as the blacksmith knows the right glow of yellow to start hammering a pot or the farrier knows exactly how much to trim to keep from hobbling a horse.

The peddler stayed a week.

When he left, I did not have a new flute.

Still, I didn't completely give up hope. We usually saw two or three peddlers before winter. The first snow came the next day. We wouldn't see another peddler until spring.

I did not come out of my room for three days. I did not speak to my father for nearly a month.

However, having foreseen this, I'd taken steps to keep myself occupied during the winter. I'd not been able to afford one of the three flutes the peddler had for sale, but he did have a small woodcarving kit that I traded for doing all his laundry during his stay. Before the snows grew too deep, I collected all manner of sticks, reeds, and branches. The time I'd spent playing in previous years I dedicated to woodworking. My hands blistered, bled, and calloused. I slept little, working at night by feel as I'd played by feel, as I'd closed my eyes and felt the music well inside me, burning and pushing to be free on the air. However, I didn't carve and whittle all the time. In those moments when I didn't, I held the bone, feeling it, studying it, knowing it with my hands.

VII

When the snows finally began to melt, I was ready. One morning, just after Father had gone to the fields, I made a bedroll, bundled my warmest clothes into a pack, and gathered a bit of food I thought would last a few days: dried meat and fruit, cheese, bread, a skin of small beer. The remains of Grandfather's flute were tucked away at the bottom of my pack, and the dragon bone was in the bedroll.

"What are you doing?" Mother asked as I came out of the pantry.

"Leaving for a few days," I replied.

She opened her mouth, but I held up my hand.

"I need music, Mother," I said. "You and I both know I'm never getting a flute from a peddler. I'm going to make my own, but I need to be completely alone. I have to go to a special place, where nothing will bother me, so I can get it perfect."

"The dragon cave." It wasn't a question.

I nodded and waited for her to forbid me.

Instead, she sighed. "Knowing you, you'll just run off the moment my back is turned, and won't even have the benefit of having food." She hugged me. "Your father is going to be furious."

I returned Mother's embrace. "Let him be. He'll recover by the time I return."

"We can hope," Mother said. She kissed me on the cheek. "Be as careful as you can."

"I will."

And before either of us could dissolve into tears, I left.

The air was brisk, swift and biting on my nose and cheeks. It was such a change from the warm autumn breeze the last time I'd made this journey. Townsfolk were about their chores and business, including many children. My clothes and pack made it obvious that I was going on some kind of journey.

Word spread ahead of me, as it does in every small town and village I've ever known.

By the time I reached the last house in the town proper, Hugh, Eric, and Gregory were there, waiting. I hadn't seen any of them in months. They'd grown over the winter and had developed a bit of facial hair, though not enough to make them look like men. Rather, with their feet spread wide and fists on their hips, they looked like boys attempting to play at being men.

The brothers mocked me, trying to get a rise out of me. Their words had no effect. What were words compared to the last pains they'd given me. I paid them no mind as I walked north past the last house in the town proper.

Getting to the dragon cave took the whole of daylight. In the hills, snow still clung to the earth in patches here and there, especially in the valleys and ravines where I'd normally travel. The land where the snow had melted away was slick and muddy. Only the few places where large rocks pierced the earth offered sure footing, and I came to treasure these rare moments of easy travel.

Shadows stretched over everything by the time the cave loomed above me. The air turned even colder, made worse by the wind that came as the sun sank behind the horizon. I hurried to start a fire, cursing myself for forgetting a lantern. My fingers shook, not only from cold, but also with a bit of fear. Again, I felt the huge skeleton and the charred armor turning to look at me as I struck flint against steel.

At last, I got the fire going, despite my unsteady fingers and the mostly wet wood I'd gathered. I built it large and warm and laid my blankets out to soak up the heat. Oddly, once the fire lit the cave, I didn't feel as if I was being watched by that same, ever-present stare. I looked around for signs that any animals might be using this cave as shelter in the winter, and found no evidence of this, not even bat droppings. In any other instance, I might be surprised, but not here. For a time, I looked out into the night, listening to the wolves howling to each other and to the owls with their haunting calls. These two would have normally scared me beyond sleep, but I knew they would not bother me here. Glancing back at the skeleton, I did not blame them. Eventually, as the fire burned low, I rolled up in my blankets, put my head on my pack, and drifted to sleep.

The next morning, I broke my fast on cheese, dried fruit, and bread. I melted a bit of snow in my metal cup for something to drink. I couldn't stand small beer in the morning, and unfortunately I'd forgotten tea. So much forgotten when I'd believed I'd planned so well. On the other side of the coin, my mind had been on other things, well, one other thing – the task I'd set for myself and the reason I'd returned to this place.

After I finished eating, I laid out my woodworking tools.

I'd gathered quite a collection of knives, drills, hooks, and chisels. When I'd taken this up at the beginning of winter, Father had gone about the town, trading small casks of his plum ale for tools. I suppose it was his way of attempting to bridge the gap that had grown between us.

With my tools laid out, I took the dragon's toe bone into my hands and closed my eyes. I let my fingers wander over it as I had all winter. I knew the touch of it, every inch, all the tiny nicks that covered its surface. Even with this familiarity, I needed to know it better. I felt I had one chance at my plan. If I failed, I don't believe I'd have had the heart to try again. So I studied the bone for that entire first day. I did reach for my tools a few times. Each time, I left them be. I was not in any rush. True, I might eventually get hungry, but that didn't concern me much. My task would be completed or failed long before true hunger became a danger to me.

The next day I took my tools to the bone. It took me the better part of the day to remove the knob from the other end of the bone and smooth out both edges.

I suppose I could go into every detail of how I carved and whittled my new flute. It was the greatest thing I've ever done, and now that I'm writing of it, each moment of the task becomes crisp and clear in my mind. Even after all these years, I believe I could do it again. But I will not tire you with every little cut and slice. Four days later, I finished the flute midmorning. Well, I'd finished cutting and carving. I did not know if I'd actually completed the task I set for myself.

Three and a half days of work rested on my palms. I'd been so careful, sometimes taking hours just to decide how much or how little to shave off the edge of a finger hole. Now I had to test it. I've never been so afraid of anything in all my life.

Timidly, as if I were leaning in to actually kiss Frances on the cheek, I brought the dragon bone flute to my lips. I inhaled deeply through my nose, held it in my lungs for a few moments, and then blew out through pursed lips.

The sound that filled the cave was the most perfect note I'd ever made, ever heard from a flute or any other instrument. My heart sang, and

I forgave my father. If he had gotten me a poor peddler's flute, I'd have never heard this note, let alone have been responsible for creating the instrument that sounded it.

However, one tone does not an instrument make. I placed my fingers above the holes. The true test would be to play an entire song. I let my breath slide across the flute and began to play.

The flute did not create music. It created bliss. The sound that came from it was purer and truer than anything I'd ever heard. Though my breath and fingers went through the familiar motions of the songs I knew, the flute seemed to make them solid in some strange way, as if this flute were playing the first music the world had ever really known. I wish that I were a poet so that I could truly explain what it was like in the cave, creating such beauty. I am not, so I'll cease trying to convince you to understand something that cannot be grasped by the mind, only felt deep down in the places where one knows the love of a husband or wife or mother or father.

I played for hours. When I exhausted all the songs I knew, I improvised, having done it often enough wandering around the town, skipping my feet to whatever melody came from my heart. In that moment, I played a mixed melody of sorrow and wonder. Sorrow at the loss of my grandfather's flute, and wonder at the treasure I'd created. With my eyes closed, I played and played. As tears rolled down my cheeks, I played and played.

Finally, hours later — perhaps days, for I had no knowledge or caring of time with the flute at my lips — I finished. I'd played all the sorrow and loss out of my heart. The flute left my lips, and I sat in the quiet. In the wake of my song, the whole world seemed a bit quieter than before, still, as if everything around, even the stones, were afraid to move because the song might start up again.

I stood up and walked up to where the dragon and knight were frozen in time, forever killing each other. I glanced at the place where the toe bone had been before I'd taken it so many months before. Had it only been months? It seemed so much longer than that, felt like I'd gone through so many changes.

Holding the flute up to the skeleton, I said, "Thank you for this gift. I know I took a part of you away, and I apologize, but please know that I will treasure this always, and a part of you will help me bring a bit of magic back into the world.

"I thank you as well," a voice boomed in the cavern.

I screamed.

Long, loud, shrill, I screamed.

VIII

Some have called me a prideful woman, and they would be within their rights. Considering some of the things I've done and seen, I believe I am justified in that pride. My confidence suffers not a bit when I admit that I screamed like a small child being set upon by rabid hounds, such was my fear.

Part of my fear came from that booming voice, but only a part.

The rest came from the shimmering form that had surrounded the dragon's skeleton. It was silvery-white and appeared as if it might be the dragon's true form, or at least what it had been in life. I couldn't make out the details, as the shimmering wavered, showing nearly solid form one moment and almost completely transparent the next.

The one thing I could see was the eyes. They were bright, glowing orbs that remained solid, or at least looked solid, and they shone with an intellect older and wiser than I could possibly know. They seemed so human and so alien at the same time.

The shimmering head looked down on me, the way I'd imagined it had when I'd been sitting by the fire. My scream caught in my throat because my breath stopped. It seemed as if some primal reflex told me that if I didn't move, I might be safe, it might not notice me. So I didn't move. Not a bit.

"You have brought me joy that I thought I would never know again," the voice rumbled. "Again, you have my thanks."

So many desires battled against each other in my breast that day. I wanted to speak, to say something, anything, to this creature addressing me. I wanted to flee, but my feet seemed rooted to the floor. I wanted to beg for my life. No amount of thought would overpower that deep need to stay still, that basic understanding my body had that to stay still was to live.

After a few moments – it was waiting for me to respond, I suppose – it began to chuckle. The sound of it wrapped around me like an embrace, calming my fear with a gentle caress of amusement.

"Fear not, little one," the ghostly wyrm said, then chuckled again. "Apologies. Listen to me, the ghost of a dragon, telling you, the human child, not to be afraid. As if the mere telling of it will make it reality, as if my words hang with the truth of music. I might as well command the seasons to reverse."

Strange as it might seem, however, the dragon's voice did soothe me a bit, at least enough so that I felt the tension leave my muscles. I managed a curtsy, and with that familiar movement, my manners returned.

"I was not so much frightened," I said, "as I was startled, sir."

"Madam," the dragon replied.

"I'm sorry?" I asked.

"If you are going to give me a human, gender-based honorific," the dragon said, "then it would be madam, not sir. In life I was female."

"Oh, well then, it is my turn to apologize," I said.

"With the gift of music that you brought me, I have no choice but to accept and forgive you. What is your name?"

"Elzibeth."

"Well then, Elzibeth, give me one more song before you go. I believe your task is complete, and I recall that humans are social creatures."

I took a deep breath. For a moment I'd actually forgotten the town, the people, and my family. They'd faded from my mind in the face of this wonderful creature speaking to me. I knew I'd have to go back. As much as I desired a life of sitting here, playing my new flute, hearing what stories this dragon might have to tell, I knew it was not to be. Home was calling, and I couldn't ignore it forever.

So I put my flute up to my lips and played for the dragon who had given me this most wonderful thing in the world. I didn't play any of the songs I knew. I played of what the flute meant to me: life, joy, and freedom. Sitting here, putting these memories to paper, I'm left empty as I try to describe these things, again wishing I'd been born with the gifts of a poet. Just know that I filled the cave with a wonder and beauty that day that few humans had ever heard, such that when I stopped playing, the feeling of the music lingered a bit, like an echo but solid, giving weight to the air. Then, even that faded, as if carried away on a breeze.

The Dragon spoke no more. With nothing else to be done, I gathered my things and began the journey back to town.

IX

Night had fallen by the time I finally walked between the houses. It was a quiet night, as most were. Light from candles and lamps shone through the windows of some houses, but not all. We were not a raucous people, but it was spring, and the snows had melted, so many would be stretching stiff legs and backs as they began to prepare for the planting. Most people also gathered in the tavern, reacquainting themselves with their neighbors from across town and those that lived farther afield. A walk that normally took half an hour the rest of the year could take several hours during the winter, depending on the snow, so most people stayed at home during the winter.

As I came upon the tavern, I heard bits of conversation and laughter floating into the night's air. I sat on the steps and listened. Some people spoke of farming and what livestock they'd lost over the winter, while others gossiped about budding romances. I found myself wondering how soon I would be included in that circle, and surprisingly, I turned a few thoughts to Frances and how the winter had treated him. Then, I heard what I'd been waiting for, and all other thoughts vanished. Hugh's deep, mocking laughter rolled out of the tavern. The sound of it made my skin crawl.

I entered the tavern, shutting the door a little more firmly than I needed to. People nearest the door turned their heads to see who had come in. Their conversations stopped when they recognized me. This quiet spread through the tavern as I walked between the tables to the huge fireplace. It wasn't the first time I'd made my way to that centerpiece of cobbled stones and mortar. We didn't have many minstrels who came to us, one, perhaps two a year at most, but a few townsfolk knew their way around an instrument and could manage to keep a melody with their voice, or understood how to tell a grand tale. When these people wanted to perform, they went to the fireplace, and tradition dictated everyone else give them attention. In return, the performer would not take up the whole evening, giving one to three performances at most. I'd first performed here in my seventh summer, sitting on my grandfather's knee.

When I reached the fireplace, I turned and looked directly at Hugh, Eric, and Gregory. All winter, as I whittled and carved, as my hands blistered and bled, I'd imagined all the terrible things I'd do to them, ways I'd get revenge for them breaking my flute. In that moment, when I saw them staring at me with narrowed eyes and tight mouths, I realized that this was the worst thing I could do. This was the perfect revenge, because they'd played their hand too strong last fall. They'd bullied me to the point of getting adults involved and so broken the children's law, so now the other children saw it as fair and right to get adults should those three get out of hand again. I'd known that from the few conversations I'd had over the winter. This meant I was relatively safe. It also meant my new flute was safe, well, as safe as could be with those three.

The flute came to my lips, and I began to play. "Skipping Through the Meadow" seemed a good first choice. It was a light, airy tune that went with a children's circle dance. More to the point, it was simple. Even as I sounded the first notes, trickles of sweat began to crawl down the back of my neck. It was warm by the fire, but not that warm.

Just like back at the cave, the music seemed to fill the empty spaces in the room, but not with a weight that pressed down. This time, the music seemed to lift people up. I played with my eyes open, mostly to avoid anything the three brothers might throw from the back of the room, but my attention did not remain on them. I saw people sitting up straighter, weaving a bit from side to side in time to the song. Some people started clapping along. More joined them. I had to play louder to be heard over the clapping, stamping, and pounding on tables. Geoffry, the tavern owner, and his wife, Gayle, moved through the common room, nearly skipping, grinning like this was their first night of business.

Somewhere in the middle, I stopped playing "Skipping Through the Meadow." The song didn't end. I kept playing, fingers dancing over the holes. But as I played, the spirit of the music became more important than the rigid structure of the song. The freedom and childlike wonder became the focus, and soon the music soared out on its own, as if skipping weren't enough anymore. The music took to the air and flitted over the meadow. Then that wasn't enough, and we who were caught in its wake were carried aloft to soar above the clouds. High notes and low intermingled, and I realized that this song must be what it was like for a dragon to fly, soaring and diving, weaving on the strange gusts of winds that must blast about high in the air.

Oh, sun, and moon, and stars, I'd forgotten how wonderful that sounded. Even now, I can hear my music in the back of my mind, how it seemed to take us all out of the tavern to where we could feel the wind on our faces. It's taking every bit of my will to remain here at the table, writing down my tale and not running off to make music again. I'm sure I remember how. But it's not the time for me to indulge myself.

As I played, the song took hold of me, and I became a mere vessel by which the music forced its way into our world. The song took on a harder edge as we flew from the skies down to the earth, toward a cave.

A few people in the tavern gasped as the notes grew deep and ominous. Smoke billowed into the common room in two nearly solid tendrils. One of these billowed into a dragon, wings unfurling as it soared above people's heads. The other became a knight strutting out of the fireplace with lance and shield.

The music clashed and so did the smoky visions of the dragon and the knight. They battled all through the common room. The crowd seemed to hold its breath as the music rose and fell in time with the ebb and flow of the fight taking place right about their heads. The knight and dragon spun and danced as the music carried them from one corner of the tavern to another. Finally, the knight managed to get inside the dragon's guard and thrust his lance into the dragon's breast, just as the dragon let fly a blast of smoky fire. The song came to a slow end as haunting low notes echoed and the smoke thinned.

I can't tell how long I played, but by the time the music ended, I was drenched with sweat. People stared back at me with strange expressions. Eyes were wide, and more than a few mouths hung open. In the near-silence that followed my performance, I heard feet shuffling under tables and one person coughed uncomfortably.

At this reaction, or maybe lack of reaction, I felt suddenly very alone and perhaps a little afraid. I had no idea how the townsfolk were going to respond to this sudden bit of magic, real magic and not some traveling performer's sleight-of-hand tricks, thrusting itself into their lives.

I got up and headed for the door, exiting as I'd entered, without a word, explanation, or apology. Eyes followed me. I did not look, but I'm sure the eyes that looked at me hardest, asking the most unspoken questions, belonged to Hugh, Eric, and Gregory.

When I finally reached the door, a journey that seemed even longer than the music I'd played, someone finally started clapping. I turned. Frances stood on a chair in the far corner of the room, slapping his hands together over and over again. Someone else started clapping over by the bar. It was my father. Others joined them, slowly at first, but then more and more. Voices added cheers and laughter to the rising din, and a few people pounded their mugs on tabletops.

I couldn't stop myself from grinning. I took a deep bow like I'd seen the minstrels and traveling performers do.

When I left the tavern, only three people weren't clapping.

After that, I went home. Mother embraced me and asked how I was, all the time checking over me as if doubting my word. I showed her my new flute. She asked me to play something for her. I played "Red Mountain Rose," a short piece, sweet and airy. Nothing strange happened; the fire remained the fire, and the song ended when I wanted it to end, though I must say, it sounded sweeter and crisper than any instrument I'd heard in all my days, before or since.

When I finished the song, Mother kissed both my cheeks. I hugged her and then went to my room, put my new flute under my pillow, and slept.

X

Over the next few months, I became quite the local celebrity. Rare was the night I was not at the tavern playing for at least a little while. Nothing happened like that first night; the smoke never came alive again. However, even without the extraordinary strangeness of my first performance, the townsfolk still loved the music I made with the flute. Well, all save for three, and the greater my small fame grew, the more those brothers glared at me from the back of the room or from behind everyone on the village green.

As time went on, Hugh, Eric, and Gregory grew grimmer and grimmer whenever we were forced to spend time together. They never did anything as blatantly hurtful as that day when they broke my flute, but they did seem to bump into me a bit more than anyone else, and while they were always quick to apologize, it seemed that I staggered from those chance encounters more and more frequently as time went on and my slight reputation grew. I took this all in stride. They weren't really hurting me, and I made sure to avoid being close to them, especially those times when we might be completely alone.

Time passed. Planting came and went with nothing out of the ordinary. Summer gave way to autumn and harvest, which then went into winter. People got hurt, but no more than usual and in no extraordinary ways. Animals died. Babies were born. The only thing that really changed was my playing, and that took the better part of a year for me to notice. Over time, I'd stopped playing the regular songs I knew, and more and more I took to playing about emotions or the feelings that come with a particular event.

One evening, late in the harvest, the tavern was quiet. Normally, end of harvest was a joyous and boisterous time, and that year should have been more so. It was the most successful harvest in memory. But despite that, Hugh, Eric, and Gregory's father had died. While their father had been working in the fields, a snake had startled his horse. The horse panicked, and while kicking about trying to get away from the snake and get free of the plow, it had kicked their father in the head. He'd most likely been dead before he'd even begun falling.

As was tradition, we held a wake for him in the tavern, body laid out on a white sheet, the one he'd be buried in. I didn't even really feel like being there. Mother and Father had made me go to show my respects to a member of the town passing, regardless of my personal feelings toward his sons. He'd never done me harm nor wrong, and they were right. So I took my flute, paid my respects, and then went and played quietly in the corner, not really close to the fire, because I didn't want to take the attention from the wake at that time. Songs and stories would come later, but not yet. Now was the time for quietly honoring his passage. I'd just planned to have a bit of soothing music just at the edge of things as people spoke their final words to the dead.

Eric came over to me. I stopped playing. A slight tension ran through the tavern. I noticed that Hugh and Gregory tensed more than anyone else, each glancing at the other with questioning eyes. Hugh shrugged, which I took to mean this wasn't some planned piece of taunting or humiliation they'd set up in order to feel better at my expense. That made me relax a bit, not completely, but a bit. When Eric stood in front of me, he couldn't quite meet my eyes.

"Could you," he said just above a whisper, "play something for my da'? Maybe something to ease him into his rest?"

I nodded, put my flute to my lips.

My song began as a lullaby. Soft notes flowed through the tavern. Soon though, the tone of the song shifted. I played of the balance between the seasons and between life and death. The lullaby transitioned into Spring, new life creeping into the world. Summer, full of fire and adventure, filled the tavern with deep, sharp tones that embraced its heady heat. As the heat settled into the crisp crackling notes of drying leaves and aching bones, Autumn took Summer's place. Winter came in after, cold and haunting, a mix of crisp high notes of the biting winds and the low, drawn sounds of endless white blanketing everything. As Winter seemed to end the song, just as after months of seemingly endless snow and ice and cold threatens to end life, the light, airy breath of Spring filled the room. I ended the piece with a rolling set of notes showing that hope remains even in the darkest of the coldest winters, that just like the seasons, life and death are a cycle, a continuous journey.

The tavern remained quiet for a long while after that. Then, as people seemed to take heart in the coming of life, townsfolk began to see Hugh, Eric, and Gregory not as their father's sons, but rather as the continuation of their father. People bought them drinks and congratulated them on the fine qualities each of them had received from their father. It became a joyous occasion, a celebration, and Hugh, Eric, and Gregory were at the heart of it.

Late in the night, when most people there were well into their cups, Hugh grabbed my shoulder and spun me around.

"My father loved dancing," Hugh said. "Play us something to dance to."

Cheers of agreement roared through the common room. Tables were moved aside, clearing a wide space in the center of the tavern. Men, young and old alike, scrambled to ask ladies to dance. As people took places and faced their partners, I began the first traditional song I'd played in months, a happy country dance. Those not dancing clapped along and laughed as too-drunk dancers stumbled through the movements.

One dance turned into another, and then another. People laughed and stumbled and jeered at each other. From my vantage point away from the dancers, I saw more than a few bottoms getting pinched – and not just ladies' bottoms.

During the fourth song, the tavern door burst open, crashing against one of the tables that had been pushed back. This startled me out of my playing. Someone shrieked in surprise.

Frances stood in the doorway, pointing up to the sky. Even in the candle and lantern light, it was easy to see the color had drained from his face.

"Dragon," he said. "In the sky. Dragon. Against the moon."

XI

Everyone rushed out of the tavern, including myself. People were talking, and I listened to snippets of their conversation.

"Really? A dragon?"

"How amazing."

"...probably a bat."

"...protect the livestock from..."

"...boy is daft..."

But they all went to see. At first no one saw anything. Then, a figure flew past the bright, blue-white orb of the moon. A long sinuous body, with wings that stretched and flapped, hung for a moment, illuminated in the sky. A few heartbeats later, it dove into the darkness of night. Gasps and cries of astonishment filled the air as I fled the town.

After I'd run for about half an hour, I began to realize what a poor choice I'd made, but I was young, foolish, and prideful. Once I'd set upon the journey, I refused to go back. Besides, someone might stop me. Still, even with the bright moon, once I got beyond the familiar herd paths, I seemed to find every hole and crack in the ground.

My grandfather used to say, "Desperation breeds creativity." After the third or fourth time I tripped, I realized that if I wanted to make it to the dragon cave without twisting or spraining an ankle, I needed to try something different. Well, I had myself and my flute. Three times I'd done something beyond explanation by playing my flute, each time with a different effect. Each time it was without intention. Who was to say that I couldn't direct an effect from whatever power the flute had?

So, I began to play. My song was light and airy, fleeting and quick, the perfect tune to make a journey seem shorter. I skipped and danced along with the tune, feet missing each and every dip and crack that might have tripped me. A wind picked up, always at my back, and it seemed to help speed me along.

As the early light of predawn crept into the eastern sky, I danced around a hill to see the dragon's cave gaping open before me. I stopped playing. When the music faded, so did the energy it gave me to keep moving. Exhaustion crashed down on me. My knees buckled, and I fell onto my backside amongst the dust and shrubs. I tried to get up but didn't have the strength. I tried to crawl toward the cave, but I only managed to sprawl into the dirt. My eyelids were heavy, closing despite my mind screaming at me that I needed to stay awake and get into the cave. My fatigue won over my will, and I fell into a deep, dreamless sleep.

Sometime later, I woke to someone shaking me. I blinked the dryness from my eyes, shook my head a bit to clear the sleep away, and looked to see Frances shaking me.

"Oh, thank the gods," he said.

"What are you doing here?" I asked, sitting up.

"When I saw you run out of the village, especially after we all saw the dragon flying around, I knew you were coming here," Frances said. "I thought..." His voice trailed off.

"Thought what?"

I stared him right in the face. He blushed and wouldn't meet my eyes. I snorted a brief laugh.

"You thought you were going to save the damsel from some nasty fate worse than death, didn't you?"

"No," Frances snapped at me. "I just worry. You're too reckless. One of these days you are going to get into trouble that you might not be able to get out of, trouble worse than Hugh, Eric, and Gregory."

I stood up and looked down at him. "Well, you might be right, but you aren't my keeper."

With that, I turned and headed toward the dragon's cave. I heard Frances scrambling to get up and follow me. He was sputtering something that might have been partway between an explanation and an apology, but I didn't pay him enough mind to really determine which.

He followed me into the cave, and promptly stopped talking. I glanced back at him. Frances stood looking at the skeletal dragon, mouth agape, eyes wide and blinking. I had to bite the inside of my lip to keep from snickering at him. Granted, about a year before, I'd been the one terrified of the massive skeleton, and Frances hadn't screamed like I had.

In the back of the cave, I discovered exactly what I'd feared. Those three perfect stones, red as any ruby, blue as any sapphire, and green as any emerald, had shattered. The remains of those stones lay scattered across the cave's floor. This was what I'd been afraid of seeing, and had absolutely no idea how to handle.

When I turned to leave, Frances was still staring up at the skeleton.

"Frances?" I said.

"Uh, yes?" he replied, not taking his eyes off the dragon.

"Remember me asking if you planned to save the damsel from a fate worse than death?"

"Yes. Why?"

"You might just have your chance."

That actually got his attention, and he looked at me. I waved my flute to the mouth of the cave. He blinked at me a few times and looked to where I'd gestured. Three drakes stood just outside the cave: one with scales red as any ruby, one with scales blue as any sapphire, and one with scales green as any emerald.

XII

Frances let out a sound partway between a squawk and a shriek. My heart sped up, my stomach felt as if I'd swallowed snow, and my breath came in short, quick blasts.

The shock I felt at these creatures looking back and forth between Frances and me faded much faster than I would have expected. I think part of it came from noticing that the little dragonlings looked massive at first, but after taking in the sight of them for a moment, I realized their bodies we actually no bigger than a large dog. They seemed to be so much larger because of their long necks and tails and how they spread their wings out and up. What really helped me remember myself was probably that day so many months before when I'd spoken to their mother's ghost. In hindsight now, I realize that the ghost might not have actually been about to do anything to me, being a ghost, but the idea of a dragon ghost scared me even more than three, potentially very hungry, drakes.

Frances pulled his knife and moved to place himself as well as he could between me and all three drakes. I couldn't help but laugh. I can't properly describe the ridiculousness of the sight. A scrawny boy just on the edge of being a man stood proud and defiant like a knight, with only a sturdy but tiny work knife to defend the damsel fair. I laughed louder when Frances turned to look at me. His expression had not a bit of fear in it. Rather, he looked at me with such self-righteous indignation that I couldn't help but laugh even harder and louder.

The drakes seemed puzzled by this. Their sinewy necks stretched out to look at me without Frances in the way. The blue drake cocked its head to the side as it regarded me, then it sniffed at the air, head rotating in all directions. After a few moments of watching us, the red and green drakes put their heads together. The red sucked in a lungful of air. I saw its chest expand as I heard the air rushing through its teeth.

All humor left me. In my mind, I saw it letting loose with a blast of flame. The fire might not be anything compared to the conflagration that its mother had used to kill the knight, but it would be enough to ignite poor Frances.

The flames didn't come. Instead, the drake let loose with a rolling series of sound that went low to high. I caught the feeling of the wonder of what new sight might be just around the next hill. The green responded with three notes, agreement with confusion.

I lifted my flute to my lips and played the same three notes the green had. Well, at least as best I could, considering the limitations of my flute. Funny, the thought of my flute being limited, as it had a greater range than any instrument I'd ever hear of.

All three heads whipped around to gaze at me, three sets of golden eyes staring at me, unblinking. The three of them piped a short sequence of notes back and forth in a rolling melody. Years before, a pair of minstrels had come to the town; one played a fiddle, and the other played a mandolin. Nearly every song they played was a bit of call and response, similar to this.

I played again, but this time, I did not copy exactly the sounds I heard. I added a bit of my own sound into the mix of notes.

That stopped them again. Their heads rose a bit, and they studied me.

We stood there in the cave, looking at each other. Their heads wove slightly side to side, and every few moments one would sniff.

"Frances," I whispered, "get behind me."

"But," he said in his normal tone of voice.

All three necks snapped like whips, and the three drakes focused their attention on Frances.

"Now," I whispered again.

How could I tell what they would make out of the hard and harsh tones of our spoken language? True, the dragon's ghost had spoken to me in my own tongue, but was that a thing of ghosts or something the dragon had learned after however many centuries it had lived?

"Right," Frances whispered.

He moved backward slowly, and I noticed that he did not lower his knife. I suppose it's lucky that the drakes were not old enough to know what that meant. Then again, their knowing might have saved some trouble later, and the course of my life would have been very different.

When Frances got behind me, I put the flute to my lips. I played my song. Not a specific song that I had written, but the song of how I came to be able to speak to the drakes. I played of three bullies who had stolen the voice from my throat, and my quest to retrieve it.

As the notes slogged through the songless winter, a chill breeze blew about, biting through my clothes. It gathered up twigs, leaves, and dust, swirling them around the mouth of the cave. When I came to when I found their mother and the knight, the debris flowed around me as the smoke had that first night in the tavern, the dragon and knight dancing and weaving around each other until finally killing each other. When this happened, the three drakes let out a high pitched whine of such utter sadness and loss that tears began to roll down my cheeks. I matched this note, joining in their pain. Then, slowly, I continued my song, slowly descending from that high-pitched wail to a low, sober span of notes as I slogged through that tedious winter, chewing and clawing into scraps of wood, trying to make a new voice for myself, to find a new song. I played of the wonder of finding my voice back here at the cave, and of how their mother's spirit had given me her blessing. I finished with nearly the same song I'd played the night before at Eric's request, of how spring emerges from winter, and how even with death, life continues.

As my final note trailed off, the drakes took up their own song. Gone was the pain they had cried earlier. Their song began with crisp notes that popped and cracked in the air, speaking of the wonder of breaking into a free and wide world. Together they wove a melody of hearing my song the night before and flitting through the air, in between trees, and up to the clouds searching for it. Such strange and wonderful things this world outside of the shells held. They ended with the rising sun, warm on their scales, and how they found something to eat, a cow or sheep, maybe.

After the drakes finished, all five of us, Frances, myself, and the drakes, stood regarding each other.

"This could be very bad," Frances said in a low voice, not quite a whisper.

I nodded. "We have to keep them hidden and teach them how to live."

"What?" Frances turned to me. "They're dragons. Oh, they might be young and cute now, but they're going to get bigger." To emphasize this he pointed back to the massive skeleton behind me. "We don't have any idea how long that could take."

A deep breath escaped through my pursed lips. He was right, though I'm sure it might take a bit of time before they really started to grow, and by that time, I might be able to convince them to move on to less populated areas. Even with Frances talking logically and reasonably about the drakes, I knew I could not turn my back on them. My song had brought them out. Somehow, someway, it had reached them out here, and pulling from my song of life coming from death, had caused them to hatch. Also, their mother had given me music again. I couldn't just abandon them. Of course, they might have been fine, they were dragons after all, but how could I be sure? No. I couldn't betray their mother and the gift she'd given me.

"I'm taking care of them," I said.

"But, Elzibeth," Frances started.

"But nothing." I had no interest in hearing whatever reasonable cautions or arguments he had against my doing this. "I'm doing this. I welcome any help you might give me, but only if you can do so without telling me what kind of foolish child I'm being, or anything even remotely close to that. If you can't do that, then go home, and by gods and goddesses, keep quiet about this."

"Of course I'm going to help you," he replied. Then he muttered under his breath, "It's the only way I can make sure you don't get yourself killed." I chose to ignore that comment.

XIII

Now, I could go into great details about the adventures we had that winter while we taught the dragons how to hunt and what to hunt, but those adventures have little actual bearing on my tale overall. The most important thing we did that winter was convince them to leave herds of sheep and cattle alone. This was our greatest challenge. Why should they ignore such easy prey, especially when winter snows made finding other food so much more challenging? When that question arose, I played for them again the song of their mother fighting the knight, and that if they hunted the humans' food, armies of hard-shelled humans would come seeking the drakes. By midwinter, we had finally managed to get them to understand. Little did I know that these lessons had come too late, that events had been set in motion the night I'd played the dirge at the wake for Hugh, Eric, and Gregory's father.

Let me now take you months later, a few weeks after the snows melted, as the first knight rode into the town. He came in the early afternoon. Frances and I saw him as we returned from the dragon's cave. The knight sat atop his massive horse, armor shining in the afternoon sun even under a layer of road dust. He took one of the three rooms above the tavern and started hunting dragons the next day.

Two days later, another knight came. Two came the day after. Within a fortnight, we'd lost track of the knights coming and going between our town and the others in the area. Word had traveled over the winter, as word does, and now dozens of armored soldiers – some knights, some just would-be heroes – had come seeking fame and glory by being the one to slay the dragon.

Frances and I did our best to remain as unobtrusive as possible. For Frances, it wasn't really a difficult task. For me, well, I had a reputation, and within the month, men in armor with swords on their hips came around asking me questions. I was, after all, the girl with the magic flute. Most of these men, the real knights mostly, respected that I didn't want to talk to them and let me be about my way. I contented myself with playing only in the middle of the night, hidden away in my room, and only with human songs I knew. I would not risk calling the drakes by playing a song from my heart. Such a song would surely bring them to the town, despite warnings to remain away.

One afternoon, as I was returning home from taking Father his midday meal, a man stepped in my way. His breast plate, while marked with nicks and dings – and one spot on his left shoulder had been pounded out after something had pierced it – wasn't poor quality as was the armor of some of the soldiers and fortune seekers who had come. We'd learned very quickly to judge the quality of the man by the quality of his armor –

the better he kept it, the better the man. A few exceptions existed. In a small handful of the knights, the better he kept it meant the better he thought about himself. Still, while those few were pompous, and if the other knights hadn't been about they might have taken advantage of their station, they didn't get too out of hand in the company of their peers. The sellswords and mercenaries were a different breed altogether. At least every few days, the town put one of those men on trial for theft or for beating up one of the townsmen, and once, a knight killed a sellsword for rape even before anyone could even begin planning a trial.

"You're the girl with the flute," he said. It wasn't a question, more like an accusation.

"I play a flute now and then," I replied, trying to move around him. I'd gotten very good at the half-answer.

He moved to block my path.

"Please, sir," I said. "My mother is expecting me."

I curtsied and tried to move around him the other way. Again, he cut me off.

"You can take a moment to answer my questions. The sooner you do, the sooner you can return to your mother. Now, does this power you have with music come from you or is it something in the flute?"

"I don't know what you mean, sir." I'd also become very good at lying, head down, gaze cast to the dust, a little curtsy added in, just for a little extra show. "I really must be going."

"No."

He grabbed my wrist. I fought against him, but his grip tightened around my forearm. The more I struggled, the more my skin burned against his gloved hand.

"You are going to stay and speak with me."

I dropped the basket I held and slapped him with my free hand. Even though his head snapped to the side, when he looked at me, red-cheeked, I could tell that I hadn't fazed him in the least. He looked from side to side, and when his face came back to look at me, the corners of his mouth turned upward in a humorless smile.

Pain flared all along the side of my head. The man let go of me, and I dropped to my knees. I blinked tears, and as my mind caught up with my senses, I remembered him slapping me. Part of me wished it had been Hugh to slap me again. Part of my reaction was due to the sudden pain, but a lot of it was just from the calculated way he'd made sure no one was watching and that he'd struck without anger, just to let me know that he could hurt me, and would hurt me.

He knelt down next to me on one knee, took up the basket I'd dropped, and placed it into my hands.

"You will tell me what I want to know. The only question is how much pain you, or perhaps your family, will suffer before then." He helped me to my feet. "Your mother is waiting. Run on home."

I did, just as he said. When I got there, I threw the basket into the kitchen as I passed and fell onto my bed weeping. Mother asked me what was wrong, but I wouldn't lift my face from my pillow. The side of my face had to be red and swelling. It still burned, still throbbed. She'd tell Father. Father would make me tell him what happened. Then Father would go looking for the man, and the man would hurt him, maybe kill him, because Father would start trouble and the man seemed used to more trouble than Father could ever make for him.

After a few moments of trying to comfort me and get some semblance of an explanation, Mother let me be. "If it's those three boys again, you let us know. We've got troubles enough these days without them causing more."

I remained there, face in my pillow, until I fell asleep.

Hours later, I awoke. The pain had retreated to a dull ache. Night had fallen, and my room was shrouded in darkness. Someone was tapping at my window. I sighed and stumbled to the window.

"What do you want, Frances?" I asked as I opened it.

"Not just Frances," the hard man from earlier said.

I tried to back away, but he grabbed me by the shoulder with more speed than I could fathom.

"Small town people are so easy," the man said. "For one small silver coin, Frances here led me right to your window."

I craned my neck and saw Frances' slight form in the shadows. I also saw three larger shadows coming up behind the man.

"Is this him?" Frances asked.

I nodded.

"Do it," Frances said, taking two large steps back.

One of the larger shadows rushed forward. The hard man frowned, released me, and began to turn. His hand went down to his belt. Before he could finish turning or draw his sword, a dull *clang* echoed in the night outside my window. The hard man staggered, shaking his head. The two other larger shadows came in. I saw Hugh, Eric, and Gregory swinging shovels again and again, beating the hard man about the arms, chest, and shoulders. He didn't have his breastplate on. Such a garment would have severely limited his stealth. I believe I heard bones snapping and cracking as the brothers beat on him, especially after he dropped to the ground.

"Enough," Frances said after a few moments. He knelt down next to the hard man. "You know nothing of us. We protect our own." Frances looked up to the brothers. "Take him somewhere and let him consider this evening."

Eric and Gregory each grabbed a foot and dragged the hard man into the night. Hugh marched a few paces after them, shovel held ready to strike.

"Are you alright?" Frances asked once they were gone.

I nodded. He reached in the window and caressed my cheek. Then he followed after the brothers.

I finally managed to get back to sleep, but not without wondering what had become of the hard man. Had they killed him? Part of me hoped that they had, but another part of me hoped that they had not taken themselves down that path. Yes, the brothers had been bullies, but I didn't want to think them capable of murdering someone.

XIV

The next day, I found Frances and was about to ask what had happened to the hard man when I heard someone snarl, "You!"

The hard man came around a corner and headed for us. He moved stiffly, and the left side of his face scrunched with pain every time he took a step with his left foot. His sword was in his hand. Frances and I both froze. Ambushing a soldier in the dark of night was one thing. Seeing the hard man coming toward you with a naked blade is another thing entirely.

Before he reached us, a knight stepped between us. Even with his back to us, I could tell it was a knight. His armor gleamed in the sunshine as he took a wide stance. His sword was out, and though the knight held it casually at his side, he stood in such a way that made me realize that he was prepared to use it.

"Hold," the knight said, his deep voice resonating with command.

"Stand aside, boy," the hard man said. "This doesn't concern you."

"Oh, but it does," the knight said. "While my peers have been hunting dragons, I've been hunting you. You're the one terrorizing young ladies looking for this girl with the flute. Well, I've caught you, and you've drawn steel against the innocent. Lay your sword down, never return, and I will spare your life."

The hard man tried to push past the knight. With even more speed than the hard man possessed, the knight had disarmed him and taken him off his feet. The knight placed the tip of his sword at the hard man's throat. The hard man's sword was a good three paces away.

"Now that you have laid your sword aside," the knight said, "you may comply with the rest of my request. If I ever see you within a hundred leagues of this town, your life is forfeit."

The knight backed away, keeping his sword pointed at the hard man. The hard man got to his feet with several grunts and groans.

"Thank you for my life, my lord," the hard man said, without a trace of hardness left in him, and then he left. I never saw him again, not that I remained in my home much longer than that.

The knight turned to us, Frances and me, and gave a slight bow. "I am Sir Phillip, and I am your servant, my lady."

Sir Phillip was beautiful. While he was a man, he was a young man, perhaps twenty or so. He had chestnut-colored hair and deep brown eyes that seemed to smile with a pure, genuine delight of life. I blushed at receiving the attention of such a man.

Sir Phillip sheathed his sword, and offered me his arm. "Shall I escort you home?"

I nodded dumbly and placed my arm in his. He took me home and introduced himself to my parents, explained what had happened, and assured them they need not fear the man any further. Father and Mother both insisted my savior stay for supper.

"No, no," Sir Phillip said. "I couldn't possibly impose."

But my parents would not be dissuaded. While my father and Sir Phillip argued politely about him staying for dinner, my mother was already putting another place setting at the table. In the end, I made the difference in swaying Sir Phillip.

"Please, Sir Phillip?" I said, looking up at him, doing my best to keep the color out of my cheeks. "It's the least we can do for you saving me from that man."

"How could I possibly refuse such beauty?" Sir Phillip put his hand to his chest and sighed. "But I insist you call me only Phillip. I've learned that the *Sir* part only really matters at court."

And so he joined us.

I spent most of the evening quiet and blushing. Father pestered him with questions about being a knight and more importantly about his prospects of starting a family. This made me cover my face with my hair. Of course it is every father's duty to see his daughter well married, but this was going too far. Sir Phillip was far too high above my station, beyond anything I could even dream of reaching. As it was, even though I was reaching the age of marriage, I hadn't really considered it, mostly because my music filled my thoughts almost every moment. Until the drakes had hatched, that is.

After dinner, as Mother and I cleaned the dishes, Father and Phillip retired to the front room. I did my best to listen in, and Mother didn't seem to mind that this made cleaning up take nearly three times longer than normal. They spoke of normal things, Father bragging mostly of what a wonderful young lady I was. Phillip replied to all the praises I received with some earnest variation of, "I had definitely noticed."

After a bit, Phillip interrupted Father, asking, "I've been following that man for some time. In each town, he keeps raving about a girl with a flute. That this girl knows the secrets of the dragons."

My heart sank into my stomach. I knew what was coming next, and that as much as I hated it, I couldn't do anything to stop it.

"Oh, that would indeed be Elzibeth," Father replied. "She has a flute that seems to be magical. Made it herself last winter. Seen and heard the strangest things when she's played it." Then his voice rose. "Elzibeth, get your flute and play something for our guest."

I took a deep breath and chewed the inside of my cheek. How much trouble would I get into if I refused? Then again, how many questions would it raise if I did refuse? I knotted my hair into my fists until finally, I relented. I went to my room, got my flute out from under my pillows, and took it to the front room.

Phillip stood when I entered, his gaze falling on my flute.

"That's quite beautiful," he said.

"It's just a plain flute," I said.

"Sometimes ordinary things hold the greatest beauty," Phillip replied. "A flower, a sunset, or a flute made by loving hands. I've never seen that kind of wood before. Is it native to this area?"

I said nothing at first. I'd not mentioned it to anyone since that day Hugh had broken my grandfather's flute, but I heard the whispers and the rumors people spoke when they thought I was too far away to hear. They all knew I had claimed it was a dragon bone. My refusal to talk about it might have been part of the fuel to fire this local piece of gossip. Even in that moment, I couldn't speak of it.

"Girl," Father said, "our guest asked you a question."

I just stared into the fire. I opened my mouth and tried to speak, but could not. In the end, I gave Sir Phillip a polite curtsy and fled to my room. Behind me, Father apologized over and over for my rudeness.

"Oh, think nothing of it," Phillip said. "She's had quite the time of it over that flute. Were I in her place and some raving mad mercenary came at me with a sword because of my flute, I don't think I'd be inclined to share much about it, either. I'm just glad I managed to intercede when I did. Well, I should be off. I need to make sure that villain is actually gone."

With some shuffling and much thanks from Mother and Father, Phillip left. Thankfully, Father seemed to heed Phillip's words and did not come to admonish me for my behavior.

Later that night, I heard a tapping on my window. Frances. I'd forgotten all about him. I struck myself in the forehead several times and wondered if I might have the will to actually succeed in smothering myself with my pillow.

Feeling like the worst friend in the world, I went over and opened the window.

"Frances, I'm—"

"Who is Frances?" Phillip asked.

I jumped back a bit, flailing in my surprise.

"I'm sorry," Phillip said. "I didn't mean to scare you. I just wanted to hear you play something on this flute. Just one song. Please?"

So there I stood, alone in my night clothes, moon and starlight shining through my window. The most handsome man I'd seen in my whole life asking me to play for him. Even in the center of a scene that seemed straight out of a fairy story, I was still going to refuse, until he looked at me and asked just above a whisper, "Please, Elzibeth?"

He spoke my name as if it were a holy benediction, and I was his. He could have asked for my virginity then, and I would have gladly given it to him.

I took my flute and placed it to my lips and played "Lovers at the Well." It's a short little song with a dance set to it. Even under the enchantment of this moment, I knew better than to let the music fly free. Still, I did embellish the song a bit, adding just a bit of a twirl and an extra few notes at the end. What could it hurt to impress the knight a bit? After all, he'd been so kind.

When the song was over, he reached in through the window. I placed my hand in his, and he drew me closer, never taking his eyes from mine.

"Thank you," Phillip said, and kissed my knuckles.

I shivered from the touch of it. He pulled me even closer to him. In two steps, I came face to face with him, only my wall separating us. He leaned in and kissed me, his lips to my lips.

Phillip left after the kiss, and I went to bed. Again, I'd forgotten all about Frances.

And I'll leave the kiss at that. I still have so many emotions wrapped up in that kiss, from the time it happened, to the arguments I've had with Frances about it, to how I felt about it after the events of the next day. No, I will say this: today the strongest emotion I feel is the shame at how much that kiss hurt Frances. He'd been watching from the shadows, with Hugh, Eric, and Gregory, to make sure I wasn't going to be bothered again. Even today, I wonder if he ever truly forgave me for that betrayal that was not a betrayal, for no words had been spoken, no agreements made.

XV

I looked for Phillip the next day but couldn't see him anywhere. I also didn't see Frances, but I didn't know that because he was the furthest thing from my mind. By the time I took the midday meal to my father in the fields, I'd begun to lose hope of seeing Phillip again. A deep ache began to form in my chest, just below my heart.

As I returned home, I heard cries and cheers from the other side of the town. Some few people were even sounding horns. I hurried that way, hoping that the excitement might draw Phillip. When I got there, I saw that it was Sir Phillip who was drawing the excitement. He rode into town, a pack horse trailing behind him carrying a slumped form, red as any ruby. Everyone in the town, commoners, sellswords, and knights alike were cheering Sir Phillip. He grinned, reveling in the attention, waving his bloody sword in the air for all to see. Then I noticed the blood on his armor. He had transformed into the most hideous creature I had ever seen.

A burning fury replaced the growing ache. My jaw ached from clenching back my scream of outrage. My mere screams would not be enough.

I pushed through the crowd to stand in front of Sir Phillip. I took my flute and placed it to my lips. Normally, in those days with the knights and soldiers and all, I'd taken to leaving my flute hidden at home. That day, I'd carried it around with me, just on the off chance I found Sir Phillip and he wanted me to play again.

"Hello, Elzibeth," Sir Phillip said. "I wanted to thank you—"

As he spoke, I placed the flute to my lips and blew out a low note that matched my anger, the fury in my heart, the heat of rage as red as any ruby. The sound of it drowned out his words. People around us stepped back.

Phillip shouted something at me, but I played louder. I wanted him to understand the hurt he had caused me. I wanted him to know the hellfire of my scorn, and the only way I knew how to do that was through my flute.

People moved back again. I saw Sir Phillip mouth my name, but I couldn't hear him over my anger and the sound of my single, prolonged note. He said something else, but I kept playing. Soon, his mouth opened in a scream. His horse reared up. Sir Phillip fell to the ground, writhing in the mud. The mud steamed and bubbled where he rolled in it. And now the smell of cooking meat filled the air.

I stopped playing. Sir Phillip had gone from screams of agony to whimpers. His thrashing turned to twitching as the skin on his neck, where it touched his armor, blistered and peeled. A few moments later, both his twitching and whimpering ended. The only sound in the wake of his death was the popping and hissing of his skin and the mud he lay in.

Before anyone else could recover from the shock, I fled. Long and fast and hard, I ran. At first, I had no idea where I was headed, but soon I found myself approaching the dragon's cave. There, I found the green and blue drakes wailing in their sadness.

I joined them in their song, adding my flute to their dirge. Then I shifted the song from one of weeping loss to one of flight. I played again of humans with their hard shells and long claws that pierce even dragon hides. I played of the armies coming to find the drakes and that they would not be safe in these hills. I played until the two drakes took to the sky and flew north until I could see them no longer and heard no more of their sorrowful song.

Then, I fled.

XVI

I ran again, this time without a destination. I walked and ran the rest of that day, through the night, and all the next day. I couldn't stop. That the tale of Elzibeth and her cursed flute would be told, I had no doubt, and it would grow with the telling. I needed to stay ahead of it if I was to have any hope.

As the sun set that second day, my mind caught up with my emotions. The realization that I'd killed a man hit me. I cried all through that night, but I didn't stop running, not until the small hours of that morning when despair and exhaustion overcame me. I had just enough presence of mind to crawl into a thicket to sleep out of open sight before my eyes closed.

For a month I traveled, avoiding any contact with humans. I ate what plants I could find in the wild. At times, the flute tempted me. I could have used it to lure a rabbit or some other small game into a trap, and I could eat well on meat. That I had nothing to start a fire with didn't bother me. I was half-crazed from hunger and grief. Even raw meat would have been better than another day of wild berries and grubs scavenged from a fallen log.

One morning, a week into my second month, I woke and knew I was not alone. First it was the smell, cooking bacon and oatmeal. Then I heard the bacon sizzling in a pan and the fire popping and crackling. I bolted into a crouch, ready to run.

"Good morning," Frances said.

I opened my mouth, and though it had only been five weeks since I'd spoken to another person, it also seemed a thousand lifetimes ago.

"Are you hungry?" he asked.

I nodded.

He gave me a bowl with oatmeal and bacon in it. I ate them greedily, and he gave me more. This second helping went down just as quickly. Frances watched me, patiently, as he ate his own breakfast.

"How did you find me?" I asked.

"The blue drake," he said. "Don't worry. Now that he knows you're safe with me, he's going to stay away from people."

"How do you know?" I asked. I'd always been the one to translate between Frances and the drakes.

"He actually speaks our language fairly well," Frances replied. "We knew you needed taking care of. I've been following as best I could, while they've been scouting for you. They aren't big enough to carry me yet, or I would have caught up with you several weeks ago."

"Why didn't they let me know?" I asked, thinking about all the meat I could have been eating if they'd helped.

"The drakes didn't want you to be mad at them for disobeying you. Anyhow, they are gone now, gone far away from people, now that I'm here."

"I don't need taking care of," I said, though my words sounded hollow in the face of my ragged clothes and the smell of bacon grease on the air.

"Of course not."

And so we traveled together for several years.

We never spoke of my kissing Sir Phillip, or what I'd done to him the next day. We rarely spoke of the drakes, and when we did, it was only by their color, as in, "Remember when Green broke through the ice trying to land that one day?" We spoke of Red least often. Every time we did, I would cry for hours afterward.

Finally, we came to a place where we thought we might live, a city far beyond any place that had heard of Elzibeth and her cursed flute. We married and started raising a family. I never played the flute again and did my best to stay away from anything that might tempt me to take it back up again. I don't know, but part of me believes that a pair of dragons, blue as any sapphire and green as any emerald, are out there, waiting to hear the call of that flute on the wind.

XVII

Elzibeth left the story of her childhood on her kitchen table amongst the candlesticks. It had taken her so much longer to write it than she'd expected. There was so much in that tale, more than she'd been able to put into the words. Then again, she wasn't a poet or a storyteller. She'd been a musician many miles away and years ago, but that was a different kind of thing altogether.

After completing the tale, she'd gone into her small garden behind the house. It reminded her of home, of her mother's vegetables, and of her father working in the fields. By the light of a single candle, Elzibeth had dug up the map case wrapped in oilcloth. She'd taken it up the stairs to the room she'd shared with her husband for their entire marriage. Oh, how she missed him. She missed him even more than the music. If she hadn't had him, the music would have overpowered her caution, but that's how it is with love: It gives us the strength to do what we could normally never do.

Lying in bed, Elizabeth took the flute out of the map case. She caressed it, letting her fingers become familiar with it once more. She had no idea how long she sat into the night, reacquainting herself with her old friend, just as she'd never really had any idea as a child how long she'd sat in a field playing her music.

Finally, Elzibeth raised the flute to her lips and played. She played as if she hadn't had the flute buried in the garden for decade upon decade.

She played for hours of the wonder and magic that her life had known. She played of three little drakes and one brave boy who grew into a braver man willing to share his life with her. She played of the sorrow she'd caused him with an unwitting kiss, and the sorrow she'd caused her parents by vanishing, and the sorrow she felt for never really feeling sorry that she'd murdered the man who had used her to kill her friend. Finally, she let the last notes of her song echo of how she'd missed the music.

The song ended. For a time, Elzibeth, her bones weary, sat in the silence that always seemed to follow the end of a song. It lingered on, and on, until she heard a tapping at the window.

Tap. Tap. Tap.

Quiet.

Tap. Tap. Tap.

Quiet.

Elzibeth got up from the bed, went to the window, and opened it.

A single eye filled the window. It was blue as any Sapphire.

"We've been waiting for you to sing again."

You can follow Elzibeth's grandson's adventures in:
"Legacy of the Dragon Bone Flute"
Available in eBook for most major eReaders.

Familiar Choices

"Please, Master," I begged. "I am willing to die if the need is great enough, but don't sacrifice me like this."

My master looked up from the last stages of her ritual. It was still difficult to think of her as a *she*. She had been male until a rival wizard cursed him, transforming an old man respected by his peers, into a young woman and a laughing stock of the magical community. Her powers hadn't diminished at all, but no one seemed to take the appearance of a girl in her middle teens as a wizard seriously.

"I'll have my revenge, Smoke," Master said. "This way I can get them all at once."

"Due respect, Master, but this path to vengeance seems unfair on my part."

"You knew the risks when you agreed to the pact," Master said, and returned to her work.

"Committing me to suicide was never mentioned," I retorted.

Master snapped, "You will follow where I lead. Else wise you will be in danger of breaking the pact. "

"I will comply," I said, meekly.

Through the pact we assist each other in various way. She gains strength through my mystic connection to nature, and I gain the means to live beyond my normal life span. The pact is designed to benefit both mage and familiar but now it will be my death.

Master had brought us to the center of a blasted wasteland that once belonged to her order. The once-beautiful landscape was destroyed by a cult of death wizards. Gabrielle was the only survivor.

The ritual was nearly complete. Soon it would be time for my sacrifice. A sacrifice I wished not to make, my first duty is loyalty.

"Forgive me mistress," I asked humbly, "but I still fail to see the necessity of this ritual."

Gabrielle looked upon her cursed body then glared at me. She cast me a wild look, full of insanity. Those eyes, with their harsh beauty were the only trace of Gabrielle's former body. The intense madness in her eyes was out of place in the youthful features of a human male. Only her eyes held a trace of her lost Fey beauty.

"It's the only way to make them pay, Smoke," he snarled. "The death cult; Zaniphar, for cursing me with this body!" She emphasized this by motioning to where her breasts once were. "Stephan for running away with that hussy!" she spat the name of her former love. "Not to mention all the others. This is the surest way to make them all pay!"

As you might be able to tell, things have not been going well for Gabrielle. In her eyes, her entire life has been destroyed. I wish she could see things as a cat. Cats never worry about the past. There is no way to change what has already been. One should look toward making the future better.

"We can solve these things another way," I said. "Must I explain a cat's view of things again?"

"No," Gabrielle commanded barely containing her fury. "I'm very well aware of that lecture. I am not a cat. I am a human. How many time do I have to tell you it might do you well to see things as a human does?"

Knowing she really did not wish a response I remained silent. If I had answered she would have punished me. I contented myself in that I had lived well for much longer than most cats ever dream of living.

Soon the preparations were complete. We stopped for an hour so Gabrielle could eat and rest before the summoning. During this time I tried to convince my mistress of the mistake she was making. Every time I spoke she silenced me with a small spell of pain.

Gabrielle stepped up to the circle and began the ritual. I watched from hiding. My role in the ritual would be small but necessary. I sat and patiently waited as Gabrielle suffered through the casting for ten hours. Blood, sweat, and tears flowed from her as she strained to complete the spell.

As the last words of power were spoken, and the final component cast, the circle began to glow. I watched as the light began to take shape. Over the next few minutes the light began to dim, as a form grew more pronounced. The glow finally faded and the form was fully defined.

In an oddly horrific way the creature before me was beautiful, from a human point of view. There was something that was even pleasing about it to me as a cat and that frightened me terribly. Desire pulsated in a strong aura along with a compelling sense of trust and friendship. The demon smiled wickedly as it viewed the surroundings.

Before it had time to acclimate to the situation Gabrielle spoke words of power. Bolts of energy shot from her hands and struck the demon squarely in the chest. It cried out in pain and surprise as it flew back.

As it stood my mistress continued her attack. Spouts of flame erupted from the ground around the demon.

"The demon easily canceled her spell., with the wave of a hand. "What the hell did you do that for?"

"I need you to do some things for me," Gabrielle said and summoned mystic chains to bind it.

"Then why the show of strength?" it asked. "Let's get down to negotiating the contract, so I can perform these tasks, and we can both be happy. "

"It's not that simple," Gabrielle said. "I don't want you having any ties to me once this is over. I like my soul just the way it is. I need you to submit completely, do these things, and then leave."

"I would have thought you would be smarter than that after such a long life," the demon said. "You know the only way to get me to submit is to defeat me."

Gabrielle smiled. "I know."

"Fine," it said and shattered the chains.

The fight was on neither my mistress nor the demon were holding back. They threw spells, enchantments, and invocations at each other. For hours the fight went on with neither gaining the upper hand. Soon they forgot about strategy and skill and began channeling raw, unfocused magical energy at each other with reckless abandon.

"Now, Smoke!" Gabrielle yelled.

I didn't attack. When I failed to make my appearance on the battleground my mistress faltered. Gabrielle fell before the dark creature.

"You have my thanks cat," the demon said as it bound her.

"When you commanded me to knowingly kill myself, the pact was ended," I said. "In the years I served you , I learned many things. After you told me of this plan ,I contacted this one and made a bargain."

"How did you bargain with this demon?" she asked. "You do not have a soul."

"True," I said. "I offered yours."

I would have said more but the demon dragged her away to where ever it is demon go. Now I was free to go where I would and live as I please. Just a cat should live.

The Half-Faced Man

I love this story. I mean, I REALLY love this story. Even before it received an honorable mention from the Writers of the Future contest, I've loved this story. This one pretty much wrote itself, start to finish. I think this is my strongest short story to date, which is why I've included it in this volume; my core fan-base deserves to have this one in their library, no matter how big or small that library might be.

Like "Jaludin's Road," this one takes place on a continent to the south of the events in the Tears of Rage *sequence. I meant for the* Lands of Endless Summer *to have a much different feel than the typical fantasy world. I think I've succeeded.*

In the greater timeline of the world, these events happen roughly in the same time frame as the events of "Jaludin's Road." One day I hope to return to these characters, but part of me fears that I wouldn't be able to do them any kind of justice in a second go, and yes, I have considered characters from both tales crossing paths. This presents its own problems of making sure none of the characters overshadow or outshine the others. Someday…

"She sees it all the right way," the Half-Faced Man said to Master Daybreak as they watched the duel arcane in progress.

Master Daybreak, easily a full head taller than anyone else in the Rising Dawn Coffee and Tea house, had to lean forward to hear over the cheers and cries of the crowd. I heard because I'd developed the skill of sifting through the noise of the common room to overhear whichever conversation I wished.

"Dueling is like traveling in the desert," the Half-Faced Man continued. "Winning is the oasis. If you notice other things – the heat of the sun, the grains of sand worming into your boots, your burning throat when you try to swallow nothing, the call of the crowd, the way your mind, not your head, but your mind, aches as you try to breach his defenses while not letting him shatter yours – you are done. It's so simple. Most people make it too hard. Keep it like walking through the desert. When she's in there, all she sees is the sand. Intuitively, she comprehends the simplicity: one foot in front of the other, one spell after another. You can't teach that. She's going to be a legend someday."

The Half-Faced Man spoke of Ba'ishyra, probably the most talented woman to ever set foot in the Rising Dawn's dueling circle.

"Like you were?" the Master asked.

"I was never a legend." The Half-Faced Man walked away.

I recall the evening Ba'ishyra first entered the Rising Dawn. It was my fourteenth summer, that awkward stage between being a child and becoming a young woman. Only a small handful of our patrons paid her any notice. The Half-Faced Man was dueling at that time, being unusually flashy in his spells. Bolts of fire, shards of ice, and blasts of sand-filled air whipped about as the Half-Faced Man and Amadan the Limper showed off for a group of wizards and shamans no one had seen before. They played this flashy game to lull newcomers into believing this was how they normally dueled. The regulars bet only a token amount amongst themselves, which was also part of the spectacle. The outcome of the duel had already been decided; the regulars would make up any losses once the strangers began stepping into the circle.

I'd seen it all before. This lady, on the other side of the coin, was unlike anyone I'd ever seen in The Rising Dawn. She gestured to her guard, a hulking man, shaved bald, dressed in silks and painted leathers. He leaned forward, and after she whispered command, he remained at the door while she made her way through the smoke and the noise. I envied her freedom from the wandering hands I had to slap away.

The far corner always remained dark enough to obscure the wealthier patrons who came to see the street duels, which were always more exciting and unpredictable than the sanctioned duels nearer the Sultan's palace. I went to the corner and asked if I could serve the lady. Up close, I saw past the silks and jeweled earrings and envy gave way to pity, despite her finery. Though she was a young woman, perhaps twenty or so summers, her body was shaped like a bottom-heavy pear, and her face and breasts looked as if someone had flattened them out. She asked for tea and water.

Ba'ishyra became a fairly regular fixture of the Rising Dawn, usually sitting alone in that dark corner with no veil because her family came from the Kandian Free Cities to the north. Sometimes, when Ba'ishyra had trouble finding an escort for an evening, she would come to the Rising Dawn and wait for the Half-Faced Man to finish dueling.

I'd watch her as I wiped the tables, carried drinks and food, and slapped at hands that reached for my hips and breasts. Even today, when wiping down my own table after a meal, my arms and hands take on the routine patterns I'd used over and over in my days at the Rising Dawn. Ba'ishyra would watch the duels from those shadows, especially those fought by the Half-Faced Man, with only a slight smile – the secret kind women use to make men's heads spin with suspicion, curiosity, and many times, arousal. Ba'ishyra's smile did nothing to soften her features, and so did nothing to solicit the third response from anyone save for the Half-Faced Man. The regulars would whisper to themselves, when she was well out of earshot, that she might find more escorts if she adopted the veil women wore deeper in heart of the Empire. I overheard them because I was invisible as I served up sin by the cup and the bottle: wine, sweet punch, coffee, and to our less adventurous patrons, tea.

I do not wear a veil. I was not born to a family deserving of such an honor. If ever there was one whose blood flowed without memory of the gods, it was mine.

The Half-Faced Man's name was Tahyr. Our regulars called him the Half-Faced Man, though never where he could hear, because of the very obvious phantasm that shimmered and glowed over the right side of his face. It was a mirror of the other side of his face, if that mirror had been made of leather and paint. He maintained that phantasm even while dueling. It was a subtle way of warning his opponents. Any worthy opponent would know such a thing was a waste of will, best conserved for defeating one's opponents. That didn't matter to Tahyr. He could only be beaten if he wished to be. He was a master of the arcane gifts that each of the gods taught, and he understood each language so completely it was as if the gods themselves whispered to him while the spells, enchantments, and incantations flew across the dueling sands in the Rising Dawn. Rumors hung on him like mosquitoes over an early-summer pond.

"He was once the High-Mage to a sultan or prince wounded in a duel and cast out for being too unsightly for any court."

"No, he bargained with a demon, his face for the power he now commands."

"You are a fool. Were he demon cursed, we could see the signs, but the wine doesn't spoil near him and the flames don't flow toward him as he walks by. He is a small god come to amuse himself by toying with mortals."

"You're the greater fool. The gods can only use the powers of their own divine gifts. He commands the blessings of at least four, perhaps more. He is a fallen saint, cast down for reaching too high in his god's realm."

"Gods and goddesses! You know nothing. He is…"

And so on. I often wondered: if he could create a phantasm to cover his face, why make it so obvious? In watching his skill with the arcane arts, he could have easily hidden the flaw with few, if any, being the wiser. I could not think of an answer, but I was young then.

He defeated so many men, that they could not believe he was merely human. He would never defeat them with the first duel or the second, but rather with the fourth or fifth, at the point where the coins had piled high. The regulars would no longer duel him, except coppers or perhaps the smallest of silver coins. He would only accept these wagers if the Rising Dawn were empty save for regulars. They challenged him to these duels to learn from him, to experience the deftness of his power, the cunning of his technique. I would find something to do during these duels that kept me in the front room, just so I could watch. These duels usually lasted moments, a handful of breaths, but they were spectacular despite the brevity. At the end of each of them Ba'ishyra would sigh, then applaud, and then sigh again.

After a few months, Tahyr began taking Ba'ishyra to the room he rented from Master Daybreak, the small one at the very back of our third story. The room cost Tahyr little. It was so small that nobody else wanted it, and because Tahyr was good for business. People came to watch Tahyr goad foreign sorcerers and wizards into duels with large piles of coin at stake. These people also indulged in the sins the Rising Dawn had to offer.

One afternoon, while I was preparing for the midday meal, Ba'ishyra came down the stairs. She took a table, waved me over, and requested simple breakfast fare. We do not normally serve breakfast at this hour. I glanced at Master Daybreak. He nodded.

"And send something up for honorable Tahyr," she said.

The Master nodded again. I shrugged and went into the kitchen to brave Cook.

Stew was already simmering in the pot over the fire there, so big that I could still hide inside it during those few times it wasn't being used for cooking.

Cook glanced up from portioning out bowls of salad. Seeing me, she returned her attention to the figs, dates, and goat cheese that would top the deep-green lettuce today.

"Ba'ishyra wants breakfast," I said. "And a second plate for the Half-Faced Man."

"Well they can both be hungry until—"

"Master said," I interrupted.

"Master said? Oh, of course, if the Master said. Master Daybreak also said, 'No one breaks the rules. Not ever!'" Cook stomped her foot the way Master Daybreak always did to emphasize the seriousness of his point. "Oh, but flash the Master a bit of coin, or maybe even a smile with the promise of coin, or something else if you're a comely thing, and new rules get placed over the old rules."

Cook went on like this as she made up two plates with bread and fruit with cups full of nectar. She regarded these plates as a smith might look over a pot just after forging but had not dowsed it with water to cool. She put slabs of cheese, one white and one a deep yellow, on each plate. With a nod, she handed me the plates, a small tea pot, and a cup.

I placed one of the plates, the tea pot, and the cup in front of Ba'ishyra, then took the other up three flights of narrow stairs and to the back of the hall to the small door that led to our smallest room. I clapped twice.

"Leave it by the door, Sweet One," Tahyr said from inside.

I did.

When I returned to the common room, Ba'ishyra waved at the chair across from her. I looked to the Master. He frowned. Ba'ishyra caught this, held up two good sized silver coins and placed them on the table. Master Daybreak chewed on his massive lower lip for a moment, then nodded. I sat across from her.

"What is your name?" Ba'ishyra asked.

"They all call me Sweet One, lady," I replied.

"I did not ask what they call you."

I opened my mouth, some polite deflection on the tip of my tongue, until I saw the expression in her hard, mahogany-colored eyes. Most people carried their expressions throughout their entire face. Ba'ishyra did not. Her face was still like ice – even in the desert, I had seen that strange substance twice – with her unblinking eyes harder than I'd ever seen them.

"Shayanira," I replied, my voice so low I sounded meek to my own ears.

"Shay-ah-near-ah." Ba'ishyra spoke it slowly, as if tasting. "Shayanira." Shorter that time. "Shayanira." My name danced across her tongue over and over again, in over a dozen variations.

"The name suits you," Ba'ishyra said at last. "Do you know what it means?"

"My mother said it means strength in beauty."

"That's close. It means, 'the hidden strength that does not allow beauty to fade.' Would you like to be friends?"

The question was so unexpected my breath caught in my throat. I had other girls, and one boy, that I spoke to, and even played with in those few minutes we weren't working at our shops and stalls, but I would never think of any of those other children, most of them years younger than I, as friends.

Again, I glanced to Master Daybreak. Ba'ishyra must have noticed my gaze shift away from her face. She glanced to the Master as well. I looked between those two, and to my surprise and delight, Ba'ishyra's left eyebrow raised the span of two fingers on her forehead, while her right eyebrow remained in place. I'd only ever seen one other person do that trick, a storyteller who bought a night by the fire in exchange for an evening of tales. Nobody fought any duels that night. After a few moments, Master Daybreak nodded.

"Yes." My voice cracked. "I would like to be friends."

Ba'ishyra's cold face broke into a smile, and while it did not make her need a veil any less, it did make her a bit more pleasant to look upon.

"Master," Ba'ishyra said. "Could you fetch a cup for my friend? I'm sure she would like some tea as well."

Master Daybreak passed behind her on the way to the kitchen. When he was directly behind her, he gave me a look that told me, in no uncertain terms, that I would be safe so long as Ba'ishyra attended the Rising Dawn, but the moment he realized that she had taken her custom elsewhere, I was doomed to pay for this demeaning reversal of stations.

For the rest of that morning, Ba'ishyra spoke on inconsequential things that people speak of when they first meet: likes and dislikes, little tidbits of our pasts, and pleasantries that meant little or nothing in the grander sense of our lives. Having wandered through the crowds of the Rising Dawn for so many years, I'd learned to read what people actually meant, even though they weren't speaking of that subject at all. In this conversation, I learned that Ba'ishyra was lonely, which, as I look back, wasn't hard to notice considering how she and I had started our friendship.

We spoke every morning she stayed with the... Tahyr – now that Ba'ishyra and I were friends, I couldn't think of her lover as the Half-Faced Man anymore – which meant some weeks almost every day, other weeks one or two days or not at all. As time passed, our discussions became more like real conversations. Sometimes, Tahyr would come down from his room early, and he and Ba'ishyra would go for a walk. I grew to love those days, for while I enjoyed the time I spoke with my new friend, I had to scurry that much faster to attend to my work once she left.

Two nights after our first conversation, Ba'ishyra started dueling. She engaged in three low stakes and low power contests, nothing to take notice about other than she was a woman. Women duelists come in from time to time, mostly pale-skinned things from those barbaric kingdoms across the northern sea, or from far to the south, where the deep desert sun charred their skin in its intensity. I wondered what sins these people committed to have All Father Sun curse them so. Only once in the Rising Dawn's history had a woman from our city stepped into the circle, and that had been in the Master's grandfather's time. During Ba'ishyra's duels, my throat nearly closed while my heart hammered in my chest. Oh, how I wanted my friend to show these men with their wandering hands that we too could wield power. She lost three duels that first night, and with each loss, I choked back tears.

She kept dueling though. Weeks passed. Ba'ishyra got better. Soon she won about half of her duels. With most of those, it seemed the victory came more from luck than her skill.

One morning, after Ba'ishyra and Tahyr had gone for their walk, Master Daybreak sent me off to get fresh flowers for his grandest table, an expense he put out for only his most important guests, and even then only for tournament nights. Those only happened when master duelists from far away would come and try their hand at the best our city had to offer.

The city had one flower shop; most flowers grow poorly in this part of the desert. I loved this errand, because I knew the secret way back into the garden where the flowers grew. I would go spend a few moments just smelling the scent of all those growing things. This time, as I slinked in that narrow space between the flower shop and jewelers next to it, I heard voices. I held my breath as I crept closer, terrified of being caught and thinking that if I grew much more, I would not be able to take this passage any more. Looking into the garden, I saw Tahyr and Ba'ishyra in a duelers' circle drawn in the center of the garden, the lines of power drawn between the lilies and the lilacs. Energies surged between them. I'd seen Tahyr dueling enough in my time to know when he was serious or when he was sucking some poor fool in just to take his coin. This was the hardest I'd ever seen him working his magic. Sweat beaded off both of them; their clothes stuck to them as second skins. Tahyr's phantasmal face had been replaced by a mundane leather mask.

When they finished, Ba'ishyra glanced over at me and winked.

Tahyr must have seen it, for he glanced in my direction. He smiled. Unlike Ba'ishyra, whose expressions only touched her mouth and her eyes, Tahyr's smile brightened the entirety of his face, at least the side not covered by the mask.

"Again," Tahyr said.

Without any other warning, he spoke words of power. The plants closest to Ba'ishyra sprang to life, reaching for her, thorned vines lashing out. She countered by calling fire from her left hand while sending shards of ice flying at Tahyr from her outstretched right.

I watched the whole of that duel, a grueling experience even for me. The subtleties and intricacies of their spells defied anything I'd ever seen. Watching taught me how masterfully Tahyr had hidden his talents from everyone. Even in those duels where he seemed to struggle, he never let on the true extent of his power, skill, and cunning. Exhausted for them, I hurried back to the Master with the flowers, hoping that my lateness wouldn't warrant too severe a beating, but seeing them duel like that was worth paying that price.

That night, just before the tournament was to begin, Ba'ishyra came in, dressed even finer than usual. With her was a man, older by far and powerful – maybe not a sultan, but someone born with at least a small piece of All Father Sun's radiance. I could tell not by the clothes he wore – any man may put on fine robes and hang jewels from his turban – but by the light of life that shown in his eyes. He seemed more vitally *alive* and *aware* in ways that everyone else in the Rising Dawn was not. seemed to have that same unfortunate quality as Ba'ishyra where his flattened face was just a bit above homely. In his case, it didn't matter. He was a man, and unpleasant features do not tarnish a man's prospects nearly as much as a woman's, and an air of potent dignity surrounded him that anyone in his presence knew he expected to be obeyed.

Master Daybreak came forward, bowing, scraping, full of compliments and endless blessings. I had to suppress a smile at the Master attempting to keep his head lower than this most important guest's. The man nodded at all the proper places as Master Daybreak led them to his finest table, the one raised in the southwestern corner of the common room. Once they sat, the man leaned forward and smelled the flowers I had gotten that morning. He said something to Master Daybreak which resulted in a beaming smile, more bows, and likely more praises, compliments, and blessings to the great man and his descendants. The man said something else. The Master's smile faded. They looked at me. I suddenly felt hot.

Master Daybreak waved me over.

"Sweet One," the Master's voice sounded as if it might be the true source of our sweet wine. "You are to serve this table, and only this table this evening."

"Yes, Master Daybreak," I replied, then turning to our grand guest, I dropped to my knees and bowed low, almost to the point where my forehead touched the floor. My friendship with Ba'ishyra was the only thing that stopped me from complete prostration. "Many thanks for granting such an honor to this unworthy one."

"If you are worthy to be my daughter's friend," the man said, "you are worthy to serve my table."

He asked for simple fare, cheese, bread, and nectar before the dueling began. When I got to the kitchen, Master Daybreak grabbed me by the shoulder, though not as tight as I was accustomed to when he was angry. And he was angry. His eyes were as wide and wild as Aunt Moon when she hangs full in the sky, and his mouth curled into Uncle Night's snarl when one of his siblings foils yet another of his schemes.

"One mistake, and… and…" he searched for some terrible threat, "well, I don't know what, but you will regret it."

He shook me, and even that didn't have the same force I was accustomed to. Normally, my neck would ache for some time after he whipped me around. I bowed low but remained standing. Dropping to my knees would have been overly respectful and likely seen as me being impertinent.

"Your guests will know nothing but peace and pleasure with my service."

Master Daybreak stared at me for a moment. When he realized I was not making fun of him, he reached out again and ruffled my hair.

The tournament began with Tahyr facing Ba'ishyra. When the Master called her name, her father's face contorted into nearly the same face of displeasure that the Master had directed to me in the kitchen. Ba'ishyra leaned to her father and kissed him on both cheeks, as a man might do, then lifted his right hand and kissed a huge ruby on the ring he wore – a ruby, All Father Sun's stone, symbol of honor and power. Once she stood in the duelist circle, her father waved me over and had me sit next to him. He didn't say anything, didn't even look at me as his daughter and Tahyr faced off against each other.

I held my breath and gripped the edges of the table. The grandest duel of tonight's tournament was going to happen first.

I should have known better.

The whole thing was over before anyone could blink. Just as the judge called to begin, Cook was at the door to the kitchen, screaming something. Being accustomed to those ravings, I didn't turn away, unlike most everyone else including Tahyr. Ba'ishyra blasted him out of the dueling circle with one simple gust of wind. Several of our regular duelists snickered, while the visitors shook their heads, clearly disgusted at Tahyr for allowing himself to be distracted so easily. When Tahyr stood, I saw him wink his good eye at Master Daybreak, who nodded slightly in return. All other eyes seemed fixed on Ba'ishyra. I added my head to those shaking, but not for the same reason. My mind saw the next few days as Tahyr won purse after purse from those who witnessed this shameful defeat.

"Brilliant," Ba'ishyra's father said. "No wonder he's caught her eye so." And then he added in a quiet tone that was probably meant for him alone. "Pity."

He and I sat and watched together in silence until Ba'ishyra lost in the fourth round to Amadan the Limper.

The tournament ended with one of the charred-skinned strangers – we called him Anvil, because few here could pronounce his name, and he stood in the duelist circle like an anvil, short, stout, and unmoving while spell after spell shattered against him – stood victorious. He defeated Amadan the Limper in a duel that lasted well over an hour.

As this stranger celebrated, Ba'ishyra stepped forward and challenged him. Anvil's dark face tightened in confusion and fury.

Tahyr and Master Daybreak leaned against the wall near the kitchen, smiling, whispering with heads together. The cunning and brilliance of this scheme hit me with the suddenness of a sandstorm. While considered unseemly to challenge the winner of a tournament the same night as his victory, it was not so uncommon that it would be completely unexpected. By tradition, the victor could decline any duels and not suffer any shame by the refusal. But sometimes there is a great gaping chasm between what tradition dictated and what men believe, especially if a challenge came from a woman, who even though she made it to the fourth round, was still a woman.

The Anvil accepted.

As the duel progressed, Tahyr spoke to Master Daybreak, commenting on Ba'ishyra's subtlety. She hammered Anvil with spell after spell, forceful and subtle, blasts of fire and wind as well as curses and hexes. But these only served to distract from her most insidious spell, one working its way through the sands beneath his feet, slowly moving the Anvil inch by inch toward the edge of the circle. This worked because she also moved herself, creating the illusion of being stationary in the circle.

I feared for the riot that would ensue when Ba'ishyra won, but the reaction was nothing more than stunned silence as Master Daybreak traversed the room, collecting the winnings.

When I looked at Ba'ishyra, she wasn't smiling as I would have expected after such a victory. She was looking up at her father. He nodded once and left. I couldn't read the expression on her face, which remained unchanged even to the point when she and Tahyr headed up to his tiny room.

The next morning, I sat at a table, quietly sipping tea, waiting for my friend to come down.

"He doesn't make love to me," Ba'ishyra said, flopping down on the bench next to me.

I sprayed tea across the table. I blinked rapidly and my mouth opened and closed as I sought some response to this.

"He hasn't ever. Not once. He's a fool for beauty, even with his face the way it is, and so he cannot, or will not love me. Can you believe that with all the sins in all the men's hearts throughout the five deserts, the one man who captures me cannot bring himself to slake his lust with me for even one night? He holds me and kisses my cheek and neck; he brushes my hair while reciting works of the great poets. I suppose that was enough in the beginning, but now I want more from him. I don't even want his heart anymore. His body would do, even for a night."

I looked at her, really looked at her. Her cheeks were flushed, and her bloodshot, sunken eyes would not quite focus on me. She wobbled in her seat. I leaned in and smelled her breath.

Ba'ishyra smiled and met my eyes. She leaned in closer. Close enough for me to feel her breath on my lips. Close enough for the stench of wine to churn my stomach. "Are you making an offer?" She giggled.

I pushed her back. "You're drunk."

This was the first time in all the time she'd been coming to the Rising Dawn that she'd allowed herself to descend in the sin we offered.

I further overstepped my station then, by waving to her eunuch. He stood in the corner of our common room, waiting to escort her to where ever it was that she went while not at the Rising Dawn. The eunuch stared at me blankly. I returned the gaze without flinching. The left corner of his mouth curved upward in the hint of a smile. I snapped my fingers the way I'd seen Ba'ishyra do time and time again. The smile blossomed into a grin, and he came over. Together, we took her back to the Half-Faced Man's room.

Ba'ishyra protested, but was not in any condition to offer any real resistance.

I pulled the door open, causing it to crash against the wall. The Half-Faced Man bolted upright in his bed, the shimmer of arcane power forming around his hands, that strange, half-mask covering his face. Bottles littered the floor of that small room. The side of his face twisted in anger until I kicked a bottle across the room at him. Rage gave way to shame. It was the first time in my life a man had would not meet my eye. My breath quickened with the feeling of such power.

"You allowed her to get like this," I said. With the Eunuch's help, I carried her three steps to the bed. The Half-Faced Man rolled aside just in time to avoid her flopping down on top of him. "You care for her."

"But—" the Half-Faced Man started, but I cut him off. The muscles on the left side of my forehead flexed while the right side remained relaxed, raising a single eyebrow. Oddly, I didn't feel like smiling in celebration of that personal victory.

The Half-Faced Man opened his mouth again, and without lowering my eyebrow, I straightened up even more and cocked my head to the side. It had been so long since I'd stood at my full height in the presence of another person, it surprised me to discover I was a bit taller than him. The Half-Faced Man closed his mouth, eyes downcast.

Ba'ishyra stumbled out of the bed and staggered toward the door. "I don't want him to care for me."

I stepped forward before she could leave the room, placed my hand on her forehead, and shoved her backward. She probably would have landed in a sprawling heap if the Half-Faced Man had not caught her. I stepped out of the room, shut the door, and leaned against it. One of them tried to escape, but I pushed hard against the door. I know that in some other lands, doors open into the room, a silly thought, for doors that open inward are far too easy to break down or kick in.

"What?" I demanded of her eunuch. He stood in the center of the hallway, smiling.

His smile broadened into a grin and he spread his hands in front of him.

"Sweet One!" Master Daybreak called from downstairs.

I looked at the eunuch and gestured toward the door. He nodded and braced against it.

I hurried down to attend my duties.

Later, when Ba'ishyra came down, squinting against the afternoon brightness, I grabbed her hand and led her to the duelist circle. I stood her on one side and then went and faced her from the other. She blinked at me and looked around, mouth opening and closing. I hoped she was as confused as she appeared. I didn't want her to dance around my question.

"Why are we friends?" I asked.

"What?" She looked at me as if attempting to puzzle out an complex spell.

"Why are we friends?"

Ba'ishyra looked at me as so many of our patrons did. Her chin rose a bit, and her eyes gazed down at me from behind her nose, as if that could shield her from the poverty that clung to me. I'd seen her turn that particular gaze at many people in the Rising Dawn but never to me. She turned to leave the circle.

"No." My voice snapped. Her foot hung between the sand of the circle and the stone of the rest of the floor. "You owe me the honor of answering me."

She brought her foot back into the circle and faced me. The haughty look no longer clung to her features.

"Apologies," Ba'ishyra said. "I am not myself this afternoon." She sat down and looked at her knees. "I don't know. At first, I thought to buy a pair of ears that had no choice but to sit and listen to me, as none of my own station care to know the girl who needs a veil but doesn't wear one." Her mouth turned downward and cheeks tightened. "Then I grew to know you. You treated me better than anyone. Now I love you as I would a sister of my father's blood."

Her head sank again. I walked across the sand, sat down and held her. Part of me wanted to throw her friendship away, such a deceitful beginning was unworthy of me, but that was too harsh. I realized I also loved her as a sister, and so I hummed softly to her and stroked her hair as she cried.

Months later, the morning before the next tournament, Master Daybreak sent me for flowers again. I made my way into that small space between the buildings to smell the flowers for a short while before returning to the Rising Dawn. Ba'ishyra and Tahyr were there practicing. Watching them, I couldn't help but smile at what scheme they had planned for that night. I stayed longer than I should have, getting lost in the intricacies of their duels. One duel they fought involved nothing more than curses; they had to determine and cleanse themselves of each curse in turn. This type of duel almost never happened at the Rising Dawn. Curses were usually too subtle a magic for spectators to appreciate. I'd seen so many duels, I could almost see the lines of fate that they wove around each other, like a great tapestry that threatened to rip itself apart.

Once they finished that duel, Ba'ishyra went over to him, and said in a low voice, "I want to see your face."

Tahyr turned away from her. "No."

She got closer to him and placed her hand on his shoulder. I could barely make out her words.

"I know you don't feel the same, but I'm in love with you. I want to know you. *All* of you. Please?"

I fled.

Later, when Ba'ishyra returned to the Rising Dawn, I could tell Tahyr had shown her what lay beneath his phantasm. She wore a veil across her face, which only enhanced the way she couldn't look at anyone or anything for too long.

I knew that focusless gaze because of an incident a year earlier when a duel had gotten out of hand. Sometimes, those with purer blood come down and used street duels to settle something personal that, for whatever reason, both of them believe will only be settled by the death of one or the other. Two men with this agenda came into the Rising Dawn, disguised as common practitioners of the arcane arts rather than those of purer blood. Their duel was quick and bloody, and before anyone could intervene, both men were horribly dead and not at all recognizable. The Rising Dawn had closed for nearly week while we all cleaned up the mess. For a month or more afterwards, none of us, clients or workers, could look on anything in the place for more than a few moments without reminding ourselves of what bit of bloody wreckage had affixed itself to that surface.

I went to comfort Ba'ishyra, but she held up her hand. I swear to the gods and goddesses, she tried using some power to keep me away. Refusing to let my friend keep me away, I somehow moved through it. Her body tensed when I embraced her, then relaxed and she fell against me, weeping. Master Daybreak yelled my name from the kitchen several times. I ignored him. He came through the door, a giant spoon held like a weapon. I looked at him with the same expression I'd fixed on the Half-Faced Man months before as I deposited a drunken Ba'ishyra in his room. His mouth crinkled into a frown, and he crossed his arms. I could almost see the battle in his mind, to confront me on this insolence or to acknowledge this change between us. With a quick, deep breath he gave me a curt nod.

Tahyr returned later. For the first time, the phantasm covered his whole face, and it showed a caricature of his face, serene in its peacefulness or peaceful in its serenity. Tahyr and Ba'ishyra avoided each other, and though they looked at each other frequently, it was only for an instant at the longest, both quick to turn away lest the other notice that attention.

The next tournament ended unlike any in the history of the Rising Dawn, unlike any in the history of our whole City. Master Daybreak spent days after quietly fuming in his room behind the kitchen and ranting about the injustice of it all. Months passed before he was able to speak without anger about how Ba'ishyra the Sly had managed to defeat Tahyr, the Half-Faced Man, when he was trying to win.

In the final round, Ba'ishyra stood against the Half-Faced Man, having defeated every other opponent in the span of a few breaths. Ba'ishyra placed a phantasm over her veiled face – the image of herself as she might be had she received the best qualities of her parents rather than the worst. Seemingly in retaliation, the moment the judges cried, "Begin," Tahyr dropped his phantasm, showing his face with his mundane mask covering his face. Had he faced off against anyone other than Ba'ishyra the Sly, that tactic might have worked, but I recalled his words from the last tournament, "all she sees is the sand. You can't teach that. She's going to be a legend someday."

Ba'ishyra molded her phantasm, showing one half of her face as we normally saw it every other time she came into the Rising Dawn. The other side of her face became a mangled mirror of the Half-Faced Man: a tattered piece of skin that had once been an eyelid flapped against a sagging, watery mass that hung out of the socket, sickly gray with splotches of green that did not quite match the color at the center of Tahyr's eye that we could see. The cheek of that horror had been chewed to stringy ruins by the row of jutting fangs that had somehow replaced the teeth everyone else has. Silence echoed in the space after the collective gasp of shock and horror, broken only by two people retching in the corner.

Tahyr stepped out of the circle. He dropped to his knees and touched his head to the floor. In the silence that followed, we could hear Ba'ishyra's footsteps grinding against the Rising Dawn's stone floor as she walked over to Tahyr. She let her phantasm fall away.

She addressed us all. "I love this man. I love his face. Not his duelist face. I see the face he hides like the man he hides deep inside that none of you will see or know."

Tahyr didn't move during this, but I noticed wet spots on the stone floor beneath his face.

Ba'ishyra knelt down and whispered into his ear. "I love you, you stupid fool." In the quiet, we all heard her.

The she left without collecting the winner's purse.

Throughout the rest of the evening, people left in ones and twos; the few who spoke did so in the smallest of whispers. We knew that we had been present for one of the great, epic duels. Even now, I cannot resist correcting the falsities about that night when I hear them. When people hear I was present, I tell the story of that night as true and as plain as I can. Amadan the Limper does the same. Even Master Daybreak could not bring himself to exaggerate that story.

To his credit, Tahyr managed to rise from knees while some people were still there. He put his normal phantasm back over his face and had two cups of sweet wine before leaving, not to his room but out the front door.

Two days later, Ba'ishyra's eunuch came to the Rising Dawn with a bundle tucked under one arm and a letter. He gave both to Master Daybreak and bowed low. The Master waved me over and handed the bundle to me. It was silk, soft and smooth. I caressed it as Master Daybreak read me the letter.

"My dear Shayanira. These are all the items dedicated to my art of dueling. I no longer need them. They are yours, as is anything that remains in Tahyr's room. Keep them or sell them. It makes no difference to us, so long as somehow you use them to enhance the wonder of your life."

When he finished, he handed me the letter and left the room. I'd never had anyone write to me, never knew anyone who could write that would waste paper on me.

Master Daybreak returned with coffee, an expensive drink rarely gifted on the staff, which we shared. We sat in quiet for some time.

Finally, he asked "What will you do?"

I considered. "I believe I'll continue preparing for this evening's service after I put these away."

Gathering the bundle, I went to small alcove I used for sleeping. Two of the stones there could be pulled up, and that's where I kept the few treasures I'd collected over my life.

"Sweet One," Master Daybreak said. He coughed, clearing his throat, then smiled. "Shayanira. I don't think Tahyr will return. Why don't you take his room?"

I chewed my lips for a moment. I looked into the Master's eyes, searching for any hidden obligations that he might attach to this offer. When I saw none, I nodded. By some silent agreement, Master Daybreak and I revealed nothing of what had happened to Ba'ishyra and Tahyr.

One month from the day we last saw Ba'ishyra and Tahyr, the Rising Dawn hosted another tournament. Word of the last tournament had spread, and people came to see if the Rising Dawn would be home to even more legends. As was usual, one of the strangers who had come just for the tournament allowed his hands to wander across me in places I'd rather not let them wander. I took the power from one of Ba'ishyra's treasures and slapped the man's hand away with a tiny charge of lightning. He yelped and jumped away. People around him laughed. Face reddening, he raised his hand to me. Amadan the Limper, who had stayed close to me all evening despite the crowds, grabbed the offender's hand before he could strike.

"Is this man bothering you, Shayanira?" Amadan asked. "Shall I remove him?"

The whole room quieted. Even the regulars watched with interest.

"No." I tried to sound bored despite my churning stomach. "I'll settle this in the circle, if he's brave enough."

"I have nothing to prove against an unveiled creature like you."

"What if I offer something you seem to desire? Should you win, you can touch me where you like, how you like, until the dawn rises again. Should I win, I get the entire contents of your purse."

"Done," he said, and pushed his way through the crowd to stand on one side of the circle.

A young man I didn't recognize escorted me to the other. As I stepped into the circle, he gave me a hopeful smile. He was pretty enough, but I could not afford distractions right now. I kept my face plain and prayed that no one noticed the heat rising in my ears.

The stranger and I faced each other across the circle. He nodded at me with a smug smile, perhaps trying to intimidate me. I did not return the gesture; rather, I reached into my sleeve, pulled out a veil, and drew it across my face. A chorus of whispers rippled through the regulars, remembering Ba'ishyra's last tournament. My opponent shifted his feet at this, looking from me to the crowd and back again. He swallowed hard. It did not surprise me that he had heard the tale of Ba'ishyra and the Half-Faced Man.

Tahyr's words came back to me, "all she sees is the sand." I had seen many miles of sand wandering the streets of this city on errands for Master Daybreak. I had wandered the deserts before the Master's wife had taken me in. My years of serving in the Rising Dawn had taught me how to keep putting one foot in front of the other while avoiding distractions.

"Begin!" Master Daybreak called.

I composed my first spell and readied two others, seeing nothing but sand.

An excerpt from *FIRST CHOSEN*
Book One of
TEARS OF RAGE

Tears of Rage *is my BFF (big fat fantasy) doorstopper series...only, I have intentionally kept the books on the shorter side, so they aren't really that big and fat and so I can keep putting them out a little more frequently than some other fantasy series I could mention. As I write these words, I have four books in the series out, with some work done on book five. Book five,* A Rise of Lesser Gods *will complete the first major story arch of the series. I have three arcs planned in all, which means the whole thing should be finished in fifteen to twenty-ish shorter books, rather than seven to ten massive tombs. Here's a taste of book one,* First Chosen.

ONE

Julianna sat at breakfast on the morning of her twenty-first birthday, the traditional day of Komati adulthood, and just as with the sickness when she was fourteen, the gods threatened to take this day from her as well – unless, of course, Julianna defied the gods. And why shouldn't she? It was her life, her memories of a day she would carry until she died.

Julianna leaned forward, clutched both hands to her stomach, and made a gagging sound. At the other end of the table, Aunt Maerie nibbled on carefully cut bits of pastries while Uncle Alyxandros sipped at his tea and read a letter. Breakfast had been a simple affair, consisting of porridge, fruits, and tea. They had to save room for all the food at the introduction supper when Julianna would officially meet Duke Martyn Collaen, a boorish oaf of a man who had expressed interest in a political marriage between Julianna and himself.

"What better way to enter into the adult world," Aunt Maerie had said, "than to accept the hand of one of the wealthiest and most powerful men in Koma."

The thought of being courted by Duke Martyn, a man nearly twice Julianna's twenty-one years, made her stomach churn. She gripped the table with her right hand, and groaned, "Gods and goddesses."

Aunt Maerie's fork stopped halfway between the plate and her mouth. She set the fork down without as much as a *clink* on the plate and folded her hands together. Her lips formed a thin line as her face tightened so that Julianna could see every one of the worry lines in the old woman's face – lines that Aunt Maerie claimed came from watching over Julianna.

Uncle Alyxandros looked up from his letter. His gaze met Julianna's, and she thought she saw the left corner of his mouth creep up a bit. As always, she could gain no insight from his deep brown eyes.

"Julianna." Aunt Maerie stared straight ahead and her lips barely moved. She spoke in the same, almost singsong tone she used when her undersized dogs wouldn't perform their tricks properly for guests. "I won't tolerate that language at—"

"Maerie," Uncle Alyxandros said.

"Alyx, do not attempt to defend her—"

Uncle Alyxandros cleared his throat, cutting off Aunt Maerie's protests. She opened her mouth, but he waved his letter toward Julianna. The instant she had Aunt Maerie's attention, Julianna took her hand from the table and covered her mouth.

"Permission to be excused?" Julianna said between quick breaths. "Please?"

The crow's feet at Aunt Maerie's eyes softened and her lips relaxed. "By all means, dear."

A brief twinge of guilt twisted into a knot a few inches behind Julianna's naval. Aunt Maerie had spent a considerable amount of time arranging this dinner with Duke Martyn. Many other high ranking men from other noble families would also be there – on the chance that Duke Martyn did not take a fancy to Julianna. Then Julianna recalled a party not even two months ago. Duke Martyn's hand seemed unable to resist pinching the breasts and bottom of every girl, and even a few of the boys, who served him that night.

"Thank you." The words came out in a quick whisper as Julianna bolted from the table.

In her haste, she knocked her chair over. The crash startled one of the new servant girls, who dropped a tea set. Shards of white porcelain and hot tea sloshed across the floor as the girl danced away from the shattered tea pot and cups. Julianna gave neither the accident nor the gaping-mouthed servant any attention as she fled the room. Her maid followed behind her.

Just as Julianna had planned, one of the downstairs maids waited right outside the door. Just like the girl who had dropped the tea pot, this maid had only recently come to the estate in the past few months. Aunt Maerie hadn't had time to burn their faces into her memory yet, which made them perfect for helping Julianna avoid Martyn Collaen. The maid stood with a bowl of watery gruel that also contained just a bit of bile from inside a lamb's stomach.

"Are you sure, my lady?" the girl asked.

"Do it," Julianna said. The illusion of sickness had to be perfect.

The maid dumped the noxious mixture on Julianna's sitting dress and the floor in front of her. As the mixture soaked into the fabric, the girl squeaked and fled.

Julianna made vomiting noises. She had spent many parties, balls, and dinners listening to men vomit up their excess liquor. Sometimes, she'd even sought out opportunities to listen to this activity in order to imitate those noises. One never knew when one might need to invent an excuse not to attend an outing or an appointment. The maid shoved the bowl into a nearby plant just as Aunt Maerie followed Julianna out of the breakfast room.

Behind Julianna, Colette and Aunt Maerie came out of the sitting room.

"Aunt Maerie," Julianna said in her weakest voice. She gestured at the mess all over the front of her dress.

Aunt Maerie brought her hand up to cover her nose. She looked about, up and down the hall. "You! Girl!"

The maid who had helped Julianna hadn't quite gotten around the far corner. She squeaked even louder as she stopped and turned around. Julianna felt that she might actually vomit. Had Aunt Maerie seen?

Aunt Maerie waved at the mess on the floor. "Run to the kitchens, get some hot water, and clean this up."

The girl curtsied and hurried off. Julianna took a breath, not realizing she'd been holding it.

"Oh, Julianna," Aunt Maerie said, taking in the sight of Julianna. "Your favorite dress."

It wasn't Julianna's favorite. She hated the vile thing, though she had worn it more frequently than any other in the past month. Aunt Maerie had urged Julianna to add variety to her wardrobe, claiming that the dress did nothing to enhance Julianna's complexion or her beautiful eyes. Julianna had countered by reminding Aunt Maerie that no one besides her, Uncle Alyxandros, and the servants ever saw Julianna in the dress, so it didn't matter how unflattering it was.

Julianna made several gagging noises as if she were going to vomit again, and then started off toward her room. After five paces, she clutched at her stomach and leaned on the wall. She wanted to hear any words her aunt and her maid might exchange.

"After her, Colette," Aunt Maerie said. "Your mistress needs you."

"Shall she be needing me to bring her breakfast?" Colette asked.

Don't overdo it, Julianna thought, though she could see the image of Colette's slightly faraway look as the maid spoke with Countess Maerie Vivaen. Colette was a more practiced deceiver than most of the high ranking lords and ladies that frequented court. Most servants were. It was a requirement of their position.

"Can't you see she's ill," Aunt Maerie asked. "She needs washing and a bed, not food. See that she gets them."

Colette dropped into a curtsy. "Yes, Excellency."

Julianna thanked all the lesser gods and goddesses at once. Half of her ruses and deceptions would never have succeeded if Colette did not play the part of the simpleminded maid so well.

A moment later, Julianna felt Colette's soft but firm grip on her arm. Together, they headed toward Julianna's suite, stopping every ten to fifteen paces for Julianna to feign another attack of her unsettled stomach.

Once they rounded the first corner, their pace quickened. They hurried past servants who were packing the multitude of paintings, tapestries, and stone busts that populated the walls and corners of her aunt and uncle's summer home.

Summerrain, a small estate of forty-nine rooms, had been in Aunt Maerie's family for over a dozen generations. It harkened back to a time when barbaric men still tried to unseat each other from horseback using lances and other weapons without the least bit of finesse. Aunt Maerie had done her best to disguise the inner antiquity of the estate by having the floors carpeted and the walls covered by as much art as she could. One of the servants' houses had been converted into an artist's house. Throughout the late spring and summer, Julianna had been forced to sit for a painter or a sculptor at least once a week. Aunt Maerie seemed to believe that Summerrain's halls could only be brightened by cramming them with as many renditions of Julianna and Uncle Alyxandros as possible.

When Julianna reached her rooms, she attempted to wriggle her way out of the sitting dress. Normally, this would not have been a challenging task, but she had an appointment, and every moment from her departure from the breakfast table to leaving the estate had been painstakingly planned. In the practice sessions at taking this dress off in a hurry, Julianna had forgotten to account for the vile concoction that soiled it. Her schedule only included time to quickly wash her body, but not her hair.

"Mistress," Colette said. "You're taking too long."

"I know that," Julianna snapped.

She stopped her wrestling match with the dress and went over to the bride's chest at the foot of her bed. It had belonged to her mother, and unlike many of the bride's chests young ladies used these days, this one was made to come apart. Each side, the top, and both bottoms – there was a false bottom about seven inches above the true bottom – were made of forty-nine interlocking pieces of carved ivory.

Young ladies used these chests to store anything they felt they might need for their wedding. When a man wished to marry a girl, he would ask her to gift him with her bride's chest. She was honor bound to grant him that gift. However, she was not required to give him the chest intact. If a lady disassembled the chest before giving it to a man, he had seven days to reconstruct it. If he did, she was honor bound to marry him. If the man truly repulsed the girl, she could always keep one piece from each surface so that finishing the chest became impossible. When he returned the uncompleted chest, she could then choose to reveal the seven missing pieces or not. That was the first challenge a Komati man must pass in his quest to win a bride.

Julianna opened the chest. "Colette, get the knife."

A knife lay hidden deep in the chest just above the secret compartment.

Colette thrust her hands into the chest, drew out the knife, and handed it to Julianna. From tip to pommel, the weapon was just a hair longer than Julianna's forearm. For the most part, it was a nondescript weapon. The hilt was a dark brown wood that nearly matched the dark brown of the leather sheath. The blade had a blood groove the length of Julianna's middle finger on one side. Aside from that, and the reddish tint of the blade, the weapon's only distinctive feature was a single word etched into the blade opposite the blood groove.

Kostota.

Julianna didn't know what the word meant, but every time she looked at it, she felt that she should know. She'd once shown it to Uncle Alyxandros, and he had quietly suggested that she might want to keep the knife hidden away, or better yet, dispose of it entirely. Julianna could not do that. It was one of two things she'd received from her mother. The other was her eyes. Her deep, piercing gray eyes were extremely rare in girls born of Komati blood, and they were nearly nonexistent in girls from other lands. It was the first of Julianna's features that most men complimented, and in doing so, they earned the first coin of Julianna's contempt. Complimenting her eyes was far too easy.

The knife sliced through the material of the dress, and in a moment, Julianna was free without any damage done to her hair. She tossed the dress into the chamber pot.

"Burn that horrid thing," she told Colette.

"Of course, Julianna," Colette replied. Then she pinched her nose with one hand as she balanced a tray holding a bowl of water, soap, and a washing cloth in the other. "But I know how much you loved it. I'll fetch the seamstress to commission a new one that is exactly the same."

Colette had perfected her imitation of Aunt Maerie's nasal tone.

"Oh, but Aunty," Julianna said in a tone of exaggerated innocence. "I couldn't possibly wear a counterfeit of the original, no matter how perfect. It just wouldn't do."

They both laughed and then composed themselves. They had only a minute or two before Aunt Maerie came to check on Julianna. Julianna slid the knife back into its sheath as Colette began to untie the strings of Julianna's morning corset. The door opened sooner than expected. Julianna dropped her knife, kicked it under her bed, and hurried to the window.

As planned, just outside the window, there was a splash of the same concoction that Colette had spilled over Julianna's dress. From the acidic smell wafting up from that mess, it hadn't been but a few moments since one of the other conspiring servants had spilled it there. The stable boy must have been waiting for the sound of their voices. Julianna couldn't suppress a small smile.

"Oh, you poor thing," Aunt Maerie said from behind Julianna. She still spoke in that condescending tone. Julianna's smile faded, and she clenched and unclenched her fists several times to keep from turning around and strangling her aunt. "Duke Martyn will be so disappointed."

Julianna turned around. "I can go." She kept one hand on her stomach and the other near her mouth. "Give me a few moments to recover."

"And allow you to embarrass me, your uncle, and yourself by rushing from the feast table, or worse, vomiting all over the high table at the main course?"

Julianna noticed where Aunt Maerie had placed herself in that list. Whenever she spoke of more than one person, Aunt Maerie always listed them in order of their importance. Oddly enough, Aunt Maerie usually named herself first.

"You will stay," Aunt Maerie continued. "Your Uncle and I will still attend and make our apologies to His Grace, *Duke* Martyn Collaen, Lord of Storm's Landing and Autumnwind. Did I mention that he has a seat on the Komati's advisory council to Governor Salvatore?"

"Yes, Aunt." *Only about forty-nine times.*

"*And,* did you also…"

Julianna stopped listening to Aunt Maerie's praise of Duke Martyn. She waved Colette to get the water and soap.

Gods and goddesses, Julianna thought. *Please let her leave.*

Instead of leaving, Aunt Maerie sat on the edge of Julianna's bed, and her foot came down on Julianna's knife. The weapon clattered against the stone floor.

"What's that?" Aunt Maerie asked and leaned forward.

Julianna stared at Colette. If Aunt Maerie found the knife, Julianna might not only lose today's activities; she might well lose the knife.

"Night below us," Julianna groaned and went to the window.

"Julianna!" Aunt Maerie cried. There was only so much profanity that she would forgive, even considering Julianna's illness.

With her back shielding her, Julianna shoved her finger into her throat. She gagged, but nothing else happened. With Aunt Maerie this close, Julianna couldn't trust her imitations. She needed to truly vomit. She wiggled her finger around, tickling her throat until her sides tightened and the porridge she had eaten spilled onto window sill and the ground outside. Julianna had never expected to go to this much trouble for a man.

"With all due respect, Your Excellency," Colette said in a demur tone. "I must ask you to leave so that I may attend my mistress."

Aunt Maerie sputtered. Julianna stayed leaning out the window, envisioning Colette gently leading the Countess of Summerrain to the door. The door closed.

Julianna stood up. Colette turned over a small sandglass that counted two minutes. As the sand poured from the top of the glass into the bottom, Julianna shifted from foot to foot. It would be so much easier to just jump forward a few minutes, but she might need the power to help her get out of Summerrain unnoticed. While she bounced up and down next to the window, watching the sand move in agonizing slowness, Colette turned down the blankets on the bed in case Aunt Maerie returned to check on them. That rarely occurred, but it had happened often enough to warrant caution.

At last, the final sands slid into the bottom of the glass. Julianna crossed the space between her and the glass in two long strides. She tipped the glass over and spread her arms. She and Colette had practiced changing from one outfit to the other twice a day for the last fortnight. By the time the top of the glass was empty again, Julianna was in her favorite burgundy velvet and black silk riding dress. Every time she looked at it, Julianna thanked the gods that Uncle Alyx could deny her nothing. All she had to do was tilt her head down, hunch her shoulders up, and give him a faint half-smile. It had worked ever since she'd recovered from her sickness when she was fourteen.

Once the dress was on, Julianna turned the sandglass a third and final time. Colette attacked Julianna's hair with brush, comb and hairpins – long, needle-like things that many men called "maiden's defenders." Julianna's dark hair was so long and thick that she needed between four and six, depending on the style of the braid. That morning, just to ensure the intricate braid remained intact throughout the day, Colette used seven. By the time the glass had emptied again, two curling ringlets fell across each of Julianna's ears, framing her face perfectly; the rest of her hair had been woven into a dozen braids that were pulled back into a bun and cascaded down her back.

Dressed and groomed, all Julianna had to do now was navigate the halls of Summerrain and get to the stables without being discovered by her aunt and uncle. Normally, this might be a challenge, but Julianna had arranged the work schedules so that all the servants who loved her more than they did the count or countess were on duty at this time. They were prepared to delay Uncle Alyx or Aunt Maerie with any number of questions or minor emergencies that could not wait.

Julianna opened the door. Uncle Alex leaned on the wall opposite her room, reading his letter. He glanced up through his spectacles. Julianna shut the door, grabbed Colette, and shifted backward in time a few moments.

"Wet cloth," Julianna said as she jumped into the bed and pulled the blankets up to her chin.

Colette gathered a bowl and cloth from the table, wet the cloth, and spread it over Julianna's head to hide her hair.

A moment later, a knock sounded on Julianna's door.

"Come in." Julianna tried her best to sound fatigued.

Uncle Alyx came in, still wearing his spectacles. He looked around the room, scanning, and finally fixed his attention on Julianna. He walked over to her bed and yanked the covers off her. He stared at her over the rims of his spectacles. Colette shrank to the other side of the room.

"Not exactly what I would consider clothes for recovering from an illness," Uncle Alyx said at last. He pulled the cloth off her head, looked at her hair, and shook his head. "It seems as though you have an appointment."

Julianna sat up. Uncle Alyx offered his hand and helped her out of the bed.

"Please Uncle Alyx," she said. "Don't make me go. This is my last chance to have a real seven birthday. My friends have planned a picnic."

He fixed her with his most disapproving stare, the one where his cheeks tensed so much it made it look like his lips were pursing to kiss something. "You know your aunt will be furious when she finds out."

To counter the disapproving stare, Julianna hunched up her shoulders, and gave him her best smile. "She doesn't have to find out."

Uncle Alyx shook his head. "There are times when your aunt may be flighty and obtuse, but she is not stupid. She *will* find out, and she *will* suspect I've had some hand in this. We'll both suffer for it greatly."

"Please, Uncle Alyx."

"Will there be any young gentlemen at this picnic?"

Julianna chewed the inside of her right cheek. "Yes."

"Anyone I know?"

Julianna ground her right toe into the carpet. "Khellan Dubhan and perhaps a few of his friends."

"*Baron* Khellan Dubhan?"

Julianna nodded. Even the mention of Khellan's name caused her ears to warm and her stomach to churn a bit.

Uncle Alex crossed his arms, sucked in a deep breath, and let it out in a long sigh.

"Well, it is apparent that I cannot keep you from being rash and impulsive, but I know viscount Dubhan and his son. Fortunately, they are both rational, level-headed men. You may go."

Julianna threw her arms around Uncle Alyx and kissed him on the forehead and both cheeks. He sighed and rolled his eyes. She'd done that ever since she was thirteen and taller than he, and he'd always pretended that he didn't like it but she knew differently. Uncle Alyx did not allow anyone do something to him that he didn't like.

Julianna gestured for Colette to follow, and they fled the room, heading toward the stables.

"If your aunt asks," Uncle Alyx called after them, "I will deny knowing anything about this."

"I'm a grown woman," Julianna cried back. "She can't treat me like a child anymore."

Uncle Alyx's laughter trailed after the two young ladies. Julianna knew better. Aunt Maerie treated everyone like a child, everyone but important people at court who outranked her in the order of precedence. Well, now that *Duchess* Julianna Taraen was an adult in her own right, she did outrank *Countess* Maerie Vivaen. Once Julianna returned from her outing, she would have a conversation with Countess Vivaen on who was and was not worthy to marry a certain duchess of House Kolmonen.

With the exception of Uncle Alyx's surprise visit, the plan to get from her rooms to the stables worked perfectly, just as they had planned it. Julianna waved her hand in frustration at the servants who curtsied and bowed to her as she and Colette rushed by. Normally, Julianna wouldn't have dismissed this show of respect in such a flippant manner, but Uncle Alyx had disrupted her timetable by several minutes. While she could have gotten them back, Julianna didn't want to risk tiring herself out before even getting to the picnic. So they hurried, not quite at a jog, but close to it.

When she and Colette reached the stables, Julianna stopped short.

"What are you doing?" Julianna demanded.

The serving boy and two of the stable hands were passing around a bottle. It was a bottle of fine Aernacht whiskey. It had been Julianna's gift to the boy for his assistance.

At the sound of her voice, all three snapped to the perfect attentive stance all who served the nobility learned to master early in their careers of service. The servant boy tried his best to hide the bottle behind his back. Unfortunately, they had already consumed enough whiskey that maintaining that rigid posture proved impossible. Each of them swayed slightly side to side, and none of them could meet her gaze, finding anything to look at besides where Julianna stood.

"Do you think that just because the nobles of this house are away that you can spit in the face of your duty?"

"No, my lady," the three of them said together.

"Excuse me?"

Julianna walked to stand a single pace from them. Gods and goddesses, she needed to get on her horse and get on the road, but she could not let this pass. The three of them stiffened even more.

"No, Your Grace."

"Better."

Julianna fixed her attention on the young man she'd given the bottle as a gift. He glanced up at her for a moment, but looked away almost immediately. She imagined what it must be like for him, with her eyes, the ones noble men were so quick to compliment, focused on him. His feet shuffled for just a moment, and then he caught himself, standing stiff again. They remained like that, a pace away from each other, Julianna looking down at him, him looking down at his feet. Moments ticked away to over a minute.

At last he said, "Forgive me, Your Grace. I will not spoil your generosity ever again."

"Accepted," Julianna replied and moved away from him. "To your duties. You can get as drunk as you want when your time is your own."

The boy bowed deeply, all trace of drunkenness gone from his movements.

Julianna turned to the two stable hands. "Our horses had better be prepared."

"Yes, Your Grace," they said in unison, and started for the stable doors. "They are just outside, Your Grace."

"Stop," Julianna said.

The stable hands froze midstep. They faced Julianna and resumed the attentive servant stance.

"You are drunk. You will *not* handle my horse while you are drunk. See the stable master. Tell him I relieve you of your duty for today. You can double your post tomorrow."

They bowed, shuffling off toward the stairs that led to the stable master's apartment. "Yes, Your Grace. Thank you, Your Grace."

She watched them walk up the steps. Once they knocked on the door, Julianna allowed a satisfied smile to break the cool mask of her displeasure. She couldn't remain angry with them. Not today, when Khellan was waiting to meet her and her friends to give her a true seven birthday celebration.

Two horses waited outside, tacked and saddled, just as the stable hands had said. When they came into sight of the horses, Colette handed Julianna a green apple. Julianna's horse, Vendyr, liked all apples, but he liked pure green apples the best. It was the only kind he would eat completely, without spilling some chewed-up mulch onto the giver's palm.

"Vendyr," Julianna said, and smiled when her horse's ears perked up, one black and one white.

All the horses at the Summerrain estate were of the Saifreni from Heidenmarch, a protectorate on the southern coast of the Kingdom of the Sun, all of them pure black with lush manes and tails. Well, at least all the horses ridden and seen by Countess Maerie Vivaen and her guests. The working breeds were in another stable entirely. Julianna's gelding was the only exception, and how the countess hated that blemish on her perfect collection. Vendyr was a rare-blood of Saifreni and Nibara, a breed from the Lands of Endless Summer across the southern sea. This mixed breeding gave him a white star on his forehead, one white ear, white socks above his hooves, and white patches on his neck and rump. This breeding also gave him strength, speed, and almost tireless endurance, thus his name. Vendyr was the name of an ancient Komati hero who had outrun the Goddess of Wind, the only mortal to ever have done so.

Now, even though his ears perked and he did the slightest dance of curiosity, Vendyr did not turn to face Julianna. She'd taken too long. Vendyr hated waiting once he was tacked and saddled. She let out a sigh and rolled her eyes at everything that had thrown off her carefully planned schedule.

While her plans did not depend on Vendyr being good this morning, he certainly could make the day harder to enjoy. Normally, Julianna would not placate him. She would endure whatever nasty little games he decided to play with her in revenge for whatever little thing she had done to slight him. Today, she didn't have time to struggle for dominance, and she suspected her horse knew it. The only question was: would he behave himself for the rest of the day if she placated him now, or spend the rest of the day testing her every step of the way. Well, there was only one way to determine that.

Just short of stomping her feet, Julianna walked right up to Vendyr's face. She offered him the apple with one hand and scratched behind his ear with the other. Vendyr whickered as he sniffed the fruit. He took one tentative nibble. Less than a heartbeat later, his lips pulled the fruit from her palm. As he chewed, Vendyr shifted his hindquarters, offering his flank to Julianna so she could mount.

Colette snickered.

Julianna leaned to her left so she could see her maid sitting on her own horse, Onyx, a pure black Saifreni. Well, Onyx wasn't exactly Colette's horse. A simple lady's maid could not possibly afford a horse in the first place, much less the upkeep. However, pretenses and appearances must be maintained at all times, so when they went riding, Colette got to ride Julianna's other horse, Onyx. In reality, Colette and Onyx had just as strong a relationship as Julianna and Vendyr.

"Really?" Julianna asked. "You find humor in this?"

Without bothering to hide her smile, Colette replied, "Of course not, Your Grace. A lady's maid is well aware of her station, and knows to keep her personal emotions reigned in at all times."

"Bah."

Julianna turned back to Vendyr. She hadn't fallen for this trick in a handful of years, but that didn't stop Vendyr from continuing to play the game: *I'll just look like I'm a happy horse, and I'll let my mistress try to mount me, and when she's halfway up, I'll move; won't that be funny to see her in her pretty dress sprawled in the dust.*

"Look, you," Julianna said, stroking Vendyr under his chin. It was his favorite spot. His lips quivered ever so slightly. "Today is not the day for this. Please, will you be good?"

Julianna knew that Vendyr couldn't understand her words, or at least most of them, but she knew he understood the tone of her voice. And after seven years, they had formed a strong bond, almost as strong as the bond Julianna had with Colette. The only trouble was that Vendyr did not recognize the order of precedence nor respect Julianna's title in any way. No horse did, no matter how much the nobility wished it otherwise. Julianna's familiarity with Vendyr served to remind her that, in many ways, the order of precedence was an illusionary construct.

As she had hoped, the tone of her words seemed to soothe Vendyr. He lowered his head and licked his lips, a sign of submission.

"Thank you," Julianna said, rubbing her hands gently over his face.

A few moments later, she sat in her saddle, waiting to see if Vendyr was going to test her in some way. He turned his head slightly to the left to look at her, lowered his head, and licked his lips again. Good. Finally something was going right this morning.

"Ready?" Julianna asked Colette.

"I was on my horse and ready minutes ago," Colette replied. Then with a wry smile, she added, "Your Grace."

Julianna blinked at her maid three times, sighed, and blinked three more times. Without any further response, Julianna kicked her heels gently into Vendyr's flanks and started off down the long drive that led to the road outside of the Summerrain Estate. By the time she reached that road, Colette rode next to her. They each urged their horses into a canter in order to make up for lost time. True, her friends would wait. After all, it was Julianna's day, but she didn't need to keep them waiting overly long.

As she left the hard task of escaping Summerrain and the last few moments of Aunt Maerie's dominance over her life behind, Julianna drew in a deep breath. She loved the dusty scent the drying leaves gave the autumn air. Now, barring intervention from some divine or infernal power, this was going to be the greatest day of Julianna's life.

TWO

Just as she had seven, fourteen, and twenty-one years ago, Yrgaeshkil stood and watched events unfold. This time she observed from a window on Summerrain's fifth floor. Few people even realized the room was here. She'd protected it through well-placed lies at corners and intersections all across the fifth floor so that even if someone managed to remember that this room existed they wouldn't be able to reach it unless they knew how to navigate the one true path of travel she'd left open.

Thankfully, she didn't have to wear the form of her detestable children, the one her husband had created for her. Today she was young, her body aged to about twenty-five years, sculpted to the height of male desire, full breasts, ample hips. Long, dark hair hung freely down her back. She reveled in the moment, as much as she could with so much weight on the outcome of the day.

Julianna rode away, down the long gravel drive that stretched from the front of the manor to the gate. Two flower gardens – each a twin of the other down to every single flower – sat on each side of the drive. This meticulous interest in the perfection of both gardens was one of several Lies Yrgaeshkil had placed on Maerie Vivaen within moments of Julianna joining this household after the debacle fourteen years ago.

"That was close," Kavala said.

Again, the scarred-faced man stood next to Yrgaeshkil. She hated how much she needed him. At least, for now. When the time came, she would rid the world of the nuisance of his presence.

"What was?" Yrgaeshkil asked without turning to him.

The door to the room opened and Alyxandros Vivaen entered as Kavala spoke.

"Julianna actually managing to escape to attend this picnic with her friends. It seems only a matter of luck that she was able to bypass her aunt's wishes."

"Luck had nothing to do with it," Alyxandros said, as he joined them by the window. "This morning has been carefully orchestrated down to the last moment. Julianna is a capable young woman, clever, and good at commanding the loyalty of those under her, but she is not perfect. I had to step in and aid her a bit. After all, this is our last chance, isn't it?"

Yrgaeshkil noticed that the mortal did not bow or show any deference as he approached.

She turned to Alyxandros, and the mortal did not have the decency to look away. There was once a time when all creatures knew their place in the order of celestial precedence. Most still did, all save for these humans. Well, the time was coming when she would remind them of their place.

"She will continue to have birthdays by seven," Kavala said.

"But they won't be this birthday," Alyxandros replied. "This is the first birthday by seven Julianna has had since the blessing by thrice has been fulfilled. It must be today, or we will have to start again, and it probably won't be with a follower of Grandfather Shadow."

"Alyxandros." Yrgaeshkil turned the fullness of her gaze on him. Even though she detested herself for it, she allowed her face to blur, putting a bit of her husband's preferred form into her features, specifically, twin goat eyes. "If this fails, you will not be able to hide from me, not in any corner of any realm."

"Why do you threaten me?" Alyxandros asked. "My part is done."

Yrgaeshkil wanted to slap this smug mortal so hard his neck would spin around on his shoulders. She turned back to the window. She could still see Julianna and her servant far down the road leading away from the estate. If Yrgaeshkil didn't turn away from Alyxandros, she might well kill him and cast his soul down into the Dark Realm of the Godless Dead for her children to play with for all time.

"Don't look at me like that, goddess," Alyxandros said. "Julianna is headed for the picnic. I have sent messages to those that needed information. I have affected today's events as much as is in my power. If this plan fails now, the fault lies with Nae'Toran and the Brotherhood of the Night."

An excerpt from:
HALLOWEEN JACK AND THE DEVIL'S GATE

Halloween Jack may be one of my all-time favorite characters to bubble up from my imagination. I started these books because when my son Mathew was ten, he asked, "Dad, can I read one of your books?" He was talking about Tears of Rage. *So, yeah, they aren't really appropriate for a ten-year-old. Luckily, I had in mind a couple of different stories that he could read… I just had to write them. I managed to crank out the first Halloween Jack book in thirty days, start to finish. It's probably the most fun I've had writing anything ever. It ties into an old Irish legend that I've been telling at Renaissance Faires for the better part of twenty years. So far, I've written two books, with five more in the works. From all the feedback that I've gotten, this is the story that sounds most like me, for those who see my storytelling show and read my books. That makes me happy, as that's what I was going for.*

TWO

John O'Brien huddled in the doorway of a bakery, holding a penny in one hand and the last gold coin of his family's fortune in the other. Snow had come early to Boston, and warmth from the ovens seeped through the door. The owner didn't mind folks standing there when the bakery wasn't open, but woe to anyone who tried to stand there during business hours. Her brother was a constable and made sure on a regular basis his sister's business was not suffering due to any sort of lowlife.

John heard a bit of shuffling behind him. He slid the gold coin into his fingerless glove and shoved that into the pocket of his coat. The coat wasn't as fine as it had been, but still the garment served its purpose and was not so worn that people refused him service when he managed to earn a bit of money by doing odd jobs no one else wanted. John was strong, able, and not anywhere near a fool. He should have been able to find work. However, no matter how hard he tried, he couldn't quite get the last of his Irish accent out of his mouth. The instant most *proper* folk heard it, they turned him away.

" 'Elp a poor soul on this cold night?" a voice asked.

John glanced back, mostly at the strangeness of hearing the Cockney accent in Boston.

The beggar was dressed more in rags and tatters than he was in clothes. Didn't have proper shoes, but rather strips of dirty wool wrapped around his feet. Grime and muck clung to his face to the point John wondered if any amount of scrubbing would ever get the face truly clean again.

"Spare somefink for a poor soul to get somefink warm in 'is belly?" the beggar asked.

John suppressed a sigh. Things shouldn't be this bad already. It wasn't even Halloween yet, and it was snowing as if it were close to Christmas. It had been this way every year since the British Empire had closed itself off from the world three years ago.

"Sir," John said, "come stand here, it's warm."

"Oh, fank yous," the beggar said, as he took John's place. "Right kind of yous. God and his angels bless you, young man."

"Just come and get warm," John said.

John wondered how the beggar was alive. He seemed more corpse than man, skin hanging loose on his face and fingers.

John actually sighed this time. He took his penny and placed it in the beggar's hand. The beggar's mouth opened, showing a multitude of missing teeth.

"Take this," John said. "No. Don't say a word." John raised his hand to cut the beggar off. "When the bakery opens, get yourself something warm to put in your belly."

With that, John walked away, leaving the beggar calling thanks behind him. John hoped he'd be able to find work of some kind soon. He hadn't eaten anything but broth and bread at the church in over a week.

As he walked, John tried to think of other warm places. Well, there was always St. Anthony's church, but John didn't want to rely on the church too much. The priests and sisters would never turn John away, he just had his pride. Too many people were asking for hand outs, and John preferred to earn his own way in the world.

Halfway down the next block, John decided to try his luck by the docks. Sometimes sailors from several ships would make a fire in the cobbled roads near the docks and trade stories, songs, and drinks. John knew a few stories. His father had been fond of old tales of Ireland and of the early Americas, especially the myths and legends of the native people. Maybe he could get some room by a fire in exchange for a story or two. The season might be especially good for the tale his father used to tell him about Jack of the Lantern. He smiled as he suddenly noticed the few jack o' lanterns he saw here and there, candles flickering behind their carved faces.

Somewhere between two and four blocks later, the back of John's neck tingled. At four-and-a-half blocks, John knew for certain he was being followed. He quickened his pace and fingered the club he kept in a hidden pocket sewn into the inside of his coat. He didn't break into a run or even a jog, but he might as well have. He glanced back. Just as he thought, his pursuers had been surprised by John's increase in speed. They'd become careless in their haste to keep up.

This was where he decided if it was a matter of fight or flight.

He spotted the four of them without any trouble. Four was two too many. Two, he could fight long enough to discourage. Three was pushing it. Four wasn't even worth trying. He'd just wind up making them angry, and the beating would be even worse.

"Now, now, Johnny O'Brien," said a familiar voice. "We saw you give the beggar something. If you did that, then you've got something to spare for us, too."

Thomas was a big lad who led a gang of four other slightly-less-big lads. They'd been giving John trouble for years, even when they had been schoolboys together. And while Thomas was correct – John still did have the last gold coin of his family's treasure – Thomas and his fellows couldn't comprehend that John had no intention of ever spending it. Nor could they comprehend that a person might give their last coin over to a stranger with less fortune for no other reason than it was the decent thing to do.

Since John had only seen four of them, it meant that Paddy had either been left behind or that the other four were driving John toward the meanest, and least bright, of all of them. John turned on his toe and ran to the other side of the street. He might not be as big or strong as the members of Thomas's little mob of miscreants, but John was no weakling. Most of the work he could find as an Irishman involved heavy labor, the kind few others wanted. He also had practice outrunning gangs like this.

"Don't make it harder on yourself than you need to, Johnny Boy," Thomas called after him. "Just give it over, and we'll be off on our merry one way and you can go t'other."

John reached the other side of the street and scrambled up a fence between two buildings. He stopped at the top and looked back. Sure enough, Paddy was running from the direction John had just been heading.

"Sod off!" John called back.

Thomas and the others were not known for being clever or quick witted. They were even less so when angry. John had used taunts and teasing to great effect in escaping these five ruffians many times before. They hadn't ever seemed to catch on to it, and John would keep exploiting this weakness until they did.

Thomas called back something unflattering about John's mother as John dropped down the other side of the fence. John didn't much care. He'd never allowed people's words to affect him.

John found himself in an alley that had been converted to a storage area. Stacks of boxes lined both sides of the alley. John pursed his lips and he squinted with his right eye. In the space of a single breath, a plan formed. He had enough of a lead. Between the darkness in the alley and his pursuers' lack of imagination, the plan should work.

He ran to the other end of the alley, pushed some snow off the fence there, and then backtracked, making sure to walk backward through his own footprints. When he got back to where he'd climbed over, John squeezed in between two stacks of boxes. He clenched his teeth together to keep them from chattering.

The moment after John squeezed all the way back, he heard crunches in the snow where someone landed. Two more followed.

"He's gone to the other end," Thomas said.

A fourth person landed this side of the fence. Footsteps crunched toward the far end of the alley. A fifth person dropped down.

"Hurry up, you daft fool," one of them called from the other end of the alley.

The fifth person over the fence, likely Paddy, grunted something and started after his friends.

John remained huddled, shivering, keeping his teeth from shattering. He had to be sure they had actually fallen for his trick.

He counted to fifty before he crawled back out.

"There he is," one of them said from the far end. "Told you asking that man was smart."

John was up and over the fence even before he could waste time being scared or worrying about his plan failing. He landed and would have been off at a dead run, except someone was standing in his way.

John blinked several times to make sure he was actually seeing what he thought he was seeing. It wasn't a person at all.

The thing in front of him could only be a demon, like the ones from the stories his father had told him before he'd died. Despite its fine clothes, the thing was sorely out of place with its red skin and single horn that curled back behind its ear. It held a device that vented steam and arched lighting between two metal rods.

"It's a pleasure to make your acquaintance, John O'Brien," the thing said in a whiny and grating voice. "It took us quite a while to find you. We're still learning our way around this new continent."

The imp – it had to be an imp, in the stories imps were the little red ones – did some things to the device, and the lightning arched faster between the two rods. Behind him, on the other side of the fence, John heard the *psshh* of escaping air and what sounded like gears grinding.

"Ummm," John said, still trying to wrap his mind around the idea that the stories might be true.

The crack and snap of wood joined the other sounds. Then came a deluge of prayers: "Saints in heaven preserve us," "Mary, mother of god," and, "Though I walk through the valley of darkness."

"It seems your friends are getting acquainted with my Steam Soldiers." The imp winked at John. "Nothing personal, Jack my boy. You just happened to be born into the wrong family."

Thoughts raced through John's mind. The top two were that he hated being called Jack and that the imp's strange device couldn't be good. As the imp kept flicking switches and turning dials, the noises behind John got louder and more frequent. That could not be good.

"You got my name right the first time," John said, and pulled his club out of its secret pocket. The oak club was sixteen inches long and an inch and a half thick. John held it firmly with his thumb and first two fingers.

The imp flicked more switches and dials, and John heard several terrified and pained screams behind him along with a giant crash of shattering wood. He didn't look, but did suspect, that noise was the fence coming down.

John rushed forward and snapped the club at the device three times. One of the dials came off at the first snap. With the second, one of the electrodes bent at an awkward angle and sparks buzzed away from the thing, fading into the night. The third strike never landed. By that time, the imp had caught on and spun out of the way.

In its haste to protect the device, the imp turned its back on John. John couldn't help but grin. He shifted his grip on the club, gripping it firmly with all five fingers. He pulled the club back behind his shoulder, and falling to one knee as he struck, John put all his body behind the blow to the imp's knee.

Now, John didn't know if the length of wood would actually hurt a demon, but he had to try. Just like with Thomas's ruffians, the demon and whatever was coming up behind him wasn't going to get John without as much effort as John could force them to make.

The club met the imp's knee with the expected resistance and the same crunch of bones and *pop* of cartilage that John was used to. John didn't like fighting. Fighting was the last resort, because in most situations he got a little banged up at the very least. Unless, that is, he caught his opponent completely off guard like this and got away before they could get up.

The imp writhed on the ground holding his leg and whimpering in pain. John spared a glance over his shoulder. Massive metallic men that looked like someone had turned a dozen locomotives into suits of armor stood over Thomas and his ruffians. The gang lay in much the same state as the imp, on the ground, groaning in pain. The armored things that stood over them had electrodes protruding from their joints, and those electrodes buzzed and popped the same way the imp's device had after John had hit it.

John supposed those would be the Steam Soldiers.

Without a second thought, John took two steps and grabbed the device. The imp still had enough wherewithal to keep a tight grip.

"No," the imp said.

"Ah," John replied. "Yes."

John pulled harder, but the imp would not let go.

"Fine." John nearly snarled the word in his frustration.

John shifted the grip on his club to two fingers again. He snapped the club twice: first to the imp's nose and then to the wrist below the hand holding the controller. The imp's fingers opened. John snatched the box and considered for a moment what to do with it.

He almost took the thing with him. Then he thought better of it. It wasn't too heavy, but it would get heavier and heavier as he ran. Also, he might be able to hide, and then these things might go away. If he took the device that controlled the armored things, whoever owned these Steam Soldiers would definitely come after him and they wouldn't stop until they got it back.

"This seems to be pretty important," John said, waving the steaming and buzzing controller above the whimpering imp. "Have fun getting it."

With that, John lobbed it up onto the roof of a building on the other side of the street, turned, and started running. He got maybe ten steps before he heard cackling laughter above and behind him.

John skidded to a stop in the snow. There was another one on the roof. Probably lots of other ones. That would figure. It was that kind of night.

He looked back over his shoulder. Sure enough, he saw an odd-shaped shadow holding a thing that flashed and popped. Moments later, other odd-shaped shadows appeared on that rooftop and the other rooftops overlooking the street.

The Steam Soldiers started moving again, coming toward John. One pointed an arm at John. The wrist erupted in steam and fire, and the thing's hand flew at John. It missed him by less than a foot. Instead of his head, arm, or shoulder, the metal hand closed around a pole supporting the porch of a haberdasher shop. Wood groaned and splintered under the grip.

Then John noticed the chain strung between the metal arm and the metal hand.

He didn't wait to see the pole come flying away from the building.

He ran headlong into the night. He heard steam venting, electricity popping, and heavy footsteps stomping behind him. Oh, and crashing wood and shattering glass.

As he zigzagged down the street, two thoughts occupied John's mind. First, where could he hide? Second, what terrible thing had he done to warrant this? Thomas and his gang was one thing, but demons and armored soldiers controlled by some steam and electric box? This would be laughable were he not living it. So instead of laughing, he ran.

After two blocks, he grabbed a street lamp and used that to spin to the right without losing any of his speed. Normally, a series of quick turns would be the surest way to confuse, confound, and otherwise conceal himself from pursuit. However, that was all contingent upon his pursuers actually being human. John was halfway down the block and very certain he could get to the other end and out of sight, when two of those Steam Soldiers came crashing through a storefront not ten paces back.

With nothing readily available to help him alter his course, John slid a bit in the snow and then dashed toward the alley on the opposite side of the street. He really didn't want to go into some place that confined, but better that than possibly having one of those things burst out of a building right next to him.

And so the chase went on for longer than John could recall. He wove through alleys and side streets so much that he lost track of where he was. His lungs burned, his legs ached, and it felt like someone had stabbed him repeatedly in his left side. Behind him, demons cackled, Steam Soldiers hissed, buzzed, and clanked, and buildings broke under the weight of their pursuit. Running was no longer an option, but at least he wasn't cold anymore.

Soon John was reduced to a loping jog. Even though he was used to long hours of strenuous work, he couldn't keep up that level of headlong flight indefinitely. Head down, body aching, his mind raced for some way to escape.

He came around a corner and found himself staring at the bakery. The beggar still sat huddled in the doorway, soaking up what heat he could.

"This is wrong," John said to himself in short gasps.

John was sure he'd been moving steadily away from here. Yet, here he was. It didn't make sense. But then, so little about this night did. He was about to turn and flee again when two of the metal monstrosities crashed through the bakery. The building groaned and collapsed, part of it on the beggar. John could hear the beggar's cries of pain, although muffled from the boards.

Then a loud *whoomph* came from inside the rubble that was once a bakery, and a giant flame erupted from the center of the wood. The blaze spread quickly.

That gave John an idea.

Most people wouldn't do anything to help someone getting beaten or murdered in the street. They would turn a blind eye and deaf ear to all the crashing and breaking wood. Oh, they might look out their window, but they'd never actually do anything to stop it, even if they didn't believe that it was real and not some strange dream. However, there was one thing almost no one would ignore.

"Fire!" John yelled with all the strength he could muster.

His voice wasn't very loud because he was panting and puffing from running, but it was loud enough that the demons stopped cackling and the Steam Soldiers stopped moving. That gave John just enough incentive to fill his lungs and yell again.

"Fire!"

This time, people opened windows and stuck their heads out into the cold night air. Other people took up the cry.

It wasn't until after people started shouting and rushing into the street that John considered that if these things wanted him so much, they might be willing to hurt any bystanders like they had Thomas's gang. As more and more people took up the cry of "fire," the demons and their metal soldiers fled into the night.

John only allowed himself a small sigh of relief before he was moving again, this time across the street. When he reached the remains of the bakery, the beggar had gone from crying out in pain to moaning. The fire had reached him and caught on the beggar's ragged coat.

People rushed about, and in the distance John heard the *clang, clang, clang* of the fire brigade bell. Fire was the one threat nobody would ignore.

John began clearing debris off the beggar, and within moments other people were helping him. When they'd gotten the beggar free, his right arm was engulfed in flames up to his shoulder. Before anyone could offer suggestions or advice, John rolled the beggar off the porch and into a snow bank. The flames sputtered out with a sharp *hiss*.

"I'm going to get him to a doctor," John said. He knew where one was only a few blocks away.

Before anyone else could protest, John lifted the beggar up and hurried away. He had, in a moment, weighed the risk of staying with the crowd and having them ask questions against moving on and encountering the demons again. At this point there were dozens – perhaps more than a hundred – people up and about to help deal with the fire. As the cry went out, more and more would be up. It was a fairly good gamble that John was safe for at least the rest of this night. Besides, the beggar had been hurt because of him. Others probably had too, but John could help this man right now.

Soon, John was pounding on the door of the doctor's office. A minute or so later, he heard locks rattle and the door open about two inches. A single eye glared at John from behind a spectacle.

"Sir," John said, "this man is hurt."

The eye looked at the beggar and back at John. The door opened. John entered and placed the beggar on the long table that filled the center of the room.

The doctor was short and frail, with only a few wisps of hair on the top of his head. While the doctor wore a night shirt, John noticed that he also had on trousers and shoes. Perhaps he'd heard the call for fire and was getting ready to go out and see if anyone required his services.

"Can you pay?" the doctor asked.

"Pay?" John replied. "This man may be dying and you're asking about money?"

"This is a business, son," the doctor said, "not a charity. If you have no means to compensate me for my work, I suggest you take him to Saint Mary's Church. The sisters there care for the sick and injured among the homeless."

"St. Mary's is halfway to the other side of Boston," John said, his voice rising. "He probably wouldn't survive me carrying him all that way."

The doctor shrugged. John looked from the beggar to the doctor, and back to the beggar. Tonight was quickly being burned into John's mind as the very worst night of his life since his parents died Halloween night almost three years ago. He couldn't even make it into a great story to trade for food or shelter because nobody would believe it.

"Fine," John said. "This should cover it."

He slipped the last gold coin of his family's treasure out of his glove and held it out to the doctor. The doctor eyed the coin, nodded, and held out his hand. John placed the coin gently on the doctor's palm, and after a moment, let go.

The instant John's fingers left the coin, a light brighter than any lamp, lantern, or candle filled the room. The beggar rolled off the table and stood straight and tall, no longer hunched over as he had been. The grime and muck that clung to his face seemed to be burned away by the light. The coat that was more rags than garment fluttered in a wind John did not feel and transformed into a pristine white robe. Two pearl-white wings sprouted from the beggar's shoulder blades.

While the beggar underwent this transformation, the doctor had pulled off the night shirt to reveal a priest's collar.

"John O'Brien," the doctor-turned-priest said, "meet Saint Peter."

John blinked. "Even with the night I've had, that was unexpected."

An excerpt from
DEAD WEIGHT: The Tombs
And
DEAD WEIGHT: Paladin

DEAD WEIGHT is my a serialized novel of a near-future, dark urban fantasy, noir, war-thriller about the United States going to war against the Unseelie court of ancient Irish Mythology. I had to think very carefully about what sections of that story to include in this collection. I get a wide range of audiences at my shows and appearances, and DEAD WEIGHT is not an all-ages story. It's got some mature content and more than a bit of mature language. The first section I decided to include started as an exercise in setting while in a one-on-one directed writing course at SFSU. I'd been working on DEAD WEIGHT with a teacher Alice LaPlante, and she wanted me to get a better handle on the faerie aspects of the world I was creating. The first section is the result of that exercise. I liked it so much that I slapped it in the front of the first installment of DEAD WEIGHT to help the reader get a good idea of how faeries and Arcadia work in my world. The second section comes from the opening of the second installment, which takes place perhaps a day or so after the first installment ends. I'm pretty sure the second section is spoiler free.

THE TOUR:
A Prologue of Sorts

...but nothing is ever lost nor can be lost.
The body sluggish, aged, cold, the ember left from earlier fires shall duly flame again.
— Walt Whitman

How should we be able to forget those ancient myths that are at the beginning of all peoples, the myths about dragons that at the last moment turn into princesses; perhaps all the dragons of our lives are princesses who are only waiting to see us once beautiful and brave. Perhaps everything terrible is in its deepest being something helpless that wants help from us.

So you must not be frightened if a sadness rises up before you larger than any you have ever seen; if a restiveness, like light and cloudshadows, passes over your hands and over all you do. You must think that something is happening with you, that life has not forgotten you, that it holds you in its hand; it will not let you fall. Why do you want to

M Todd Gallowglas

shut out of your life any uneasiness, any miseries, or any depressions? For after all, you do not know what work these conditions are doing inside you.
— Letters to a Young Poet, Rainer Maria Rilke

Military historians argue the reasons the enemy devastated the United States so much in the early years of the Faerie War. In hindsight it really shouldn't be that big a mystery; the United States simply forgot too much of the Old Knowledge. If they hadn't, they would have been much better prepared.

From the moment the white man displaced the first Native American tribe, the United States sowed the seeds of its later inability to deal with the aggression from Faerie in the middle of the Twenty-First Century. Only the artists and those who lived on the fringes of society seemed to remember, and we know how the U.S. felt about *those people*. Thus, America lacked the resources to stem the early onslaught. Perhaps that is why the Unseelie chose to make the United States the focal point of its reentry into the human world. As it is in the wake of all great conflicts of the modern era, now that the Faerie War is over, people yearn and strive to recapture the cultural mythology of all our forefathers and to make sense of a war with an enemy that we are unlikely to ever make sense of.

Some people study, spending time on the internet, in libraries, and delving into dark corners of occult and arcane bookstores, searching for the minutest details of faerie lore and legend to better deal with the world as it is after the war. Others, those who are not so academically minded, take tours.

Every day, thousands of people take pictures of the blackened crater in Washington, D.C. where the original Capitol used to stand. The crater still smokes today. They visit the fortress that sprang up in Central Park that took the military over three years of constant siege to capture. Just recently, the air space above and inside the Grand Canyon has become safe enough for people to fly through to see the last strongholds of the fey in our world.

However, unlike many previous wars, the most popular tours aren't of battle sites. This was a war unlike any remembered save in myths and legends. The most important conflicts weren't fought by soldiers. To truly understand the Faerie War, people flock to see those places where visionaries created works of art striving to repel the invasion before it began.

One of the most popular tours is in the San Francisco Bay Area. This tour, thanks to magic left over from the Faerie War, teleports people from site to site to see the artwork of a girl, a girl who saw through the cracks in reality before any other person in the world. She was the first to fight with her spray paint cans and paint brushes and pastels. Her best efforts came to nothing, because of the best of intentions of a boy who only wanted to help make his community a nicer place.

The tour begins in the girl's childhood bedroom. When people pay their twenty dollars in the foyer of the house she grew up in, the underpaid state park employee hands them a set of headphones. Each of these devices narrates the tour, beginning from the moment one reaches the top of the stairs and turns left into the bedroom. The voice is a pleasant male voice, containing a slight tremor.

"Let us begin with the south wall. It contains pictures that the artist..." nowhere in the tour or any literature is the girl named; names have power, even after so much time, to affect things in the world that are better left alone; so, as it is with every such tour, she is referred to always as *the artist* "...colored and painted in preschool and kindergarten." These contain images, different colors blending together, and of stick-figure people fighting stick-figure monsters.

"You may notice that, even in their simplicity, something about them draws you. Occasionally when the light hits a picture just right, or if perhaps, you look at a picture from just the right angle, those simple pictures might seem to move a little bit. If you do manage to notice this effect, keep it to yourself. Any time someone tries to call this to the attention of someone else, the effect stops, and the magic of that moment is lost.

"Let us turn to the west wall. These are works the artist created in elementary school. You will notice the increasing complexity and that she painted creatures that we take for granted now – in all their alien wonder. Some of the pictures are of familiar forms: dragons, unicorns, elves, pixies, sprites, and ogres. Others are bizarre creatures with a single leg, or three arms, or eyes all around their heads. The impressive thing isn't that she painted these things, even though she painted them even before the war; it's that her artwork, even at the young age that she created it, fills viewers with such wonder that they feel like a child hearing their first fairy tales again. Don't you agree?

"Allow me to draw your attention to a specific picture: two rows in from the left and five down. The one displaying a scene with a faerie lady standing over a knight on one knee."

The work is done in watercolor paint with alternating long and short strokes. The background is blended shades of green, brown, and yellow. The lady is dressed in red and silver, and the knight's armor is gray and black. The lady holds a sword with a blue blade, and she's touching the knight's shoulder with it.

"Some people claim that while looking at the lady for more than a few moments that they can feel a warm breeze in their hair and the sword's leather hilt pressing into their hands. Others will tell you that if you look at the knight long enough that you'll feel the cold edge of a blade caressing the side of your neck. Do you? Don't answer yet if you are skeptical of such things. Look for a moment without thinking too much about it, and you may feel what the artist intended you to feel.

"By now, you have no doubt noticed the centerpiece of this wall has several ribbons next to it. These are the only official prizes her work has ever received."

This picture of a dragon was colored with crayons on lined binder paper. The thirty-four vertical blue lines and the one horizontal red line are this picture's only background. The face of a dragon fills three-quarters of the paper. The scales begin with light green, shaded with gray on the outside of the beast's snout and darkening to almost black in the center. Its eyes are gold with flecks of red. Its lips curve upward at the very edges, as if this creature understands more about the viewer than the viewer does.

"Can you feel the warmth of the creature's breath on your face? Do you hear a subtle chuckling in the back of your mind? If not, don't feel bad. Not everyone does."

On the north wall the work gets more elaborate. These are the paintings — real paintings rendered on canvas — that she did in her high school years.

"Notice how these paintings show noble faerie lords and ladies hunting in woods of weeping willows with watery tears where the leaves should be and also shows epic battles between the two ruling courts of Arcadia: the Seelie and Unseelie. See how the artist chose to represent the Seelie court with bright colors and depicts them as knights in radiant armor, while she portrays the Unseelie court as grim and dark, with the relatively human-looking of them possessing demonic features. At this point, we all know these are not accurate portrayals of these creatures. The fey do not conform to humans ideals of good and evil, light and dark. They are alien creatures whose morality is something far removed from human ethics. Many people have wondered why the artist chose to portray the courts in such a way, but without being able to speak directly to her, the mystery will remain."

The centerpiece of this wall is an oil painting that the girl created during a special summer school for the arts. It's four feet by three feet and depicts a scene where two faerie armies clash around two mortal champions. Seelie knights ride unicorns and griffins into the battle, while the Unseelie ride giant buzzards and dragons. The infantries of both sides clash with sword and spear and claw and fang. The air throughout the battle is charged with magical energy. Even with all this chaos, there remains a wide circle around the two mortals who are playing a game of chess, seemingly undistracted by the conflict that rages around them. While standing near this wall, tourists can almost hear the trees crying, the tromp of unicorn, and the faint screams of the wounded on the battlefield amidst the clash of steel on steel. They smell of blood and fresh loam, and the chill wind of forests older than anything we know on earth tickles the hair of the arm. And underneath all that, they hear the tick, tick, tick, of the chess clock and one of the players sigh in displeasure at his opponent's previous move.

"This painting has drawn people to ask many questions: Why are these two people playing a game in the middle of this fighting? Do they even know the battle is there? Which of these two scenes is real? Are they even in the same place? Why do the fey leave them alone to play their game?"

At this point, the tour jumps to other locations. After the girl left high school, she became a graffiti artist. Her work appears in many secret and out-of-the-way places throughout the San Francisco Bay Area. Her paintings appear in tunnels, under overpasses, on walls of alleyways. These works generally take up the entirety of whatever surface she used for a canvas. People are ushered through the locations quickly, because the physical sensations felt in the presence of the works can become addicting. One painting in an alley in downtown San Francisco depicts a riverbed where a group of nyads (a type of water fey) and dryads (fey spirits bound into trees) are singing and playing harps, lutes, and pan pipes. This alley is always seventy-three degrees Fahrenheit, no matter the time of day or the weather, and the faint whisper of a song can be heard as if a radio is playing at low volume just around the corner. The side effects of this painting have required round-the-clock security to turn away any of the homeless who try to squat here.

The voice in the headphones accompanies the tourists to each location on the tour as both moderator and one-sided conversationalist.

Eventually the tour returns to the girl's house, and the visitors can look behind the curtain of the final wall, the east wall, which is dominated by a single piece. This is a painting of a door with a single, old-fashioned keyhole.

"This concludes our regular tour. For the expanded tour, which allows you to look through the keyhole, please see information desk for the release form and appropriate donation rates. Thank you. Have a great day, and we hope to see you again."

That is where the recorded voice stops.

Not everyone has the courage or the curiosity to sign the release and look through the keyhole. These days, most people understand that exposing themselves to anything having to do with faerie magic is a gamble and that the odds are not in their favor.

For those who do sign the waver and look through the keyhole, most will only see a beautiful, though very small, picture of the girl's parents' bedroom. It also shows her parents, dead always in the way the viewer fears most to die: hanging, burning, murder, sickness – it doesn't matter what the fear, the magic of this tiny painting always knows. However, a few very rare and unique individuals see what the girl saw. That's why this tour and others like it remain open, and will remain open so long as the government stands. Tours like these are the surest way to find artists who can take up where the girl left off.

This bears some explanation.

The barrier between realities is not equal in all places. Sometimes cracks form between one world and another. These cracks usually happen in out-of-the-way or secret, hidden places: under beds, behind furniture, in backyards hidden behind that tangle of bushes and shrubs that never seems to get pruned; and in places where children and artists gather: galleries, playgrounds, jungle gyms, avant-garde coffee houses; or where the human mind slips from the realm of normal perceptions: mental wards, crack houses, Burning Man. These cracks and holes are usually too small to see, mostly because the average human is too busy with the minutia of their banal life to notice anything of true wonder. But then, they are not the gifted ones; they are not the artists, the madmen, that the rest of humanity looks at whom they shake their heads with pity. "Normal" people don't understand these people or the pity they feel for them. They cannot comprehend that by seeing through the cracks in the world these gifted and mad artists destined for lives of hardship, unhappiness, and alienation.

In the moment just before most "normal" people looking through the keyhole would grasp what is it to live with the gift and curse these artists possess, they look away – and most of them forget.

Most.

Those few who do not look away soon find themselves creating their own works of art, whether painting, music, poetry, sculpting, etc. They see the cracks between the worlds. They see into Faerie and all its breathtaking wonder, madness, and horror. It is a timeless land that knows nothing of death. It is a realm of gnarled gardens, mountains of half-gnawed bones, and of primeval forests, lush and dark in both beauty and savagery. These forests writhe alongside concrete jungles, thick with artfully bent metal and snowflakes of broken glass. Almost-Victorian estates rest upon shorelines scattered with carcasses of sailing vessels, thousands of ships carved from the fossilized remains of giant beasts that dwarf the greatest of dinosaurs. Satyrs and centaurs frolic in meadows of red grass where the heads of human babies grow in place of dandelions. Those who have the talent to see beyond static reality take up their art as champions against the fey who still seek to threaten this world. The war may be over, but as it has for millennia, the threat of Faerie remains. Only this time, several gates between Earth and Faerie remain open. Because of that, this tour, with a tiny picture inside that keyhole, remains open in the hope that enough mad and brilliant artists will awaken to fight and hold the Unseelie at bay.

The Tour: Interlude the First

"Come away, O human child!
To the waters and the wild
With a faery, hand in hand,
For the world's more full of weeping than you can understand."
— *W.B. Yeats*

"We all make choices, but in the end our choices make us."
— Ken Levine

"This concludes our regular tour. For the expanded tour, which allows you to look through the keyhole, please see the information desk for the release form and appropriate donation rates. Thank you. Have a great day, and we hope to see you again."

Violet bit the inside of her cheek. She'd been waiting for this part of the speech since she started the tour. She knew the whole tour by heart. For years, she'd been able to recite the whole verbatim, frequently doing so on her morning walk to high school. Ever since the first time Violet had come on the tour on a sixth grade field trip, she'd wanted to look in the keyhole painting. She'd gone home that day and begged her parents to sign the release, and no matter how much pleaded, no matter how many chores she promised to do, no matter how many times she threatened to run away to one of the wild zones, her parents wouldn't sign the waver for her. She was sweet sixteen today, and when they asked her what she wanted, and she told them the thing she wanted more than anything in the world, they still denied her.

She envied the artist who had created all the works of art on the tour. She'd never had to have her parents tell her whether or not she could bring the stuff of dreams into physical form. The artist had been chosen. Violet wished she'd been chosen, wished she could be taking a stand against the faerie, but her parents wouldn't allow it.

"You have a gift," her father had said two weeks ago while discussing her birthday over dinner. "I know you want to use it to help people, but right now, you're still a child. I know it doesn't feel like it, but you'll have to trust your mother and I to know what's best for you right now."

But they didn't know. They couldn't know.

Taking three deep breaths to steady herself, Violet guesstimated the number of steps between her and her goal. It seemed about seven. She should have expected that. She'd read enough to know about the Old Traditions. She wasn't going in completely blind to the world she'd be diving into if this worked the way she thought it would. Seven steps separated Violet and the dream she'd held onto.

At the very end of her third breath, Violet jumped over the velvet rope that kept the regular tourists from the keyhole painting.

Shouts went up almost immediately.

On Violet's first step, she heard gasps of surprise, and her mother said, "What are you…"

When her second step hit the floor, the guards called for her to stop.

Third step, Father shouted, "Miss Violet Craige! Get back here this instant!" Even in her forward rush, part of her mind sneered at her father still adding Miss onto her name when he was mad at her. And then, Mother's shriek rose above everything else.

Four steps in, and more than half-way there, one of the security guards reached for Violet.

She dodged with her fifth step, moving a bit diagonally as well as forward. The angle wasn't enough to keep the guard's fingers from tightening on the sleeve of her jacket. He yanked hard on the jacket.

The jacket slid off her arms and shoulders as Violet's sixth step brought her back in line with her target. While planning this out in her mind, she figured at least one guard would get to her. She'd worn her baggiest jacket just in case.

More people called out behind her, some in surprise and some in anger. Despite her curiosity, Violet didn't look back. Instead, she went right into her seventh step and put her eye right up to the keyhole.

Time…slowed…she blinked…in the prolonged moment while blackness shrouded her vision…words echoed in Violet's inner ears…bubbling up from the memories of times past…times spent hanging out with artists and dancers…

Time becomes fluid and mutable at the slightest touch of Faerie.

Her eyes opened…

She saw a skate park. Graffiti covered the concrete where people would normally be tricking their way across, impressing themselves and each other. Only, it wasn't normal graffiti tagging. The images were murals of dark buildings: Towers, castles, and fortresses. Each building trapped away somehow: chains, boards, and bricks kept windows and doors shut, moats and forests of thorns made certain that nobody within could escape. Somehow Violet knew these things were to keep things from getting out. At one end of the skate park, a teenage girl worked with cans of spray paint and brushes to finish another of these fortifications. At the other end of the concrete, a teenage boy, wearing a Boy Scout uniform and looking slightly younger than the artist, worked on hands and knees with cleaning supplies to scrub the artist's paint away from the concrete.

And…Violet…blinked…

Now she looked down on a hill with green grass. Deep purple sky with gray-green clouds stretched across the horizon. Three people walked on the hill. The boy from the previous painting walked in the center. While he still wore the standard Boy Scout shirt, the rest of his clothes were of a military uniform. He was also a few years older. Another soldier walked to his right. To his left was a girl, but not the girl from the skate park. This one wore a gray long coat with voluminous hood. Two braids, so blond they were almost white, hung out of the hood. In her left hand, she carried a straight razor big enough to…

And…Violet…blinked…

In this scene the girl with the gray coat and the braids and the artist from the first painting stood over the Boy Scout. Again, he was few years older. He had a dark bloodstain on his chest and lay in a pool of blood. This time, rather than a still frame, the scene moved. Both girls looked at Violet. "It's your turn," they whispered.

And…Violet…closed…her…eyes.

It wasn't a blink. Her eyes stayed closed. She knew, deep down, that seeing all these paintings had only taken the fraction of a moment. All around her, guards, her parents, and other tourists were still freaking out. Violet wished she could share in their naive little panic. She'd read enough, studied enough of the Old Traditions, to piece together what had just happened, what she'd just brought down upon her head.

She…opened…her…eyes…

Through the keyhole, Violet saw the scene she'd expected to see. It was the scene everyone else normally saw: A bedroom that could have belonged to any upper-middle-class married couple. However, rather than the pair of strangers Violet expected to see, she saw her own parents laying on the bed, being torn apart and consumed by all manner of dark Unseelie creatures: goblins, boggarts, ghoulies, hags, and things so grotesque and frightening Violet didn't have a name for them. The creatures looked up, and snarled at Violet, "Welcome."

As comprehension of what happened, of what she'd done to herself, pressed down upon her, Violet pushed away from the wall and the keyhole painting.

Someone grabbed her and spun her around. It was one of the security guards. He opened his mouth and drew in a breath in the way of someone getting ready to shout at another.

The shouting never started.

Rather, some force flung the guard across the room. He hit the far wall with a bone-snapping crunch that churned Violet's stomach. She would live her whole life, and from time to time, that sound would echo in her ears.

She shook her head and blinked several times in rapid succession. This time it was the normal blinking of surprise. Everyone in the room had been blown back against the walls, though most looked to be in far better shape than the guard who had grabbed her. The exception was the man standing a few feet away.

"Hello," the wizard said, looking at her over the wire-rimmed sunglasses.

The man was in his late twenties, perhaps early thirties, and Violet could tell he was a wizard by the staff of petrified redwood – still glowing a bit from his spell – he held in his well-manicured hand. At first glance, he looked good, not necessarily handsome, or cute, or hot. In fact, she had trouble telling if he was actually attractive on his own. Most of his appeal on that first glance had to do with grooming. He wore a suit more expensive than many people's cars. Violet could tell, because her father did business with men like that.

Then, on her second glance, her throat clenched up, making breathing more than a challenge. With the pressure of what she'd become pushing down on her mind, coupled with the knowledge that if someone on Earth had actually commissioned that suit it would have cost more than most houses, her head swam. Even with the vertigo, she was not so addled that she couldn't piece together who this was.

Violet opened her mouth to say something, but she couldn't make the words happen.

The wizard had a warm smile, but his gaze held nothing but the cold of his ice-blue irises.

"His Majesty, Oberon," the Wizard said, "is very interested to meet you."

Finding her voice at last, Violet said, "Oh, so not good."

What was she going to do now?

Concerning Science Fiction in Academia

"Theme for Poetry 304"
by M Todd Gallowglas

"Everything is science fiction. From the margins of an almost invisible lit-erature has sprung the reality of the 20th Century." – J.G. Ballard

The teacher told me:

Take a poem and let it move you
To write a new work based on something true
of your own experience. So I chose to be
inspired be Mr. Langston Hughes.

How can I feel something similar to his pain?
I am thirty-four, white, born in middle-class California.
I go to school. I'm an English major because
I like to read and I like to write stories.
I am the only genre writer in my lit classes.
Or, at least I'm the only one brave (stupid) enough
to mention this to my teachers and fellow students. Time and again
they dismiss what I have to say because my approach is from:
Asimov, Herbert, Tolkien, and Ellison, (being Harlan, and not Ralph)
rather than: Melville, Hawthorn, Thoreau, and Elliot.

It's not easy to stand there and take it, when other people claim
that the writing isn't true. Though it resonates with the
same human conditions – it sees and feels, and explores and searches,
and sometimes does it better than "Serious Literature."
Some of which should be fired out of the *canon*.

I'm mostly over it now. Mostly. I see their narrow-minded view.
They do not understand what I love, and because they do not understand,
they fear, and because they fear, they ridicule
and push each genre to its own literary ghetto.

Now, I find I pity those who refuse to open themselves to genre,
they will never know the joy of reading:
"The enemy's gate is down." – Orson Scott Card
"I will not fear. Fear is the Mind-Killer." – Frank Herbert
"The man in black fled across the desert, and the gunslinger followed." – Steven King

"'Repent, Harlequin!' said the Ticktockman." – Harlan Ellison
"That we should suffer so much fear and doubt over so small a thing." – J.R.R. Tolkien
"Violence is the last refuge of the incompetent." – Isaac Asimov
"Fear of a name increases fear of the thing itself." – J.K. Rowling
"Life would be unbearably dull if we had answers to all our questions." – Jim Butcher
"By not acknowledging our fear, we fall victim to the lies we tell ourselves, and those are the most dangerous lies of all, the hardest lies to see beyond." – M. Todd Gallowglas
"You can have peace. Or you can have freedom. Don't ever count on having both at once." – Robert Heinlein

These writers and their words are my refuge and the voice
of a vast tradition worth exploring, but sadly some don't,
and that makes them somewhat less free.

That is my poem for Poetry 304

"Science fiction is a concerned art form, for even in its shallowest version, it deals with the future and the potentialities of man's place in it…I write it because it refuses not to be written." – Harlan Ellison

The above poem was inspired by Langston Hughes's poem, "Theme for English B" because I was ridiculed in a poetry literature class for being, "that scifi guy." It began when the teacher made a flippant comment about my interest in the literature of science fiction and fantasy. More often than not, students and teachers in English departments across the country often have strong opinions about what "true" writing is and what it isn't. Most of the time, they are speaking about "literature." I empathized with the narrator of Hughes's, "Theme for English B" because he feels that, as the only African American student in his class, he is not understood. Most of the time, I feel like the proverbial black sheep in literature and writing classes because I love science fiction and fantasy. The ridicule and prejudice of the other class members sting me just as much as any ignorant, knee-jerk reaction does.

Many people scoff at science fiction saying that it is nothing more than escapist fluff, and as such has no bearing on modern society. While science fiction is written primarily for enjoyment, important messages are frequently found in entertainment. As long as humans have entertained other humans, they have placed moral and spiritual values in their stories. Aesop's fables – which have lasted since the Roman Empire – are first and foremost stories to entertain children, but there is a moral lesson to be learned from each one of those simple stories. William Shakespeare also placed moral admonishments in every one of his plays, such as in *Hamlet* when we hear the line, *"To thine own self be true."* Shakespeare wrote his plays to entertain people, yet today we find his work a treasury of timeless ideas that have shaped the English language and culture for hundreds of years.

Critics of science fiction might say that we find none of these merits in the works of science fiction.

In the 1930's Isaac Asimov wrote a story about an automated, sentient machine created in a humanoid form. He called this machine a "robot." The term had never been used before, and this is only one example of how a science fiction story has affected the future. While science fiction writers did not get every minute detail right, they have predicted many things that have come to pass, enough to make a reader pause and wonder. Science fiction not only predicted space travel and mankind walking on the moon, it also foresaw many things that we take for granted today: television, computers, submarines, organ transplants, and satellites in geosynchronous orbit. In his groundbreaking 1984 novel, *Nueromancer*, William Gibson wrote about the dangers of Internet addiction when the Internet was taking its first limping steps of infancy. In the words of writer J.G. Ballard, *"Everything is science fiction. From the margins of an almost invisible literature has sprung the reality of the 20th Century."*

True, while some science fiction stories are far outside the scope of realistic speculation, they arouse people's imagination and their curiosity about things to come and as writer Joan Vinge said, *"Science fiction is the anthropology of the future."* Science fiction can mirror current issues.

For example:

Billy smiles as he slams the clip into his .75 caliber Colt ThunderGod™. His thumb flicks the safety from "wimp" to "frag". Holding it makes him feel like a man.

"ThunderGod™," Billy says, his commanding baritone reverberating from deep in his barrel thick chest. "Accept no substitute."

"I won't trust a man with anything less to guard my rear," breathes a sultry voice with just a hint of British accent.

Billy turns and soaks up the vision of his partner. Any man who spends even five minutes on the 'Net™ wants Selena™. Dozens of corporations spend millions of dollars every year on case studies to continually refine the archetypal male fantasy. Selena™ is the outcome, the pinnacle combination of physical training, plastic surgery, and extensive model and acting training. Her physical attributes and wardrobe change weekly based on a poll on her website. Today she's wearing a chainmail bikini top, a short, plaid skirt barely hanging on her ample hips, and thigh high, patent-leather boots. Her hair is coal black with white highlights shot through that look like spider webs. She's dressed just like her part in the upcoming movie STAR WARS™ XVII: PRADATORS™ OF THE MATRIX™. Billy can't wait to see it.

Logos from her corporate sponsors are strategically tattooed on her thighs, the tops of her breast, and — even though Billy can't see them — he knows there are twin tattoos just below the curve of Selena's buttocks. Billy doesn't even consider her eyes, instead, his gaze lingers on her ample double D breasts and the words "Milk: It does a body good!™" emblazoned upon them. His mouth starts watering and agrees that milk would do his body just fine.

"Are you ready to put that gun to good use?" Selena™ asks. On the word "gun" she pauses and glances down, her eyes full of promises to come.

"I was born ready," Billy assures her.

"Then let's get to it," she says with a naughty smirk, reaches over her shoulder, and draws twin katana from behind her back. The blades of both samurai swords gleam in the pale light cast by the street lamps. Each has glowing neon letters etched on the blade. "Cut through traffic with the Suzuki™ Katana™."

Billy turns toward the alley where their prey awaits. The walls are plastered with posters advertising everything from movies to clothes to video games to food to personal hygiene products that promise to make one irresistible to the opposite sex. The alley dead-ends about forty feet away. A single door is that far wall's only occupant.

Making his way toward that door, Billy scans the posters. He's going to need that information later.

Now that he's in the alley, he sees discarded wrappers form all the major fast food chains, all of them tantalizing him with the grand prize of their latest contests. Of course, these all tie into several of the movies postered on the wall. Again, he soaks all this in.

They're at the door. Billy wraps his free hand around the door handle. He takes a deep breath. The moment right before is always his favorite. This is going to be good. Just before turning the knob, he feels Selena lick his lower earlobe, and whisper, "Let's go have a little fun." The cool night air tingles against his ear where her saliva left a trail. His toes curl and all his… muscles… harden. Yeah, this is going to be really good.

He twists the knob and yanks the door open. Selena dives through, and Billy follows.

The room beyond the door's threshold is filled with over a dozen leather-clad, gun-wielding, sword-swinging Badguys™. Each of these Badguys™ is wearing logos and ads for those companies and products that compete with the ones in alley outside and those adorning Selena's™ magnificent body.

Billy doesn't bother to count. He takes aim with his .75 caliber Colt Thunder-God™ and starts blasting Badguys™. Selena™ is already cutting into them. In moments the bullets and blood are flying. Billy and Selena move through the room, violent poetry in motion. A minute and a half later, all the Badguys™ are down, the logos they wear are mangled by either Selena's™ blades or Billy's bullets.

There is one last Badguy™ in the corner groaning from a stomach wound. Billy walks over to him and empties the clip from his .75 caliber Colt ThunderGod™ into his head.

Billy turns to Selena™. She drops her swords, smiles, and reaches behind her back to undo the straps on the bikini top. Billy knows nothing's going to happen, but like every time he gets to this moment, he hopes against hope that someone forgets to...

Billy ground his teeth in frustration the moment the virtual reality program ended. He pulled the Virtual Reality™ helmet off his head and slid it under his desk, while outraged cries fill the classroom. Billy stopped doing that after the first few times. It never helped.

"Whining won't do any good," Mr. Thomas said from the head of the classroom. "You know you have to wait until high school before you meet the age requirement for virtual sexual experience."

"But I'm already fourteen," Lucy Dibiasi said.

"You don't get rewarded for being held back a grade, Ms. Dibiasi," Mr. Thomas said. "Stop laughing class and settle down. For today's assignment, I want you to write an analysis of the simulation noting the effective use of at least ten of the advertisement placements and how those products benefit our lives. Bonus points for anyone who brings one of these products to class and can effectively demonstrate its importance."

Billy powered up his Tablet PC™ and waited for the two minutes of ads to go by before opening up MS Word™ so he could get to work. One ad caught his eye, and he had the perfect topic for his paper, though he'd have to stop in the school store during lunch to pick up something for class tomorrow. Thank God his parents got him that secure credit card for school emergencies like this.

Some might ignore Billy's story, or downplay the messages conveyed because "it's science fiction." However, present-day America may be closer than anyone suspects. In the book, *Culture Jam*, Kalle Lasn, states: *"Your kids watch Pepsi and Snickers ads in the classroom. (The school has made the devil's bargain of accepting free audiovisual equipment in exchange for airing these ads on 'Channel One.')"* In *Fast Food Nation*, Eric Schlosser writes: *"The fast food chains run ads on Channel One, the commercial television network whose programming is now shown in classrooms, almost every school day, to eight million of the nation's middle, junior, and high school students – a teen audience fifty times bigger than that of MTV..."*

Advertising in schools is becoming big business, and for good reason. Like the prisoners in Plato's "Allegory of the Cave," students in our current school system sit passively at their desks absorbing information presented to them. In the early 1970's Paulo Friere introduced the "banking concept of education" which advertisers use against America's youth, laughing all the way to the bank. In *Pedagogy of the Oppressed*, Freire writes: *"The more students work at storing the deposits entrusted to them, the less they develop the critical consciousness which would result from their intervention in the world as transformers of that world. The more completely they accept the passive role imposed on them, the more they tend simply to adapt to the world as it is and to the fragmented view of reality imposed on them."*

This creates, quite literally, a captive audience on which companies focus their advertising power. It might not be very long before the advertising giants blatantly flex their economic muscles not only into education, but politics as well. Children born today might grow up to live in a bleak reflection of George Orwell's novel *1984*, where it is illegal for citizens to turn off their TV so the government can constantly pump propaganda into peoples' homes. There are also TV's on every street corner, built into walls, and even in the sidewalks. All of these television monitors go both ways, so the government can watch the watchers and know which of their propaganda techniques are working. Or perhaps the future might be more like Ray Bradbury's *Fahrenheit 451*, where books are illegal because they make people think too much and where firemen burn down houses that have books hidden in them.

Fredrick Pohl, one of science fiction's most celebrated authors, said, *"It's a pity that taxpayers don't read science fiction. They might know about the age they're buying."* Awareness of the future is the responsibility of the individual. People need to wake up and educate themselves on the future their politicians are purchasing (on credit, no less) from unborn generations, and people need to do something about it by exercising their voting power. Unfortunately, hindsight tells us that mass mobilization only happens in America during great catastrophe such as the 9/11 attacks and the devastation wrought by Hurricane Katrina, or when something happens to peoples' favorite TV shows. Every year, more letters are written protesting choices made in Hollywood than in Washington DC. (It is interesting to note that one of the largest letter writing campaigns in American History was conducted to keep the original *Star Trek* from being cancelled.) Even though we've seen glimpses of many potential futures from the writings of Orwell, Bradbury, Gibson, and others, the country's pattern suggests that it's only a matter of time before little Billy will be writing essays about the benefits of the products he sees advertised during his daily (hourly?) trip into the world of Virtual Reality™.

English teacher Harry Thomas watched as his eighth grade students attacked their keyboards. He hoped that this assignment would get some of them into the school store during lunch hour following class, or maybe after school. The school sponsors had only required that the essay list five products, but he thought ten would really get the money in their pockets burning. He could really use a bonus this month.

Harry sighed. He remembered years ago when he first became a teacher. He planned on changing the world, one student at a time. But that was before marriage and kids, car payment and mortgage. Now he was a bit more of a realist. Teachers didn't get paid enough to live on, but they could afford quite a nice lifestyle with the corporate kickbacks from sales made in the student store. And besides, Christmas™ *was coming, and he didn't want to disappoint the wife and kids.*

"*It is change, continuing change, inevitable change, that is the dominant factor in society today. No sensible decision can be made any longer without taking into account not only the world as it is, but the world as it will be. . . This, in turn, means that our statesmen, our businessmen, our everyman must take on a science fictional way of thinking.*" - Isaac Asimov

Theme for English B"
by Langston Hughes

The instructor said,

Go home and write
   a page tonight.
  And let that page come out of you--
  Then, it will be true.

I wonder if it's that simple?
   I am twenty-two, colored, born in Winston-Salem.
   I went to school there, then Durham, then here
to this college on the hill above Harlem.
I am the only colored student in my class.
The steps from the hill lead down into Harlem,
through a park, then I cross St. Nicholas,
Eighth Avenue, Seventh, and I come to the Y,
the Harlem Branch Y, where I take the elevator
up to my room, sit down, and write this page:

It's not easy to know what is true for you or me
   at twenty-two, my age. But I guess I'm what
I feel and see and hear, Harlem, I hear you:
hear you, hear me--we two--you, me, talk on this page.
(I hear New York, too.) Me--who?

Well, I like to eat, sleep, drink, and be in love.
   I like to work, read, learn, and understand life.
   I like a pipe for a Christmas present,
or records--Bessie, bop, or Bach.
I guess being colored doesn't make me *not* like
the same things other folks like who are other races.

M Todd Gallowglas

So will my page be colored that I write?

Being me, it will not be white.
    But it will be
    a part of you, instructor.
    You are white--
    yet a part of me, as I am a part of you.
    That's American.
    Sometimes perhaps you don't want to be a part of me.
    Nor do I often want to be a part of you.
    But we are, that's true!
    As I learn from you,
    I guess you learn from me--
    although you're older--and white--
    and somewhat more free.

This is my page for English B.

About the Author

M Todd Gallowglas is a professional storyteller (like on a stage with a show in front of real people) and the bestselling author of the *Tears of Rage* and *Halloween Jack* series.

As a child, Todd wished that he could be a left-handed red head, because he thought they were the most special and different people in the world. Because he was a brown-haired righty, life had forced him to create his own path to being special and different by making up stories of fantastical worlds of adventure. He even believed in these worlds so completely, that several of his teachers questioned whether he knew the difference between fantasy and reality. The jury is still out.

He wrote his first fantasy story for a creative writing assignment in the third grade. Ever since, he's loved spinning tales that take the reader off to the far future or away mystical worlds. High school was a convenient quiet place to hone the craft of writing adventure stories…while he should have been paying attention in class. Todd received a BA in Creative Writing from San Francisco State University. Throughout his time in at SFSU, several teachers tried to steer him away from writing that nasty "genre" stuff. However, they underestimated just how much Todd's brain is hard-wired for telling tales of the magical and fantastic, and their efforts to turn him to literary fiction came to nothing.

After graduating, Todd returned to his career as professional storyteller at Renaissance faires and Celtic festivals. His first professional sale was to Fantasy Flight Games, and he has a run of stories for their Call of Chthulu game line. His story "The Half-Faced Man" received an honorable mention from the Writers of the Future contest. Embracing the paradigm changes sweeping through the publishing industry, M Todd Gallowglas used his storytelling show as a platform to launch his self-published writing career. Nearly all of his eBooks have been Amazon bestsellers, and *First Chosen* spent most of 2012 on Amazon's Dark Fantasy and Fantasy Series lists.

He currently lives with his wife, three children, more pets than they need, and enough imaginary friends to provide playmates for several crowded kindergarten classes. He is currently corrupting his children by raising them with a rich education of geek culture. And still, as busy as he is, he manages to squeeze in time for some old-school table top gaming and airsoft battles on the weekends (because it's not as messy as paintball). Shiny!

Find out more about M Todd Gallowglas, his books, and read some of his rants, head over to his official website: www.mtoddgallowglas.com

Made in the USA
Charleston, SC
07 July 2016